.45-CALIBER JUSTICE

To the right of the hotel lobby was the bar. To the left, a dining room blazed with light. Through its doorway, Jim Hardin saw Lothry seated alone at a round table, a bill of fare in his hand.

Gun drawn, Jim took one step into the room. "Keep your hands where I can seem them, Lothry," he warned. "You can walk with me to the law or you can die where you sit. Either way, I mean to make you pay for killin' Jody."

Lothry sneered. "Was that his name?"

"Yeah, he was called Jody," blurted Jim. "Jody Taylor. And he was a decent kid."

"He drew on me!"

"Liar! His gun was in his holster!"

A flicker of a smile crossed Lothry's lips. "You put it there."

Jim stepped forward, aiming for Lothry's chest. "His name was Jody Taylor," he said coldly. "Remember it in hell!"

FOR THE BEST OF THE WEST—
DAN PARKINSON

A MAN CALLED WOLF   (2794, $3.95)

Somewhere in the scorched southwestern frontier where civilization was just a step away from the dark ages, an army of hired guns was restoring the blood cult of an ancient empire. Only one man could stop them: John Thomas Wolf.

THE WAY TO WYOMING   (2411, $3.95)

Matt Hazlewood and Big Jim Tyson had fought side by side wearing the gray ten years before. Now, with a bloody range war closing in fast behind and killers up ahead, they'd join up to ride and fight again in an untamed land where there was just the plains, the dust, and the heat—and the law of the gun!

GUNPOWDER WIND   (2456, $3.95)

by Dan Parkinson and David Hicks

War was brewing between the Anglo homesteaders and the town's loco Mexican commander Colonel Piedras. Figuring to keep the settlers occupied with a little Indian trouble, Piedras had Cherokee warrior Utsada gunned down in cold blood. Now it was up to young Cooper Willoughby to find him before the Cherokees hit the warpath!

THE WESTERING   (2559, $3.95)

There were laws against settin' a blood bounty on an innocent man, but Frank Kingston did it anyway, and Zack Frost found himself hightailin' it out of Indiana with a price on his head and a pack of bloodthirsty bounty hunters hot on his trail!

Available wherever paperbacks are sold, or order direct from the Publisher. Send cover price plus 50¢ per copy for mailing and handling to Zebra Books, Dept. 3372, 475 Park Avenue South, New York, N.Y. 10016. Residents of New York, New Jersey and Pennsylvania must include sales tax. DO NOT SEND CASH.

TOMBSTONE REVENGE

H. PAUL JEFFERS

ZEBRA BOOKS
KENSINGTON PUBLISHING CORP.

This book is for my sisters, Arlene and Jean.

ZEBRA BOOKS

are published by

Kensington Publishing Corp.
475 Park Avenue South
New York, NY 10016

First printing: April, 1991

Printed in the United States of America

Part One
The Palo Duro

Chapter One
Snake in the Grass

They called him Tascosa, a handle hung on him by his best pal, Lou Garrard.

His true name was Jim Hardin.

Tascosa was the place he hailed from, a speck on the map of the high plains of Texas where his dreamer of a father had settled with glorious expectations into a dugout house on a patch of rented, worthless farmland beside Little Blue Creek.

Fresh from Ellsworth, Kansas, which he figured was getting too crowded, Thomas Hardin had arrived in the Texas panhandle with his pretty wife Maggie and young Jim less than a year after the U.S. Cavalry of fearless Colonel Ranald S. MacKenzie had settled once and for all who was going to rule the Staked Plains by breaking the hold of the Comanches in a decisive battle on September 27, 1874.

Before that, only the most daring, the bravest or the foolhardiest had set foot in that territory of forbidding escarpment in northwest Texas which was hospitable only to buffalo, antelope, jack rabbit, prairie dogs, horny toads, rattlers and the dauntless Comanche who ranged unimpeded across the teeming gameland between the many-forked Red River, the Canadian and the Cimarron — but even the Indians chose not to settle where there was sparse water and nothing growing but sagebrush, grama grass and prickly shrubs.

With the establishment of peace and the way opened for

whites to settle around what had been nothing more than a fording place on the Canadian River at the intersection of a buffalo trail and the old Indian trace known as the Spanish Road, the first to grasp the possibilities in the High Plains was Colonel Charles Goodnight, a formidable man who was already a trail-blazing legend in the West.

Born in Illinois but transplanted to Texas in 1845 at the age of nine, the colonel had first tried his hand at freighting and then cattle raising in the Keechi Valley, only to be wiped out by Indian raiders. In 1860 he'd joined the Texas Rangers, serving four years of bloody battling against the Indians along the northwest frontier and learning the territory of the High Plains as well as he knew the back of his hand. Using that knowledge after the war, he'd laid out the best routes for trekking Texas cattle to markets in New Mexico, Wyoming, Kansas and Colorado. It was in Kansas that Tom Hardin had run into him and first heard the colonel waxing poetic about the potential of the High Plains for raising cattle if the land could be cleared of the Comanche.

With the High Plains made safe, the colonel moved into a place that seemed perfect for ranching. A natural corral formed by a canyon cut into the otherwise relentless flatness by the Prairie Dog Town Fork of the Red River, it offered plenty of grass and water and ample shelter from the blizzards that howled across the prairie in the wintertime, and there were abundant cedar, chinaberry and cottonwood trees for fences and buildings. A thousand feet deep, as wide as fifteen miles in places and as narrow as a few hundred yards in others, the Palo Duro ran for sixty miles beginning just east of the Canadian River fording place known as Tascosa.

Tom Hardin thought Colonel Goodnight was a great man, as indeed he was — straight as an arrow, warning Tom that the land Tom had set his mind on by the creek was a sorry spot for a farm. "Raise cattle," Goodnight advised, unavailing. Soon, on this hard scrabble land, Maggie Hardin died of a fever, leaving the raising of the boy to Tom, a job which was well done according to all who knew the lad, for Jim grew strong, straight, honest and never a shirker.

Then, on a crisp clear autumn day in 1876 as the father and his strapping fourteen-year-old son were clearing brush, Tom Hardin was bit by a rattlesnake that struck silently out of the tall grass. The deadly fangs sank deeply into the thick, corded vulnerable veins of the left wrist. Shaking off the snake, Tom yelled, "Jimmy! Come quick! I need you!"

Working nearby, the boy ran half in excitement, half in dread and found his father sprawled on the ground. "Snake," Tom moaned, nodding at the rattler slinking away.

Drawing his father's Colt Paterson, Jim shot it.

"Afraid I'm a goner," groaned Tom as his purposeful son knelt beside him.

"The dickens you are, Pop," Jim grunted fighting to stay cool and calm and flipping open his jackknife. Grasping his father's clammy arm, he sliced open the puffy pink bite wounds, squeezing the slashes to flush out blood and venom. His yellow neckerchief served to make a tourniquet.

But it was to no avail.

Tom Hardin was right; he was a goner — dead by sundown.

Two days later, the Reverend Bernard Dilbert and Jim did the burying, laying Tom Hardin in the poor earth beside his beloved wife.

"What'll you be doin' now, Jim?" asked the sorrowful Reverend Dilbert as he slipped his worn Bible into his black coat pocket. "I can't see you workin' the farm on your own."

"I reckon you're right about that," Jim said as he stared blankly at his parents' graves and rubbed his chin, feeling the barest trace of a beard which his father had taken to ribbing him about, saying that he was fast becoming a man. Jim had shot up pretty tall and filled out impressively, and folks said he was becoming the spittin' image of his old man, which made him feel good because everybody in Tascosa held that Tom Hardin was a mighty handsome man. "I'll be needin' a job, that's for sure," Jim said to the preacher. "So I s'pose I'll amble over to the Palo Duro and see if Colonel Goodnight can use an extra hand."

"That's a right good idea, son," said the reverend. "And I can't think of anybody better for any man to work for than

9

Colonel Goodnight. When do you figure on goin'?"

"Right away," Jim declared. "There's nothin' to hold me here now. No sense delayin' it."

"No indeed," said the preacher. "Life is for gettin' on with."

Chapter Two
The Colonel

Baking in the noon sun that had driven its inhabitants indoors, Tascosa paid no attention to Jim as he rode through. At Henry Kimball's blacksmith shop there was not a noise to be heard—no ring and clang of metal being hammered, no whinnying of horses being shod. Just as quiet was the general store of G.J. Howard and Ira Rinehart. The street before it was empty, and the only sounds of life were the buzzing of flies and the easy clop of his chestnut mare's hooves kicking up yellow dust. Most of the inhabitants of Tascosa were Mexicans who'd brought their *siesta* with them.

The only time he'd ever seen Tascosans approach excitement had been a couple of years before when a thief and murderer named Sostenese l'Archeveque made the mistake of killing a pair of sheepmen named Casner for their horde of twenty-dollar gold pieces and was stabbed to death by anxious Tascosa citizens who feared an attack on the town by the avenging relatives of the Casner brothers if justice were not meted out fast.

The murdered pair had had even more money on them—twenty thousand dollars—it was said, and from time to time someone went off in search of it, always fruitlessly. "They're plain fools," Tom Hardin had judged when he heard of a new outbreak of digging. "There ain't no money to be found," he had declared, stirring in Jim's head the question of whether his pop might've been speaking of efforts he might have made himself, secretly and in vain, to locate a treasure that could rescue and redeem a dream gone sour.

Quiet even shrouded the Horse Blanket Saloon, named for the cheap house whiskey which was said to be made from anything that was handy and then strained through a horse blanket into buckets and served up to customers out of a wooden ladel. Just what was the difference between horse blanket whiskey and any other kind was something Jim didn't know, never having seen the brew, let alone having it pass his lips, because his ma had disapproved of liquor of any kind. The effects of drink on those who partook of it, he had witnessed often, however, seeing men stumbling out of the Horse Blanket in the broad daylight of Saturdays when the Hardins came to town to purchase goods.

At the back of the Horse Blanket's one big room, he'd been told by sniggering town boys, there was a staircase that led up to a loft where there were sporting women by the names of Canadian Lily, Atlanta Annie and Moonlight Rose. Not knowing the precise meaning of "sporting women" and too proud and ashamed to admit it, he'd merely nodded knowingly. Later, he'd mulled it over and figured it out, then sat beside the creek in wonderment of the world and speculating on whether the day might come when he'd partake of it and discover all of its supposed attractions.

Now, peering up as he rode past the sun-baked saloon, he noted that green paper shades were pulled down at the two windows that marked the mysterious loft and wondered what the person with the alluring name of Moonlight Rose might be doing at that very moment — sporting, perhaps?

Southeastward from Tascosa, the wide, featureless prairie shimmered and thirsted beneath a climbing sun. Sweat had turned his shirt and the seat of his pants to a sopping stickiness, and beads of it glittered like jewels on his brow and dripped from his sharp nose and downy chin. He'd filled three canteens with water from the creek, two for drinking and one for soaking a big red wipe that he patted on his face and neck, enjoying the coolness as the hot air dried up the dampness.

But he felt sorry for the horse. Lady was her name. He let her set the pace, which was an easy walk that rocked him as gently in the saddle as his mother had done for him in the cradle.

At mid-afternoon he slid down to rest and cool himself in the shade of a mesquite tree and gaze wonderingly at the awesome canyon stretching before him — miles of reddish cliffs, slopes lush with tall cedars and a sprightly, meandering stream nestled at the deep bottom reached by a steep, winding trail.

He'd been to the Goodnight ranch once with his pop, but his memory of the famous pioneer who owned it was hazy, except that he had been a scary, broad-shouldered, thick-chested man with a head carried low like a buffalo. He soon found such a man supervising a crowd of sweaty cowboys who were mending a wooden fence at the foot of the descending trail. "Do I have the distinct honor of addressing Colonel Goodnight?" he asked.

"Don't know about the honor of it," answered Goodnight in a tone as gruff as his expression, "but that's who you're talking to. What can I do for you?"

"I'm lookin' for work, sir," said Jim, sliding off the horse. "Cowboy work, to be exact," he added forcefully, casting a self-conscious glance at the men who already had the right to call themselves cowhands.

Despite the shade of a broad-brimmed black hat, Colonel Goodnight squinted through the unrelenting blaze of the overhead sun and took his time answering. Studying the slender, sun-browned, tawny-haired figure fidgeting before him, he muttered, "You look a little scrawny to me."

One of the cowboys snickered.

"If I don't measure up," Jim said, bristling and jutting out the unshaved jaw, "you can hand me my walking papers."

The colonel chuckled. "Don't think I won't, either."

"That mean I'm hired?"

The colonel waited again, mulling things over. "Follow the stream about a mile," he said at last, "and you'll come to the ranch house. See the cook."

Jim stiffened. "I don't want no job in no kitchen," he

blurted, tipping back his tan hat defiantly. "I want a man's work."

"The cook," said the colonel with strained patience, "will give you some lunch. You look like you haven't eaten for a while. Nobody goes to work for me on an empty belly. When yours is full, Mr. Raphael, the cook, will introduce you to the ranch boss. Mr. Place does the hiring. If he needs another hand, he'll see about arranging some . . . man's work."

The cowboys laughed.

Chapter Three
The Cook and the Boss

As burly and black-haired as a bear, the cook slapped down a plate of Son-of-a-bitch stew. "That's the last of it, and the bread's all gone," he said, wiping his big hands on a soiled white apron stretched to capacity around a bulging belly. "And the milk's finished, too, so there's only water to wash it down with," he added, plunking a tin cup onto the uncovered plank table.

"This is fine," Jim said, remembering the red-and-white-checkered cloth his mother had always laid out for meals.

"Hardin's your name?" asked the cook, pulling up a chair and plopping onto it with beefy bare arms stacked like logs on the table top.

"My given name's James, called Jim."

"Raphael's my name. Francisco Raphael. The men call me Frank."

"Pleased to make your acquaintance, Frank."

"You any relation to John Wesley Hardin, the gun man?"

"Distant, I was told," said Jim, keenly aware of being assayed as he scooped up a spoonful of the watery beef stew that was too salty by half.

"How's the grub?" asked Frank, obviously fishing for praise.

"Tasty," Jim said with a forced smile.

"I seen him in action," said Frank. "Your kinsman, I mean."

"Is that so?"

"This was down in Towash. It was Christmas Day of '69. Wes gunned down a gambler name of Bradley, who was also named Jim, by the way. It was a pretty fair shootout with Wes comin' through it standin' up and Jim Bradley with a pair of slugs in 'im and beggin' for mercy. Then Wes spoils the whole thing by lettin' him have four more, 'parently jest for the fun of it. Now that's what I call a real mean streak. What about you, Mr. Jim Hardin?" He stood, drumming his fingers on his belly. "I see you wear a gun. You got a mean streak like your distant relative?"

"I don't think so."

The cook reared up. "An' what makes you so sure of that, may I ask?" Frank said as Jim speared the last chunk of meat that was more gristle than beef. "You're young," he said, whipping the plate from the table. "Sometimes meanness don't show till later. That's the difference between men and hosses. You can spot a mean hoss right off. You can't always do that with a man. I hope you had enough to eat, 'cause that's all there is till supper, which is at seven o'clock in the summertime, on account of the sun stayin' up longer."

"The meal will hold me fine, so if you'll tell me where I can find Mr. Place, I'll be seein' about the work I came here for."

"I'll take you to meet Aaron."

"No need. Just tell me the way."

"It's easier to take you than tell you," said Frank as he peeled off the greasy apron.

"Some men's lives are best regarded like closely held poker hands; called at your own risk." So said Frank as they rode down the canyon. Such was that of Aaron Place, he went on, as a few men with inquisitive natures had learned, to their rue. The one thing nobody wondered about was Aaron's ability, he continued. "Yep," he said. "Aaron is the best boss a cowhand could want."

His age was somewhere between thirty and forty, Frank figured. That he'd been for the South in the war was known, and he'd been slightly wounded in the attempt to recapture Galveston from the Yanks at Christmastime 1862. He had then seen the sunset of the Confederacy while riding with the troops of General Joseph Shelby's Missouri Cavalry, which held out to the last along the Rio Grande, not quitting the fight until July 4, 1865. After that, he'd done some mavericking in the Nueces Strip and learned that he wasn't cut out to be a rancher and would be happiest working for someone else. One story had it that he'd bossed the Colter Ranch in Goliad for a time, though his reason for moving on remained a question. He'd been seen in the Kansas cow towns quite a bit before winding up in Colorado, where he'd caught the eye of Colonel Goodnight.

He was handy with a six-gun and one of the most popular stories about him concerned him killing three men in Long Charlie Carew's saloon in Abilene, said Frank.

He'd also been quite a ladies man, it was rumored; especially other men's wives, it was said, which possibly explained what appeared to be a post-war lifetime of quick departures. But there were those who cast doubt on the stories of Aaron Place's romances by pointing out that little Aaron Place with his dwindling supply of black hair, bowed legs and leathery face was much too far from good-looking to be regarded as a lady-killer.

Having spent most of his life in the sun, he now faced the world with a permanent squint which had carved deep furrows of flesh that looked like the quivers of arrows at the corners of eyes that were emerald green and wary. Being short, he had to look up at the tall kid the cook brought into the camp six miles downstream from Frank's kitchen. Seated in a clearing at a folding table and hunkering over a stack of paperwork, he lifted his head and squinted toward Frank. "What have we here?"

"This fella's lookin' for work," declared the cook from atop a broad-shouldered bay. "The colonel sent him for you to look over. His name's Jim Hardin."

"You're in luck, kid," said Aaron, rising. "It so happens I'm short-handed at this time. You ever work cattle?"

"Afraid not, Mr. Place," Jim said sheepishly.

"Never mind," he said, advancing. "You'll learn. If you don't, you'll either be dead or fired. The first thing to learn is that nobody calls me 'Mr. Place.' I'm Aaron." The green eyes seemed to rake Jim as he sat his pretty chestnut horse. "Them duds won't do. Don't s'pose you've got a set of *chaparajos?*" He slapped his leathered thigh. "You gotta have chaps!"

"Sorry, sir. I don't."

"Cripes! First you call me 'mister' and now 'sir.' For the last time, it's Aaron! Well, you'll have to borrow some chaps till you can get your own. Don't s'pose you've got *anything* proper? A rope?"

Jim shrugged. "I reckon I don't."

"Well, we can supply all you need—" Aaron sighed—"but it'll come outta your first pay. Frank, introduce this fella . . . what's your name agin'?"

"Jim."

"Frank, introduce Jim to Lou. Lou Garrard's the top hand. He'll see about supplyin' the outfittin' required. He'll start you workin'." The green eyes peered up, boring like drills. "Brush poppin's the place to begin, I s'pose." Aaron's gaze drifted to the six-gun on Jim's hip. "Know how to use that iron?"

"Passably."

"You ain't one of those gunslingers the West is gettin' to be famous for? You wouldn't be hidin' out from the law? On the run?"

"Nope."

"No offense intended."

"None taken."

"That's a Colt Paterson?"

"It belonged to my pop."

"Well, at least that's one piece of equipment Colonel Goodnight won't have to supply. And it's apt to come in handy. There's tons of snakes in this here canyon. You ever eat rattlesnake stew?"

"Can't say that I have."

"Then, you're in for a treat," Aaron said, sitting down at his paper-cluttered table. "Frank, here, is an expert at makin' it."

"I'll look forward to it," Jim said without enthusiasm.

"Don't pay no mind to that stuff about rattler stew." Frank chuckled as they rode away. "Aaron's a big one for teasin' the new men. He likes to see what makes a man flinch. The idea of a meal of rattler stew usually gets a rise. You done good. Didn't bat an eye. Aaron noticed it, too. Gets you off on the right foot with him, believe me."

"Does that mean it ain't true?" Jim asked. "You don't cook up snakes?"

"Cripes! I hate the damned things!"

"Me, too," Jim muttered, with a pang of painful memory of how his father had died. "They're the most cussed creatures on God's earth!"

Chapter Four
Top Hand

If Aaron Place gave the impression of a volume of puzzles, Lou Garrard appeared to be an open book. Born and raised on a ranch on the Brazos, he was a cattleman through and through about whom no questions or doubts were whispered. The kind of youth Maggie Hardin would have described as winning in every way, he was fair-haired, blue-eyed and almost as baby-faced as Jim, save for a three-day stubble of a beard. He was nineteen years old, but anyone encountering him for the first time was conscious not of his youthful appearance but of a confident bearing and directness found in much older men. "Give me a week of watchin' you at work, Tascosa," he said as he sorted through clothing and gear of his own to lend to Jim, "and I'll know if you got the right stuff."

"And what's the right stuff?" asked Jim, his arms piled with a shirt, a short denim jacket and work pants, a pair of leather gloves and *chaparreras* that were as soft as butter and deeply scarred with scratches and gouges.

"The right stuff," said Lou, rummaging in a wooden box in the corner of his room, "is guts." Straightening, he bellowed, "Ah, here it is. Just the thing."

Flung at Jim was a slightly crushed black hat with a narrow brim bent to a point at the front. "This thing's seen better days," Jim said disdainfully.

"It'll serve you better'n the thing you're wearin'," answered

Lou. "That's a whorehouse hat. Wear that into the brush, and it'll be spiked by mesquite and thorny bushes quicker'n you can bat an eye. For workin' brush you need the right hat. The one I just gave you is it."

"Right hat," said Jim, cracking a lopsided smile as he pulled off his tan Stetson and slapped on the black. "Right stuff!"

"Now you need the right hoss," said Lou, wheeling toward the door. "That mare you rode in on just won't do. Lordy no. Just won't do! That filly might attract the attention of some dewy-eyed girl in Tascosa, but for workin' the brush you'll be needin' a hoss that's light on its feet, one that can twist and dodge and stop and turn on a coin. A hoss that can help a man root the cow critters outta the brush. I got just the one in mind. Black as midnight, which is his name."

"Black?" Jim asked.

"No, blockhead," snorted Lou, striding toward the remuda. "Midnight!"

The horse, the clothes, the chaps, and the hat were only the beginning. Now came the learning of the work. So much was different from all Jim had experienced helping his father in his vain efforts to tame unyielding land into a farm.

Suddenly, everything in life was different.

Soon Jim saw himself changing: leaner and harder in body, keener of head, sharper of eye, cooler in judgment, steadier in his decisions—better and better in all things.

All thanks to Lou, who would introduce something new by cocking back his weathered hat, hooking his thumbs under his gunbelt, rubbing his jaw and muttering, "Say, Tascosa. . . ."

"Say Tascosa," he'd asked. "Do you smoke or chaw your tobacco?"

"Neither" was the reply.

"Well, hell, Tascosa, if you're gonna hang around with me, you gotta do one or the other, else who'm I gonna bum it from?"

So Jim learned about chewing tobacco and the rolling of cigarettes.

"Be careful with the matches," Lou warned. "Get careless tossin' one away and you can spark a prairie fire that nothin' will put out. Make a habit of cuppin' the match in your hand. Lightin' up at night can set off a scare in the herd and trigger a stampede." The way to stop a stampede, he attested, was to circle 'em and try to turn the leaders back on the rest. "When herdin' 'em, never ride too close." He taught that canyon cattle were "windies", which were contrary and hard to drive. Sick ones were "downers", and long-legged ones were "leggy." Wild and woolly, it was a "Cimarron." A scrubby calf was a "doggie", and a sick adult was a "cutback." "But no matter what you call them beasts," Lou grumbled, "they're a pain in the rump."

A pretty little song would soothe them. Lou demonstrated by bursting forth with "Well, I met a little gal and offered her a quarter," sung with a sweet, gravelly voice. "She says, 'Young man, I'm a gentleman's daughter.' "

When he spoke of women it was to tease Jim. "I reckon you're a greenhorn in that department, too, eh? We'll have to see about your education one of these days."

"What about liquor?" he asked. "Are you afflicted with the thirst?"

"Never had a drink," Jim admitted shyly. "Save for some hard cider once."

"Hard cider's nothin'," grumbled Lou. But learning about drink would have to wait, too, Lou said. Whiskey on the job, he disapproved of, as did Aaron and the colonel.

There were several lessons concerning ropes. His lariat, he called his "ketch rope." When it slipped through the hand and ripped off skin, it was "hot," and a "wasted loop" was one that missed. "It's a simple thing, a rope," Lou said, coiling his, "but it's your lifeline, kid." The best way to hobble a horse in tall grass, the lesson continued, was to short hobble the front feet. "That'll let him get plenty to eat."

He was brief of speech and long on patience, taking things as they came, and when he laughed, it was usually at himself.

Then there was the matter of shooting.

Save for Aaron Place, Lou Garrard was the best man with a six-gun in the Palo Duro, and although Jim never expected to be nearly as excellent with a Colt, he longed to learn how to shoot well. Finally, on a crisp black night when they were camped far down the canyon and eating a rabbit Lou had picked off with one shot for their supper, he summoned the nerve to bring up the subject. "This is fine rabbit," Jim said, gnawing a bone. "And you got 'im with one try. That's damned good shootin'. Do you think you could teach me to shoot like that?"

"Reckon I can try," said Lou teasingly. "Seein' as how I taught you practically everythin' else you know."

So, that winter was spent shooting.

In this, as in everything else, Lou proved a patient instructor, but as the days passed, the need for him to correct his pupil quickly diminished until, rather than teaching, he found himself competing with Jim, first with set targets and then with moving ones as they scoured the prairie above the canyon for birds, rabbits and prairie dogs.

"You're gettin' to be so damned good," Lou soon declared, "it's scary."

"Aw, I'll never be as good as you," Jim answered, blushing but flattered by the extravagant praise.

"You'd be better'n I am now," said Lou, "if you'd stop holdin' back."

"I ain't holdin' back!" Jim yelled. "Why would I hold back?"

"To keep from embarrassin' the britches off of me, that's why!"

"That's bull," Jim answered, which he knew was a lie. He had been keeping a check on the Paterson because he saw that he was getting to be as good as Lou.

When March arrived, it was time to ride out to survey the camps in advance of the roundup, a job for teams of two with Lou deciding on the pairings. "Tascosa, since this is your first time at this task, you'll accompany me," he declared to Jim's satisfaction and nobody's surprise.

But on the first night out, Jim sensed there was something on Lou's mind, a troubling, and figured it was something Lou wanted to talk about and would when the spirit moved him.

Then, on the fifth night, after minutes lost in thought, Lou lit a cheroot, took a deep breath, blew out the smoke and declared, "Tascosa, I'm thinkin' of chuckin' this job."

Stunned, Jim blared, "What the hell for?"

"Boredom," Lou answered explosively. "I am so damned bored! There's nothin' excitin' about this job no more. Lately I've been havin' this feelin' I gotta break loose." He flipped the cheroot into the fire. "Yeah, I'm itchin' to git outta here. My folks allus said I was cursed with a yen for wanderin'. I ache to head for someplace . . . different."

Dry-voiced, Jim asked, "Where to?"

He shrugged. "Who knows? Anyplace at all. Anyplace but here."

"That's a crazy notion, Lou," Jim argued. "You've got a nice set-up here. You're the top hand! The colonel and Aaron give you a free hand. The pay's good. The men admire you. Hell, they love you! And you'd give up all that for a pig in a poke? What in tarnation for?"

"My feet itch. And when they itch, the only thing to do is scratch 'em. That means pullin' out. Seein' what's beyond the sunset. Who knows what awaits me?" He flashed a winning smile. "Maybe it'll be a pot o' gold."

"All you need is a little fun," said Jim cajolingly. "When we get paid, we could ride to Tascosa," he said excitedly. "They've got a saloon there!"

Lou laughed. "Saloon? When's the last time your mama ever let you set foot in a saloon? Shoot, the way I figure it, you've never been in one."

"Hell and damnation, Lou, everybody's gotta have a first time. Well, this'll be mine. You know, they've even got a whorehouse there."

"Kid, the devil's really got a hold of you, hasn't he? You in a whorehouse?"

"What say? Wanna do it? Sat'day?"

"Pal, there's nothin' that could keep me from partakin' of your first time in a saloon. And Jim Hardin in a whorehouse? What a hoot!"

"It's settled, then," Jim declared, eyes alight. Slapping his chaps with the battered black hat he'd been given, he yelped. "Yahoo! Look out Tascosa! Here we come!"

"Blessed Lord—" Lou sighed, —"what have I wrought?"

Horse blanket whiskey, here I come, thought Jim with a simple grin. "Moonlight Rose," he crowed, "look out for the Tascosa Kid!"

Come Saturday when Jim pushed through its yellow batwing doors, the Horse Blanket Saloon was exactly as he'd imagined it to be in the descriptions given by the knowledgeable town boys. A vast room fogged by tobacco smoke and lit by scorched oil lamps hanging from the ceilings, it had a long bar down one side that was crowded with Tascosan men, a handful of leathery cowboys he recognized from the Palo Duro and others he didn't know from other places. Tables along the opposite wall were occupied by blank-visaged gamblers playing faro and poker. The hard dirt floor was covered with sawdust. In the back, a steep stairway led upward.

"Well, here we are," said Lou, whipping off his hat and sweeping it in an encompassing arc. "Just the place for a man to wet his whistle and dip his wick, eh?"

The smell of drink was overwhelming even in the smoke and odors of unwashed bodies. And the noise was overpowering: the banging of a tinny piano and a steady rumble of baritone voices, cut through by the piercing shriek of a scattering of laughing women with bared shoulders, upswept hair stuck with glittery combs, and painted faces.

"Golly, look at them women," Jim whispered to Lou.

"A drink first." Lou laughed, tugging Jim toward the bar by the sleeve. "What'll it be, amigo?"

What to say? Maggie Hardin had always denounced drink as demon rum. His pop called it rotgut and a waste of a man's money. "There's only two things to say about spirits," Thorns Hardin had warned him. "It tastes awful and it leaves you with a headache!" And from the pulpit, Reverend Dilbert never failed to castigate liquor and those who partook of it.

"Make mine the same as whatever you're havin', Lou," Jim answered.

Propping his elbow on the bar and hooking his boot heel on the brass rail, Lou wiggled a finger at the bartender. "Couple

25

a ryes."

Drinking it quickly, Jim decided his pop was right about the taste—plain awful. Like the worst-tasting sulphur medicine his mother had forced down him when he had the croup. Nasty stuff, rasping in the throat, it burned its way into his gut. "Easy does it." Lou laughed. "A little at a time! That stuff kicks like a mule!"

Sipped, the second was better, smoother.

With the third, Jim felt the effect. Not a kick, though. But a sort of gentle lift and then a whirling, like being whisked off his feet as a baby and spun around his pop's head. Like then, he giggled.

Then he saw the woman.

Slowly descending the stairs, she had golden hair topped by what seemed to be a diamond coronet. A sleeveless scarlet dress that swept to the floor had silver spangles at the bottom. A band of lace frills dipped deeply from shoulder to shoulder, revealing a swell of breasts as white as milk. "Who's she?" he gasped.

"That's Rosie," answered the bartender, glancing up.

Jim gulped. "Moonlight Rose?"

"The one and only," said the bartender, looking down again.

"Golly," Jim sighed, poking an elbow into Lou's ribs. "Ain't she somethin'?"

"For a whore, she ain't too bad," said Lou. Turning to the bartender, he asked, "What's the tariff?"

"Two bucks an hour; ten, all night."

"That's pretty steep."

"All night, the house throws in a bottle."

"Well, what'll it be?" said Lou, clutching Jim's shoulder. "All night?"

"Ten dollars?" Jim muttered. "That's damned near half my pay."

Lou laughed. "It'll be my treat!"

"Aw, Lou," Jim protested, "I couldn't let you do that!"

"No arguin'," he insisted, digging coins from his jeans and banging them on the bar. "Take the money and go to it!"

The word "harlots" rang in Jim's memory in the form of the

voice of the Reverend Dilbert. Hellfire and brimstone were the reapings of those who sewed their oats with harlots, he'd warned. "Strumpets and hussies," hissed the recalled voice of Maggie Hardin. But into Jim's swirling head came no voice sounding like his father's. He'd never heard his pop talk about women at all, and certainly not about whores.

"What the devil you waitin' for?" demanded Lou, stabbing a finger into Jim's chest. "There's the money, and there's Moonlight Rose! If you don't speak up for her now, somebody else will. Maybe even me!"

"All right, all right," Jim grunted, scooping up five dollars, having decided on the hourly rate, "but I'm only takin' half and only if you agree it's a loan!"

"Sure, kid." Lou laughed. "Pay me back anytime!"

Cupping the coins in his hand, Jim lurched away from the bar, shouldering through the crowd, grunting "Excuse me! Pardon me! Comin' through!"

Then, suddenly, she was in front of him, smiling. "Well, lookee here. A new face."

She smelled like lilacs.

"And what a face," she said, petting Jim's burning cheek. "Honey, where you been all my life?"

"I've been right here in Tascosa," Jim said, his throat as raspy and rough as fresh-sawed wood.

"How old are you? Does your mama know where you are?"

"I'm goin' on seventeen," he lied. "I ain't no kid, my ma's dead and so's my pop. I work for Colonel Goodnight at the Palo Duro, and if I want to spend my wages drinkin' and spendin' my time with a woman, who's to say I cain't?"

"Well, not me, darling." Rose laughed, looping his arm with hers and turning him toward the stairs. "Certainly not me!"

Two hours later when he returned downstairs, Jim found Lou at the bar gabbing with a little man who was as bald as a cue ball, pink-faced from drinking the Horse Blanket Saloon's choicest whiskey and dressed to the nines in a fine suit and vest with a gold chain looped across a potbelly. "This strike could

27

be the motherlode," he was saying as Jim wedged in next to Lou.

"Mr. Parker," said Lou, "this here's my saddle buddy. Name of Jim Hardin, but everybody calls him Tascosa."

"Howdy," said Jim, all smiles and eager to tell Lou about upstairs.

"George Parker's my name," said the bald man, extending a pudgy hand. "Mining's my game, which is why I'm bound for Tombstone. I was just tellin' Mr. Garrard that the word I've gotten is that you can pick up silver nuggets the size of your fist right off the ground."

"Where's this?" Jim asked, doubtful.

"Tombstone, Arizona."

"Tombstone?" Jim snickered. "Sounds more like a graveyard than a town."

"The name *is* a kind of a joke! You see, the story I heard is that a prospector by the name of Ed Schieffelin set out one day from Fort Huachuca to do some scratchin' around, only he was headin' into Apache country. Well, one of the soldiers says to him, 'The only thing you're gonna find is your tombstone.' So what happens? Ed hits pay dirt, and bein' a man with a good sense of humor, what does he name his claim? Tombstone!"

"And you're headin' out there to stake a claim of your own, is that it?" Jim asked, certain that his leg was being pulled.

Parker chuckled. "Not at all, lad! A smart man of my age doesn't dig for ore. He makes his money selling picks and shovels! I'm in the business of purveying mining equipment! But if I was a young 'un like you and Mr. Garrard, I'd likely take a shot at prospectin', yessiree."

Glancing anxiously at Lou, Jim recognized the flash of wanderlust in his eyes.

"Well, compared to this spot," Lou said, "Tombstone sounds pretty excitin'. If you ask me, the town of Tascosa ain't worth warm spit." He flashed Jim a smile. "So how was your roll in the hay with Moonlight Rose? Everything you hoped it would be?"

"To tell you the truth," Jim said, blushing, "I didn't know

what to expect. But it was fine. Jest *fine!*"

"That's the entire story about women." Lou chuckled. "You never know what to expect."

"Amen to that," said Mr. Parker with a bark of a laugh as he fished out a gold pocket watch. "Say, look at the time! I'd best be gettin' to bed. I'm leavin' for Tombstone early in the morning."

When he was gone, Jim nudged Lou in the side. "Nuggets as big as your fist lyin' there on the ground, ripe for the pickin'," he scoffed. "Can you believe that?"

"Why not?" said Lou dreamily.

"Arizona! Geez, Lou, that's hunerts of miles from here! That's a long way to travel with nothin' but some cockeyed story to go on."

"And just what is there here?" Lou said bitterly. "Nothin', that's what."

"You're not thinkin' of goin'?"

"What the hell's so great around here? You and me could go out to Tombstone and try our luck!"

"I've got me a decent job. Everybody's been great to me. Aaron, the colonel, all the hands—you. I'm happy with what I got. Besides, the drive's about to start. I never been on a cattle drive. And from what I heard, them cow towns in Kansas is somethin' to behold. And the truth of it is, Lou, I was kind of lookin' forward to goin' up there with you."

"Well," Lou said, rubbing his stubbled beard, "I guess I could wait till after the drive. It wouldn't be right to yank up stakes on the colonel at this time, what with the drive all set to shove off."

"I expect so," said Jim, squeezing Lou's arm and grinning ear to ear.

Chapter Five
The Goodnight Trail

April came in hot with the Palo Duro cattle gathered, surly brutes to be driven by leathery men with sun-weathered skin as tough as rawhide, tight lips, iron muscles and searching eyes as keen as sky-wheeling hawks.

"Two hundred and fifty miles to Dodge City," said Lou across the campfire to Jim, hunched forward, his arms circling his upraised knees, while the flames sparkled in his wide eyes. "It'll take upward of three months. In that time we're gonna be a world unto ourselves," Lou said earnestly. "Each one's life depending on the other." He sighed, exhaling cigarette smoke. "It all comes down to the skills they've learned over the years and the gear they got packed into the rolls tucked behind the cantels of their saddles or in Frank's supply wagons." His eyes drifted. "Six-guns, knives, ropes and hobbles, saddles, bridles, blankets, boots, slickers, hats, kerchiefs and whatever else they deem vital."

Lou had stowed what seemed to Jim to be a half-year's supply of cheroots and cigarette makings.

"Do what Aaron Place tells you; he's the trail boss, and none better in all of Texas. And stick close to me, Tascosa," said Lou, flipping the last of the cigarette into the campfire, "and you'll get through the drive jest fine. For now, though, best get some rest. The sun seems to come up earlier at the commencing of a drive."

30

How on earth, Jim wondered as he curled up on his blanket, could anybody sleep on such a thrilling night?

His head buzzed with anticipation of the adventures that lay before them! The sights he would soon behold. Except for having been born in Kansas and being hauled from there to Texas when he was too young to notice or care, he'd not been more than ten miles away from Tascosa. A new world lay beyond the Canadian River. And what about crossing the Indian Nation? What would that be like? Would they have to tangle with savage Indians who delighted in lifting white men's scalps? The river to cross in the Indian Nation was the Cimarron. "The bloody Cimarron," Aaron Place called it. So many big waters to cross. How many creeks and rivers? The last, the Arkansas, was the threshold of Kansas, the final obstacle before Dodge City. And then he would taste the pleasures of the town he'd heard so much about from the Palo Duro men who'd already been there and liked to tease him about what he could expect to find: saloons, gambling dens, dance halls, bawdy houses. It was Dodge City, the men had promised him, that put the "wild" in Wild West. And the women? Why, the gals of Dodge would make him forget all about his roll in the hay in the rude cribs of the Horse Blanket's loft with Moonlight Rose.

"You ain't had a real whore," vowed Aaron Place, who knew all about women, "till you poke a Dodge City whore!"

Sleepless, Jim saw that the trail boss was first up, even before Frank started banging pots and pans and brewing coffee and cooking up biscuits.

At the crack of pinkish dawn, Colonel Goodnight lumbered past on his purposeful legs clad in leather chaps, his head low like a buffalo's, to sip Frank's java and talk in low tones with Aaron Place.

A moment later, Frank clanged a bell and bellowed, "Grub pile! Bacon's ready. Biscuits ready. Get 'em while they're hot!"

Old Blue would lead the way.

"Remarkable creature," explained Lou, stroking the rump of the big mulberry-colored steer. "He's sure one of a kind," he said admiringly. "The good Lord made Old Blue and broke the mold."

Calved in the Nueces Strip in the spring of 1870, the steer had been bought by Colonel Goodnight four years later, part of a string of five thousand steers from John Chisum, and Old Blue had promptly demonstrated his abilities as a leader, taking to the point of the herd that Colonel Goodnight had driven from Colorado to establish his ranch in the Palo Duro Canyon of the Staked Plains. Since, there'd been numerous lucrative offers to buy the animal, all rejected out of hand by the colonel, usually with the boast "That there steer is worth a dozen cowhands to me."

A large brass bell dangled below Blue's immense neck from a new leather collar. Attached to it was a little strap for tying up the clapper at night and when the herd was grazing. "That'll be one of your jobs, Tascosa," said Lou. "But don't fret about Old Blue bein' nasty about it. He's used to humans. Fact is, he prob'ly thinks he is one."

Each day, Colonel Goodnight took the point, riding next to Old Blue and leading the way up the trail that Old Blue knew well, the one Charles Goodnight had blazed and that bore his name.

At suppertime with the cattle bedded and Old Blue's bell silenced, the colonel would conduct a meeting to assess that day's progress and offer his estimations for tomorrow.

Past the first of the rivers they would cross—the Salt Fork of the Red—they plodded north and east, passing Fort Elliott and escorted for a few days by a company of cavalry heading out on patrol and looking for any Comanches that might have strayed from their territory.

A day later, crossing the Canadian, the colonel found Indian signs. "They're Comanche," he declared, grim-faced as he scratched in the dirt. "A small party, movin' northeast.

Best tell the outriders to keep a sharp eye out. They'll not give us any real trouble, though we can expect to lose a head or two. Let 'em have a few. Better to let some go than have the redskins swoop down on their war ponies and in their paint to take the whole damned herd. The worst threat from them will be if they somehow set off a stampede. Tell the men to be extra watchful but not to raise any ruckus over a head or two. Better to give up some rather than lose a few hundred dying up stampeding."

Every day, riding with Lou, Jim searched the ground for Indian signs, scanning horizons for dust plumes or smoke that might mark a large movement of Comanche. But without hindrance from any tribes and with fair and hospitable weather, they made good time through the Indian Nation, crossing the Cimarron easily behind Old Blue, and on the last day of April reached the Arkansas.

"The river's high," declared Lou. "Must've been a rainy spring in these parts."

Undaunted, Old Blue plunged in, beckoning his followers after him.

On the second afternoon past the river, the wind whipped up sharply from a suddenly blackening western horizon, the sky streaked with lightning bolts, and thunder claps rolled toward them like hollow thuds of a distant cannon. "This is very bad," muttered Lou.

"Keep 'em goin'," ordered the colonel, riding back from the point. "Best to keep the pace while the storm's ragin' and it's still light." When bedding them was unavoidable, he galloped to the point where Jim rode beside Old Blue. "We can't go on in this tempest," said the colonel. "Tie up Blue's bell, Tascosa."

He'd chosen open and flat ground that formed the bottom of a wide, shallow hollow, best for coping with a stampede should there be one, ordering the riders to close in on all sides to crowd the cattle together until they were so compact and solid Jim thought a man might walk from one end of the herd to the other without setting boot to ground.

Drenched and dank as the rain came down in torrents, Jim circled the cattle on Midnight. The cold downpour drummed upon his black hat, spilling from the brim when he tilted his head down or looked up sharply at the flashing of lightning that turned the dark night into a moment of instant daylight and revealed the uneasy herd and figures of cowboys in rain-sopped hats, glistening yellow slickers, soggy boots and their slippery-backed and skittish horses.

Aaron Place had divided the night riding into two watches of six hours, the change being made at midnight.

Promptly at twelve, Lou rode out as Jim's relief. "How's it been?" he whispered.

"Jumpy."

Lou chuckled. "The critters or you?"

"Cussed rain," said Jim, squinting into the wind-driven, slashing torrent.

"If it was dry," said Lou with a friendly grunt, "you'd be cussin' the drought."

At that moment, lightning rent the sky, and the thunder was instantaneous, jolting the ground beneath them as if the earth were about to yawn and swallow them. Midnight lurched, its ears back, nostrils flaring. "Easy fella," said Jim, stroking the horse's rain-slicked neck soothingly.

Then, an even more terrible sound: thousands of cattle crashing to life in the impenetrable darkness and the pouring-down rain.

"Jesus," cried Jim as Midnight quickened between his legs.

"Stampede," groaned Lou, the dreaded declaration piercing the noisy night. "Ride to the point, Jim!" he shouted. "Git ahead of 'em! Try to turn 'em back on themselves."

Carried forward by Midnight's instincts, Jim quickly reached the front of the thundering mass of shapes.

Looking back, he gaped in horror. Like trees swept by a flood, the great, long horns of the raging herd bobbed amidst the torrent, glistening in the momentary bursts and flashes of the unrelenting, goading lightning.

During one bright streak, Jim caught a glimpse of Aaron Place at the head of the herd as if he were the leader of the hellishly mad rush of terrified beeves.

And then Aaron was gone, swamped and swallowed by the river of rampaging beeves that would take all night to quell and dam up. An hour after sunrise, they found the trail boss's crushed body pinned under his dead horse.

"Looks like the horse spilled," said the colonel, kneeling hatless by the bodies. "The horse probably stepped into a prairie dog hole. Fell. The herd ran right over them." He rose, putting on his Stetson and addressing Lou Garrard. "This tragedy aside, how bad was it?"

"The whole thing could have been a lot worse," replied Lou. "Nobody else is hurt that bad. Bumps, scrapes and bruises and a few cuts. No broken bones. As far as the men go, we got off good. It appears that we've lost a couple hundred head of cattle. A dozen or so trampled."

The colonel nodded grimly. "We'll pull up for a day to bury Mr. Place and let the herd settle down. Lou, you'll take over as the trail boss."

"Hot damn, Lou," exclaimed Jim as they walked toward the chuck wagon. "I reckon now that you're the trail boss you'll be changin' your mind about quittin'! Right?"

"It's somethin' to mull over," said Lou. "Yeah, it does complicate things."

"You'll be great at it, Lou," said Jim excitedly. "Just great!"

"We'll see," said Lou. "Time will tell."

At the next dawn, docile after their rampage and obedient to the steady clang of Old Blue's bell, the herd meekly walked north again as cowboys darted at their flanks to string them out. Behind Old Blue and Jim, who was happily riding point at Lou's side, to Frank's chuck wagon in the drag, they stretched for five miles in a rising sun that was shining so brightly that Jim had to shield his eyes with his upraised black hat to see them.

Six days later on a splendidly sparkling May morning as

35

the cattle poured like an ink stain across pastureland, Jim drew rein on Midnight, hooked a knee around the horn of the saddle, rolled a cigarette, lit up and gazed across the tall sweet grass to the gray smudge of chimney smoke and the rooftops of a place that seemed as fabulous and legendary as the ancient and holy cities of his mother's beloved Bible: Bethlehem, Nazareth and Jerusalem. Spurring Midnight, he grinned from ear to ear knowing that the place in the sun to which he galloped beside Lou Garrard was their generation's Babylon, Sodom and Gomorrah rolled into one — the reigning queen of the cow towns: Dodge City.

Chapter Six
Saturday Night on Front Street

Peering in amazement, Jim beheld a throng of cattlemen, buffalo hunters and soldiers from nearby Fort Dodge shoulder-to-shoulder with jostling horses and freighters clogging Front Street at the far side of a wooden bridge that spanned the Arkansas River to both connect and separate the two parts of Dodge City—the sedate and settled neighborhoods of the permanent residents and the boisterous, seasonal visitors who roared into town with their herds of longhorns and pockets jingling with the money the cattle provided—the city's reason for being.

Square on the hundredth meridian, the bustling new cow town had sprouted beside the Arkansas from a scattering of sod huts and rude shacks that had been built by buffalo hunters before the arrival of the Santa Fe Railroad in its long reach westward. With the building of a railhead, left behind were Abilene, Ellsworth, Newton and Wichita. Now it was Dodge City that lured the herds from Texas and claimed the title of Queen of the Cow Towns.

"Never seen anything like this," exclaimed Jim. "I didn't know you could squeeze so many folks together in one place. Fact is, I never seen this many people in one spot in my whole life. It's kind of scary."

"Yeah, there's nothin' like a Sattiday night in a cow town to give a man pause," said Lou knowingly. " 'Specially Dodge City."

37

"You should know, Lou," said Jim with a grin. "You've been in so many of 'em and here last year, right? So you know where all the fun is!"

They'd paused at the bridge to read a large signboard:

DEADLINE!
Persons Intending
To Discharge Firearms
Are Not Allowed
North Of This Sign.
Violators Will Be Arrested
Charles Bassett,
City Marshal

"Looks like they don't put up with lawlessness in Dodge City," said Jim anxiously.

"Never seen a case yet where words stopped a man from doin' what he wanted once he got a bellyful of booze," said Lou, riding onto the bridge.

Proceeding up the broad, dusty, bustling street, Jim barely contained his excitement as he gaped at the garish signs fronting the flanking buildings that seemed to be both old and new at the same time: the Comique, Alcazar, the Opera House, the Lady Gay Dance Hall, the Long Branch saloon, the Green Front, Junction, Old Horse, Alhambra and Long Charlie Carew's Old Dodge with its batwing doors painted Irish green.

"This is the place we're lookin' for," said Lou, sliding from his horse. "Long Charles is an old friend of mine," he said, stepping onto the boardwalk. "I've gotten drunk in Charlie's saloons since he first went into business in Abilene. I guess as long as the railroad keeps pushin' west and openin' new cow towns, Charlie will tag along openin' fresh emporiums just like the last one."

The saloon was one vast room with a sawdusted plank floor and a ceiling of blue-gray tobacco fog pierced by hanging oil lamps that cast yellow light and blue shadows on the people and furnishings below. At the rear rose a bandstand draped in red-white-and-blue bunting with five unoccupied chairs and naked music stands. The bar ran down the right side, the tallest man Jim had ever seen presiding over it.

Standing higher than most horses, Carew was six and a half feet tall, Jim reckoned. Lanky, he loped with huge strides behind the long bar toward Lou. "Look what the wind blew in," he bellowed above the baritone roar of the saloon. "Hell and damnation, I thought some jealous husband would've planted you six feet under long before this." Eyes as green as the batwing doors shifted to Jim. "Who's this?"

"He answers to the name Tascosa," answered Lou.

"Call me anything except late for chow," said Jim, grinning broadly.

"Welcome to Dodge in spite of the bad jokes," said Carew, grasping Jim's hand. "First time here?"

"Exactly," said Jim. "Looks like a very interesting place."

"Interestin' ain't the half of it," said Carew.

"Seen one cow town, you seen 'em all," said Lou, slapping a dollar coin on the bar. "How far's that go this year, you old crook?"

"Same as last year. Only tonight your drinks are on the house," said Carew, pushing the coin back to Lou and reaching for a bottle of rye.

"First time I ever saw you buy a drink for a customer," teased Lou.

"The generosity's got nothin' to do with you. It's on account of it bein' Tascosa's first cattle drive."

"Much obliged," said Jim as he raised a brimming shot glass to his lips. "Look out guts, here it comes!"

Lou nursed his liquor, concentrating on talking old times with the tall man behind the bar, a litany of names that provoked laughs, windy tales or sad stories about how this one died or that one was killed. "What about Bat Masterson?" asked Lou presently. "Is he still hangin' around these parts?"

"Yeah, he drifted away for a time, but he came back into town a while back," said Carew, mopping the top of the bar with a rag. "I guess you could say he's had his fill on adventurin' across the frontier. He got himself shot up a bit down in Sweetwater a year ago. He was walkin' with a cane for a while, but now he's gettin' back into fine fettle. He and his brother Ed are deputy marshals these days, along with Wyatt Earp. You remember Wyatt. The three of 'em do most of the law keepin' while Charlie Bassett lolls around the office. You should see him! He's balooned to three hundred pounds, at least. Bat'll prob'ly show up sometime durin' the night, makin' his rounds. Unless Wyatt's got the early patrol duty. Course, they'll all be workin' later, once the sun goes down and things heat up. There's several outfits in town. And you know cowboys when they're paid their trail wages and decide to bust loose." He paused with a frown. "The Ludlums are also in town."

"Shoot, I was hopin' I'd miss them," said Lou grimly.

"Well, they're here," said Carew with a shrug as he turned to tend the other customers strung down the length of the bar.

"Who are the Ludlums?" asked Jim.

"Brothers. Bunch of owlhoots. I had a little trouble with 'em last year."

"What trouble?"

"Like all man's troubles. A disagreement over a woman. The worst of the Ludlums—Mickey—was beatin' up on one, and I insisted he cease."

"What *about* women?" asked Jim, glancing side long at Carew. "I reckon there are plenty of sportin' women in Dodge."

"Enough to go around a couple of times," said Carew.

Jim surveyed the saloon. "Don't see any here, though."

"They'll abound once the sun goes down and the music starts."

At that moment, as Jim helped himself to another rye, the room hushed, and every head looked toward the batwing doors.

Pushing through with the slithery ease of movement of a lion was a gaunt, heavy-boned, loose-limbed and powerfully framed man with the badge of a deputy city marshal pinned to his supple leather vest.

"That's Wyatt Earp," said Carew for Jim's benefit.

"He looks capable," muttered Jim.

The deputy drifted through the room making his presence felt, then eased toward the bar. His long face was surprisingly pale with deep-set, blue-gray eyes that appeared to take in the whole room at once. Lips drawn into a thin line were almost hidden by a heavy, tawny mustache that drooped to a massive jaw. From his hip dangled a long, heavy Colt Special, a firearm that seemed better suited for clubbing than shooting, Jim thought as Earp sidled between him and Lou, leaning an elbow on the bar. "Evening, Marshal," said Jim, feeling edgy and nervous.

"Howdy," said Earp. "Haven't seen you before. You just blow in from Texas?"

"That's right," said Jim. "Came up from the Staked Plains with Colonel Goodnight's herd."

"I know the colonel," said Earp. "A gentleman and a real upright individual. Don't do anything to embarrass him, kid."

"I'll try not to," said Jim, feeling as chastised as when his mother had scolded him.

"Hello, Charlie," said Earp with a nod at Carew. "How's business?"

"Thrivin', Wyatt."

"That's what I like to hear. Peaceful and quiet?"

"Like a church meetin'."

"Let's hope it stays that way."

"Any reason it shouldn't?"

Earp took a deep breath. "The Ludlum boys are in town and drinkin' down at the Long Branch at the moment. So Bat and me are visitin' all the places, lettin' everybody know they're here. I got this side of the street; Bat, the other." He turned now to Lou. "As for you, Mr. Garrard, you stay clear of the Ludlums this time."

"Whatever you say, Marshal," said Lou, raising his arms.

41

"I'm a peaceable fella."

Earp stabbed a finger into Lou's chest. "Glad to heard it."

" 'Scuse me, Marshal," blurted Jim, "but if these Ludlums are trouble, why not just run 'em out of town?"

"Because, young man, they haven't broken any laws," said Earp. "Unless they do, all I can do is keep an eye on 'em. I keep an eye out for all would-be troublemakers."

"Is that why you picked me out?" Jim gulped. "Did you think I was one of the Ludlums?"

"Hardly! Mickey, Mel, Frank and Sid are Kansas boys, born and bred, whereas you've got Texas written all over you; pure, greenhorn Texas." Stroking his mustache, he chuckled. "You can always tell a Texan, though not much. This is your first time on a drive?"

"Right. But my pal Lou's been on plenty of 'em," said Jim with a nod at Lou. "So, if you're worried about this greenhorn Texan, rest your mind. I'm in good hands."

Earp fixed Lou with studying eyes. "I'll be expecting you to see that this kid behaves himself," said Earp. He turned to Jim. "You go wrong by an inch, and your ass'll feel the toe of my boot. Or worse. You hear me?"

"Loud and clear." Jim gulped.

"Good," said Earp, lurching away from the bar to drift through the saloon again, pausing here and there to chat with others before stepping through the batwings again and onto Front Street.

"Do you believe that?" growled Jim. "What's he think I'm goin' to do? Shoot up the place? Stick up the bank?"

"Could be." Charlie Carew laughed, refilling their glasses from the bottle of rye. "You do look sort of dangerous!"

With the attention-grabbing screech of a fiddle, the band announced its presence and plunged into a reel. Then the leader, a tall and spare youth with a booming voice, sang, "Oh, brandy is brandy any way you fix it; But a Texian is a Texian any way you fix it."

Jeers and whistles erupted from the Texans in the audience, but the singer continued:

42

"When other folks have all gone to bed,
The devil is a-workin' in the Texian's head."

Regarding this as a compliment, the Texans roared their approval.

Tapping his toe and grinning, Jim muttered, "This is mighty fine. Yes indeed, mighty-fine."

Another reel began, and as if by magic, women appeared to clutch the arms of some of the men and pull them to their feet to dance. "Well, Tascosa, there's the women you were lookin' for," said Lou. "Whyn'tcha grab yourself one of those gals?"

"Don't dance," whispered Jim, hearing the voice of his mother: *Dancing is the snare of the devil!* "Never learnt how," he added, peering through the smoke haze at the alluring women. "Those are mighty fancy ladies, though, ain't they?"

With a lopsided grin, fueled by the whiskey, smoking the cigarettes he had deftly rolled for himself and Lou, he watched the dancing women, keeping time to the music with his feet. Jim savored everything—the crowd, the noises, the smells—the sheer joy of being in the midst of so many people having so much fun. He relished this sudden break with the relentless manliness of the trail and gave himself over to the shrill laughs of the women with their bright dresses and painted faces. Only for a moment did he let go of his happiness to remember that his friend and boss Aaron Place would never again know these joys.

But the river of splendors of this first night in a cow town, when he had earned the right to call himself a cowboy, had a dark undercurrent. It took the form of the apparent peril that came in the shape of the Ludlum brothers. Surely, he thought, they had to be a fearsome group if Wyatt Earp and Bat Masterson were expressing concern about their presence in Dodge. He pondered what had happened last year between the Ludlums and his friend. Might there be trouble again? He worried about Lou, turning to look each time the green batwing doors of Long Charlie's

43

saloon swung open, wanting to see who came in, though he had no idea what the Ludlums looked like. Could this be one of them? he wondered each time someone entered.

Is this a Ludlum? he asked himself as he observed a man in a black suit with a wheat-colored brocade vest and a Colt pistol holstered under a frock coat. Medium sized, he seemed to be in his twenties with brown hair, a small well-trimmed mustache, rosy smooth-shaven cheeks and searching blue eyes. He walked with a slight limp, making straight to the bar, but he did not seem to need the assistance of the silver-topped walking stick that swung easily from his left hand. "Wyatt told me you were in town," he said, addressing Lou. "Long time no see."

"Hello, Bat. I heard you were mixed up in that fracas a couple of years ago at Adobe Walls down in the Texas Panhandle," said Lou.

" 'Deed I was," said the man in black, laying the gleaming black walking stick with its glinting silver knob on the bar.

Lou introduced him. "Jim, meet Bat Masterson, deputy marshal of Dodge City. Bat, this is my pal Jim Hardin, called Tascosa by those who know him best."

Masterson grasped Jim's hand. "Any friend of Lou's is a friend of mine, Tascosa."

"When word reached us about Adobe Walls, Colonel Goodnight and I figured you'd cashed in your chips and your scalp was swayin' from some young Comanche buck's belt," said Lou. "Maybe even from Chief Quanah Parker's himself."

"I don't mind telling you, it was damned close," said Masterson, chuckling, his eyes alight with the glee of a man who appreciated that nothing could be so exhilarating as being shot at without effect. "I'm a city man now. Civilized."

Lou drew aside the frock coat to reveal the silver star pinned to the fancy vest. "Never figured I'd see you sportin' a lawman's badge."

"The pay's good." Masterson smiled. "And there's no heavy lifting! I like it. Some folks are trying to talk me into running for the top job come next election."

"Somehow I can't see you settlin' down," said Lou. "You've got the same malady that afflicts me — the wanderlust."

Masterson lit a cheroot. "Every man's got to put down roots sometime."

"That's exactly right," declared Jim. A little drunk, he boldly clapped a hand on Masterson's shoulder. "I've been tryin' to tell Lou that he's got a perfect set-up at the Palo Duro. Maybe you can convince him, Mr. Masterson."

"Call me Bat. Convince him of what?"

"Ever since he got to talkin' to some drummer-man about the silver mines in a place called Tombstone way out in the Arizona Territory, Lou's had this crazy notion that if he went there he could strike it rich."

Masterson exhaled cigar smoke. "Sounds mighty appealing."

"Cripes, Bat," exclaimed Jim, shaking his head. "I asked you to talk him out of it!"

"I was going to say, if you'd let me finish young man," said Masterson patiently, "that I've never been one to put much store in the pot o' gold — in this case, pot o' silver — at the end of the rainbow. And I find it hard to imagine Lou scratching around in the dirt for nuggets."

"Thank you very much," said Jim with a nod of vindication.

"What about a poker pot?" asked Lou, finishing his drink. "Care to get a game goin', Bat? Or does that badge of yours prevent it? Have you given up on the vices?"

"Not at all," said Masterson, waving the cheroot in the air. "I'll be pleased to take your lucre." He smiled toward Jim. "What about you, Tascosa? You joining us?"

"No thanks," answered Jim, shaking his head furiously. Any card playing was sinful, his mother had taught and the Reverend Dilbert had preached. "I worked too damned hard for my pay to gamble it away on cards," he said, drawing up a chair behind Lou at a round table near the band-

45

stand. "I'll settle for watchin'." Not only the game, he thought, but the door for any sign of the Ludlums.

"Mind if I take a hand?" asked a grizzle-bearded teamster who soon explained that he was stopping for the night on his way to Denver with a load of house furniture direct from Kansas City.

"More in the game, the more I pocket," said Lou confidently.

Claiming the fourth chair was a young cowboy introducing himself as Roy Fields from the Cantrell ranch near San Antonio. Reeking with rose water, he had a fresh porridge bowl barbering that plastered down his brown hair with oily pommade and a fresh blue shirt and stiff new Levi's blue denim pants.

"Suppose we allow the deputy marshal the honor of dealin' first," said Lou, passing the deck.

"I'm only in for a couple of hands," said Masterson, dealing briskly, flipping the cards out with little clicks. "It's early now, but in a little while the town'll be heating up, and my place will be out on Front Street, 'specially with the Ludlums on the loose. Wyatt told me he warned you about them being here, Lou."

"He told me they're in town."

"Fact is, Wyatt and I were hoping you'd go back out to your camp."

"I like it here fine."

"The Ludlums are not the sort to forget," said Masterson.

"I ain't worried, Bat. Play cards."

"Wyatt and I will be keeping our eyes peeled for them, but we can't be everywhere. It's Saturday night, and there'll be a couple hundred fellas out on a toot all up and down Front Street. That's why I'm in this game for only a few quick hands."

"I reckon that when the time comes for you to leave and carry out your duties I'll have cleaned you out anyway." Lou chuckled.

Assessing the hand over Lou's shoulder, Jim found a trio

of treys, the jack of clubs and the ace of spades. The teamster took three. The cowboy held pat. Masterson discarded two. "I'll take one," said Lou.

Picking up his fresh card, he arranged the ace of clubs next to the spade and called, raising the ante a dollar and watching the others fold.

"If I hadn't dealt," muttered Masterson as Lou spread out his cards in triumph, "I'd say there was somethin' fishy goin' on."

The cowboy won the next hand, but it was his only win as the fortunes of the game shifted to the teamster for two hands, to Masterson for the next and then to Lou for the next four. But they all played cautiously, wagering low and risking little. "And now," said Masterson after half an hour, sliding back his chair and picking up his walking stick, "you'll have to deal me out. Time for me to get back to work."

As he approached the batwing doors, he was met by a short, stocky youth who held open the doors and blurted cockily, "Allow me, Marshal! Pleasant evenin' ain't it?"

"It was till now, Mickey," said Masterson coldly. "Where's the rest of your nefarious tribe?"

"Oh, they'll be along directly. You know us Ludlums. We allus hang together."

"Yeah, and the day that you really do hang together can't come too soon," said Masterson, pushing past.

Laughing and letting the doors swing back, Ludlum faced the room with his thumbs hooked on the gunbelt that slanted downward from left to right to the Colt six-shooter holstered and laced to his thigh. From a slouching hat that was more brim than crown to his brush-scuffed boots, he was dressed in prairie dog brown and stood with his legs apart. A sharp, stubbled chin jutted defiantly. "Tell me if I'm wrong," he bellowed as he approached Charlie Carew at the bar, "but was me and all my kinfolk just insulted by the deputy?"

"I wasn't payin' attention," said Carew, tilting forward,

47

supported by stiltlike arms on the bar. "You here to gab or drink?"

Ludlum tipped back his hat. "You got any cold beer?"

"The ice is all gone," snapped Carew. "You want your beer cold, come back in December."

Drumming stubby fingers on his gunbelt, Ludlum sneered. "Then, make it a glass of that horse piss you call whiskey," he said, twisting to gaze to the back of the room. "Hey Charlie," he asked, squinting, "Would that be Lou Garrard back there playin' poker?"

"None other," answered Carew. "And I don't want no trouble between you two like last year. I got my prize Irish shillelagh back here behind the bar, and I'll brain the first one who causes any ruckus. Do I make m'self clear?"

" 'Deed you do, Charlie. Still, I s'pose I ought to pay him my respects."

"It's a free country," said Carew as Ludlum strode to the back of the saloon, "but you're warned!"

Standing beside Lou, Ludlum asked, "This a private game or can I sit in? I see there's an empty chair."

Hooking the leg of it with his toe and sliding it toward Ludlum without looking up, Lou said, "You want to play, cut the jabberin', sit down and ante up."

"Hey Lou," said Jim nervously, "don't you think we'd better be goin'? We got the hosses to tend to. And we still ain't found a place for ourselves to bed down. I never been in a hotel and—"

"Plenty of time for all that," snapped Lou. "If you're worried about the hosses, go an' see to 'em."

"I guess they can wait," said Jim, smarting from the harshest words he'd ever heard from Lou and studying Ludlum as Lou raked in the cards. "I'm not leavin' without you."

"Suit yourself," said Lou, shuffling.

"I'll cut," said Ludlum, reaching for the deck.

Lou dealt, giving himself a pair of red queens.

"Take two," said Ludlum, flicking out the discards.

48

The teamster took three; the cowboy, two.

"Dealer also takes three," said Lou. Holding his queens close to his chest, he added the seven of spades, the five of diamonds and queen of spades. "Lucky ladies," he said, spreading the winning hand on the table.

"Nobody's luck lasts forever," said Ludlum, smirking as the teamster took up the cards to deal. "Luck's a woman, you see. And the man she fancied last year might be dumped for another this year."

"We all know the way you have with women," said Lou, scooping up his hand. "So why don't we just let Lady Luck make up her own mind?"

Ludlum tilted back in his chair. "Whatcha mean by that remark, Garrard?"

"Whatever you take it to mean," snapped Lou.

"I don't take it politely," said Ludlum, settling on the chair and sliding it back.

"Take it anyway you like," growled Lou.

"Lou, c'mon. Let's go," pleaded Jim urgently as Ludlum rose to his feet and the saloon fell silent like the sudden, ominous quiet before a storm breaks with the crack of thunder and the sharp stab of lightning. But this thunder was a pair of pistols firing as one, and the lightning was tongues of fire from two gun barrels. Then, a terrible, motionless second as Lou stared blankly across the poker table at Mickey Ludlum gazing back vacantly. And then the scrape of Ludlum's chair sliding away and a splintering of wood as it broke.

As if he'd been yanked off his feet like a puppet on a string, Ludlum tumbled backward to the floor with blood spurting from the middle of his chest like water gushing from a spring. Bending over him, Jim gazed with fascination at lifeless eyes staring past him at the smoky ceiling. Jerking his own eyes toward Lou, he muttered, "He's deader than a doornail."

"He always was a damn fool," said Lou. "Worse than that, he always was a lousy draw. Missed me by a foot even when he pulled first. You all saw that, right? He cleared leather first."

"That's the way it was. I'll swear to it if I have to," said Charlie Carew, towering above the body on the floor. "But the best thing for you to do right now, Lou," he continued, "is to hightail it outta Dodge, 'cause the other Ludlums'll be gunnin' for you, and they won't be lookin' for a fair fight. You hang around Dodge once they hear about this and you're beggin' for a bullet in the back. I suggest you make for the Staked Plains startin' this minute."

"Reckon you're right." Lou sighed, holstering his Colt. "Only it won't be Texas." He flashed a smile at Jim. "There's a spot a mite west of the Panhandle that I have in mind, eh, Tascosa?"

"And I'm comin' with you," exclaimed Jim.

Lou shook his head. "No. You belong at the Palo Duro. You're not the wanderin' kind like me."

"I ain't goin' back there, Lou. I'm goin' with you. If the Ludlums decide to come after you, that's no time for you to be by yourself."

"Just the opposite, amigo! I'll travel farther and faster alone. Besides, Colonel Goodnight's goin' to need you! First he loses Aaron. Now I'm abandonin' him. You're the best hand he's got left."

"Lou, I'm goin' with you and that's that."

"The fact of it is," shouted Wyatt Earp, pushing through the batwings "nobody's goin' anywhere till I find out what happened here to my satisfaction. So, suppose the two of you accompany me to the office, where you'll be the guests of the people of Dodge City till morning."

"You're lockin' us up?" demanded Lou. "This was a clear case of self-defense, as the folks here will swear."

"They can swear all they like," said Earp, drawing his long gun. "In the mornin'."

When the click of the key and the squeal of the hinges of

the cell door being opened woke Jim, Wyatt Earp was a black cutout against the dull morning light at his back, peering down at him. "Time for you to git up and git out of town," said the marshal. "And don't come back till next year. And count your lucky stars that you're still alive."

Sitting up sleepily and rubbing his jaw, Jim felt the scratch of stubble; a proper beard coming in at last. Yawning, he asked, "Where's Lou?"

"Prob'ly halfway to Arizona Territory by now."

"He's gone?" Jim shouted, bolting up.

"Left around midnight."

"Without me!"

"That's the way he wanted it. And I agreed with his thinkin'. I figured it would be best for you and him to separate."

"What gives you the right to decide things for me?"

Earp tapped his thumb against his badge. "This."

"That's nothin' but tin. Tin badge. Tinhorn marshal," said Jim bitterly.

"I'll chalk that talk up to your youthful age," said Earp.

"I'll follow him, you know. I'll ride like hell to catch up with him."

"You'll wind up lost the first day. That man's not goin' to leave a trail for anybody to follow. Not for the Ludlums and certainly not for a greenhorn such as you. Besides, I'm not lettin' you loose on your own. Bat Masterson will accompany you out to your camp and turn you over to Colonel Goodnight, who's puttin' up quite a bit of bail money to get you out of this calaboose."

"Bail money? How can you get bail money for somebody who ain't done nothin' unlawful?"

Earp tapped his badge again. "This little piece of tin gives me that authority."

Defeated, Jim sank dejectedly onto his cot. "Know what you are, Earp? You are a snake."

"Perhaps so, kid. Perhaps so."

"Do I get time to buy me some breakfast?"

"If you want to chance running into one of the Ludlum boys just to stuff yourself with steak and eggs. . . ."

Jim grunted. "I get the point, Marshal. Where's that crippled deputy of yours? Where's Masterson? Sooner I get outta sight of you, the better."

"Bat's waitin' out front with your horse. That's a mighty fine mount you have. A real black beauty."

"Lou gave 'im to me."

"For what it's worth, I'm sorry about your friend's troubles."

"It *was* self-defense."

"That won't cut any ice with the Ludlums. They'll be looking for you, you know. They're a vengeful bunch. That's why the only thing I want to see of you is the north end of that black horse of yours, with you on it, headin' south. Texas is the best place for you and as fast as possible. You've got a good job workin' for a real good man. Why throw that away for a pig in a poke?"

Recalling that he'd said the same thing to Lou, Jim barked a laugh. "Yeah, what you're sayin' makes a lot of sense," he muttered. "Even if you are a snake."

Chapter Seven
The Letter

As if things weren't bleak enough returning to the Palo Duro without the companionship of the man who'd taught him to be the cowboy he'd longed to become, Jim endured the harshest weather in memory. Gripped by searing drought that dried up the streams and parched the grass, the Staked Plains were then hit by an early winter of howling blizzards and deep, stranding snows. Hundreds of cattle that didn't die-up from thirst in the summer froze to death in the cold, so the herd that Jim bossed north to Dodge City the following spring was half the number that Lou and Old Blue's bell had led up Colonel Goodnight's trail the previous season. The second year was the same, if not worse, and Jim wondered if nature itself were protesting the absence of Lou from the high plains, unleashing a third season of miseries that took the form of unrelenting rains that flooded streams and turned them into snake-infested, bug-swarming, sickness-provoking lakes and bogs. But these torments and the work of being the colonel's top hand had transformed the green boy who had ridden point with Lou up to Dodge City into a tough, sinewy young man capable of meeting any challenge the Staked Plains cared to throw his way.

Whiskers that he'd despaired of ever seeing on his chin, he now had to shave regularly. But he'd allowed a full and rather handsome mustache to sprout, though he kept it neatly trimmed because Moonlight Rose told him she couldn't abide what she called "beer-soaked, t'baccy-stained straggly lip hair."

There was even a fair growth of hair on his chest, which was fuller and deeper now, as his shoulders were wider, arms stronger and legs more agile and capable whether herding cattle, dancing a two-step on the dance floor of the Horse Blanket or cavorting with Rose in a big brass bed upstairs.

He was two inches taller than the last time Lou had laid eyes on him before he bounded into his saddle to escape the murderous wrath of the Ludlums that fateful night in Dodge.

Had Lou not killed Mickey Ludlum, Jim ruminated as the fierce elements ravaged the plains, it would have been Lou and not him rising to the top of the heap to boss Colonel Goodnight's ranch.

As top hand, he had the colonel's permission to use the fancy writing paper that was ordinarily for business purposes. Kept in a small cedar chest in the tack room of the main barn behind the main house, it was almost as stiff and heavy as cardboard. A heading was embossed in royal purple at the top:

The JA Ranch
Palo Duro Canyon.

In slow, deliberate hand, he wrote the date:

Friday, May 6, 1881

Below it he wrote "Dear Lou" with a scratchy nib of pen on paper that made his blood run cold.

"As I take pen in hand," he wrote, "I see that it has been more than a year since I wrote you last time."

He paused to dip the pen in the blue ink of a heavy brass inkstand carved with the ungainly and downright ugly figures of longhorn cattle and wonder if that letter or any of the others he'd written had ever reached Lou. No replies had been received.

"It's hard to believe it is goin' on four years since we was in Dodge City and the last time I seen you," he wrote, grinning

54

over the memory of that unforgettable night and letting his mind wander through the amazing events that had occurred since.

"You'll be right proud of me, I'm sure," continued the letter, "because Colonel Goodnight has made me his top hand—the boss of all the men who work for him in the Palo Duro. It's a mighty important job, and I want you to know that if it wasn't for you and all the stuff you taught me back when I was a lowly greenhorn, I couldn't have gotten to the top the way I have."

"Yeah, Lou," he said aloud as he read what he'd put down on the paper in his big, bold, careful penmanship, "I'd be nothin' without you."

"You'll get a kick out of this, Lou," he wrote. "We had these English visitors at the ranch who were here doin' business with the colonel. Well, one was at supper with us at one of the range camps last week when this English dude makes up his mind that he wasn't goin' to sit next to some smelly cowboy all covered with blood from castratin' bull calves. So he ups and moves his plate to the other end of the table. The hand he was referrin' to was one of the new boys, Hank Smith, who never did take to strangers. If you'd been here to know Hank, you'd've liked him. So Hank got even with the insult by loopin' a rope on that Englishman's tent pole that night and yankin' it down. The Englisher was fit to be tied and demanded the colonel fire Hank, which he did; only he rehired him once the Englishman was gone. The colonel called the Englishman an overbearin' son of a bitch. Ain't that a hoot?"

What a damn fine man the colonel is, Jim thought, pausing in his writing.

The paper had been barely touched, he noted, frowning. *What else is there to say?* he thought.

There was Apple Axe! "You remember him," he wrote. "The fat bartender at the Horse Blanket Saloon? Well, he got his left eye poked out by ridin' drunk into a yucca plant about a year ago. That empty socket was disgustin' to see, believe me! So after receivin' lots of complaints from customers, Apple Axe sent off to someplace in Chicago and got himself a glass eye. But the darned thing didn't fit too well, so he tried packin' it with a wad of cotton, which left him with this white fringe stickin' out. The result was somethin' hideous. Even worse than him without an eye. So he finally gave up on glass eyes and started wearin' a black patch. Anyway, he got himself shot and killed the other day for a reason I didn't hear."

There are too many shootings in Tascosa these days, he thought grimly, wetting the pen tip once more.

"Tascosa's even wilder than ever," he wrote, "and all of us feel sort of nervous when we ride in on Satiday nights for a little likkerin' up at the Horse Blanket, some card playin' and, of course, for the women."

This was the stuff Lou would tease him about if he were here, Jim thought, smiling with pleasure. Lou had appreciated nothing better than ribbing him about women.

"Moonlight Rose—you remember her!—has taken a real fancy to me," he continued, "so it's with her that I spend my time (and my money, ha! ha! ha!) when I go to town. But sometimes when I'm with her, all I want to do is talk. Ain't that amazin'? And she lets me ramble on and on without complaint. Fact is, I suppose, she's pleased to get the rest. Ha, ha, ha!"

There was something more between himself and Rose, Jim thought as he looked over what he'd written. Was it love? Could a man be in love with a whore? That was a question he could ask Lou about in person but not in a letter, he decided.

"A change of subject is in order right about here," he said out loud.

"Tascosa's been on a real boom," he penned. "There are some new ranches that opened up, and there's so many folks pourin' into town to do business they even put up a hotel called the Exchange that has three bedrooms and a spacious dinin' room that's also used as a ballroom for dancin' on special occasions."

56

He stopped a moment to bark a laugh and remember a joke, which he hurriedly put in the letter. "One of the new hands, a kid named Jody Taylor, told this one. Why is my new britches like a cheap hotel? No ballroom! Of course, I expect there are lots of grander hotels out there in Tombstone with plenty of ballrooms. Maybe I'll stay in one if I ever get out there for a visit!"

He lifted pen from paper again to stare blankly into the dim corners of the lamplit tackroom as a wave of cold loneliness suddenly overcame him. What might have happened if he'd chosen not to return to Texas? he wondered. Suppose he'd ridden out of Dodge City back then with Midnight pointed westward? How would it have been if he'd caught up to Lou and gone to Arizona too?

What was Lou doing at that very moment? Where was he out there? Was he in Tombstone or might that wanderlust of his have started itching again and drawn him farther away? To where? California? Down Mexico way? Or was he still there in Tombstone, bellied up to some bar in some saloon? Could he be thinking of his old pal Tascosa, perhaps? Did he miss not riding into Tascosa and carousing with the Tascosa Kid?

Shaking off the thoughts, he resumed writing. "Things can get a bit testy between the reg'lar folks who live in Tascosa and the newcomers. Which brings me to the story of old man Chase and the ruckus that he started last spring when some owlhoot fresh up from the Nueces Strip came stumblin' drunk out of the Horse Blanket and seen this duck waddlin' in the road and promptly shot its head off. Well, that got old Chase's ire up, so Chase says to the owlhoot, 'From now on you'd best keep the peace around here and leave that gun of yours holstered.' With that the Texan let go a shot into the ground between old Chase's feet. So Chase wheels round, stomps into his house and returns with a double-barreled shotgun and blows that owlhoot right out of the saddle. And the law didn't do nothin' about it. So, you can see, if a duck ain't safe in

Tascosa these days, who is? Anyways, whether Tascosa is wild or not, tomorrow is Satiday and the last one before I have to make my annual summer's ride around the entire ranch—there's a million acres to the colonel's holdings now, Lou. Can you believe that? So Jody Taylor and some of the boys and me are goin' into town, where I will leave this letter in the keepin' of Moonlight Rose to give to the westbound mail hack next time it passes through."

He paused, closing his eyes and smiling a little as he stroked his fine, trim mustache and thought about seeing Rose again. How long since the last time? Several weeks!

"In the hope that this letter reaches you soon and finds you well, I will close now," he wrote quickly. "Got to get me some sleep so's I'll be wild and woolly and ready for anythin' when we hit Tascosa tomorrow."

He signed it, "Your friend, Jim Hardin, known to you as Tascosa."

On a long, elegant envelope that went with the fine stationery, he penned:

Mr. Lou Garrard
General Delivery
Tombstone
Arizona Territory

Just past noon the next day, with the letter carefully stowed in a saddlebag draped behind Midnight's neck, he rode into Tascosa with six of the hands. A mix of old faces and new, they were all older than he except for Jody Taylor, a wild fifteen-year-old from the Rio Grande country of Texas who'd been hired two years after Lou had lit out from Dodge for Arizona. Lou would have taken to Jody, he expected, just as he'd taken to greenhorn Jim Hardin.

"From the way you talk about him all the time, this Lou Garrard must'a been the greatest cowboy there ever was," remarked the young Texan as they proceeded toward Tascosa.

"Well, Jody—" Jim chuckled—"I reckon he was at that."

"From what I been told about what happened up in

Dodge," said Jody, drumming fingers on the Colt .45 strapped to his narrow hips, "he was pretty damn good with a six-gun, too, hunh?"

"The best," answered Jim.

Jody shook his head, smiling crookedly, his sky-blue eyes alight with excitement. "The word I hear around the ranch is that you were better."

Jim snorted. "That's bull."

"Frank the cook says Lou Garrard admitted so himself!"

"Jody, if Lou ever said anything like that," Jim answered, "he was just bein' kind."

"I'm pretty good with a six-shooter myself, you know," said the kid.

"I didn't know."

"They say Tascosa's a pretty wild place," said Jody, his eyes glinting with excitement and bringing back to Jim's mind the first time he'd accompanied Lou into the town. It was a sharp flash of memory of the mining equipment drummer spinning stories of Tombstone and the light that shone in Lou's eyes as he drank it all in. "How's the women there?" asked Jody, jolting Jim back to the present.

"Tascosa ladies are friendly." Jim chuckled. "For a price."

"I mean to get me one," declared Jody. "And blast the cost."

Dusk was gathering by the time they tied their horses at the crowded hitching rail in front of the Horse Blanket, and Jim turned to Jody. "Let me give you some advice on how to enjoy your time in Tascosa and live to come back again," he said, noting how Jody's face screwed up into the same kind of frown his own father had witnessed many times when he was about to lecture his son, and surprised to hear himself sounding remarkably like a mixture of his father and Lou. "Keep a tight rein on your wallet, your fly buttoned and your gun holstered."

Swaggering onto the plank sidewalk, Jody laughed. "Don't go frettin' about me, boss. I can handle m'self just fine!"

Boss! The word had a fine ring to it, thought Jim as he

followed Jody through the batwing doors and into the uproar of hard-worked men working hard at letting loose. His elbows pried open a space in the phalanx at the long bar. "Business appears to be thrivin'," he greeted the bartender.

Tall and spare, which was unusual for a Mexican, he was known only as Cibola and had replaced Apple Axe, ruling the regulars and transient rowdies with the authority of a toma-hawk stuck under his belt and a handy sawed-off shotgun nes-tled in a sling under the bar. "Been goin' full blast for three days and nights," he said. "There's a bad bunch playin' cards in the back. Four of 'em. The ones in the duster coats. They're all good fer nothin' long riders. The one with his back to the wall is number one. Name of Lothry. I knew him down in Eagle Pass couple of years back. He's a half-breed. Part Apache, part Mexican. He'd cut his grandma's throat if there's money in it. Those with him are his gang. I hear they're wanted for a string of robberies and murders on both sides of the border. I been keepin' my eye on 'em. But so far the lid's managed to stay on." He set down an empty pony glass. "What'll it be for you?"

"Rye," said Jim. "And bigger'n that," he added, pushing away the shot glass and peering through the boisterous room to the four hardcases in the rear. "Is Rosie around?"

"She left about an hour ago headin' for the Exchange to catch forty winks," said Cibola, pouring whiskey into a tall glass. "She said she'd be back around six." He drew out a gold pocket watch, snapping open an intricately engraved cover. "It's four now."

"Then, I guess you'd better keep the ryes comin'," said Jim with a shrug.

"We aim's to please!"

"Look, Cibola," whispered Jim, leaning across the bar. "I want you to do me a favor and keep tabs on how much liquor is bein' consumed by that kid at the far end." He nodded to-ward Jody, who was slanted against the bar with a hand rest-ing on the grip of his Colt. "He's greener than he'd care to admit, and I don't want him gettin' so soused that he winds up rolled in the alley. Or worse, what with that owlhoot quartet in town."

"I'll brain him with my tommyhawk if I have to," Cibola grinned, patting the weapon lovingly.

"Just bootin' him out will do," said Jim. "And if he gives you any trouble, just send someone up to get me." He winked and jabbed a thumb in the direction of the ceiling. "And I'll take care of the matter."

Moonlight Rose appeared at six, drifting teasingly to the bar in her fanciest — and Jim's favorite — frilled, flare-skirted, bosom-revealing dress. "Well, lookee here what the cat dragged in." She sighed, looping his arm in hers. "Been so long since I seen you, I was beginnin' to feel slighted that I wasn't invited to your funeral!"

"I'm alive and well, Rosie." He laughed, hugging her hard against him. "And horny as a bull."

"Well moo, moo, moo." She laughed, tugging him away from the bar and toward the stairway that led up to a gallery with a row of doors to tiny rooms used by the sporting women, including the one where he'd been with Moonlight Rose the first time. But since that day, like him, she had improved her station in life and now claimed the large, airy front room with a commodious brass bed and gilt mirrors. The green-shaded windows overlooking the street were the same ones that had fascinated him as a young lad bursting with the stories he'd been told by the town boys of what went on behind those shades — tales that had stirred the wild imaginings of the child who'd grown into the boss of the JA spread, biggest in the Palo Duro.

Although it was a sultry night, the shades, as then, were pulled down, and the windows were closed against the busy street's inquisitive eyes and ceaseless noise. Yet even with the stifling of the glass and the shades they could not miss hearing the shot that rang out less than half an hour after they'd entered the room. Nor could they not hear the urgent shouts in

61

the street below. Then the thumping of heavy footsteps running across the gallery. The banging of a fist against the door. And Cibola's shouting. "Hey, Jim! You'd better git downstairs. It's that kid of yours. He's been shot!"

He'd been drinking but wasn't drunk, Cibola blurted as Jim raced across the gallery. He'd gotten into a card game with the four long riders. Won a few hands. Piled up a bunch of cash. Quit while he was ahead.

"I guess the four of 'em followed him outside," exclaimed Cibola as they dashed down the steps. "I was busy and didn't notice what was goin' on. Next thing I heard was the shot, and then somebody rushed in sayin' Lothry'd gunned down a kid in the street."

"In the back," muttered Jim angrily as he gently turned the body over. Face-up and with arms flung out, Jody's eyes were wide open but lifeless, like those of a cast-off rag doll. A big red stain marked where the bullet had ripped out through the chest.

A silent crowd formed a grim circle around him.

"Anybody see it happen?" asked Jim, looking up angrily, his voice trembling pleadingly.

"I did," said a young boy excitedly. "They was four of 'em. Strangers to me. Wearin' duster coats."

Jim bolted to his feet and grasped the boy's shoulders. "Did you see where they went?"

Wide-eyed, the terrified boy nodded sharply. "They's, they's, they's—"

"C'mon, boy, spit it out," yelled Jim, shaking the boy.

"They's in the hotel," sobbed the boy, pointing across the street to the Exchange.

"Good boy," said Jim, striding away.

To the right of the small lobby was the hotel's bar, unpeopled by anyone resembling the four Texans. To the left, a dining room blazed with light. Through its doorway, he saw Lothry seated alone at a round table, a bill of fare in his hand.

Gun drawn, Jim took one step into the room. "Where's

62

your buddies, Lothry?"

With an expression that was a cross between puzzlement and alarm, Lothry looked up, riveting his gaze on the gun pointing at him. "Out back seein' a man about a horse."

"Which one of you killed the kid?"

"Don't know what you're talkin' about," said Lothry, laying down the bill of fare.

"Keep your hands where I can see 'em," warned Jim. "I been told it was you that killed the kid."

Slowly, Lothry turned in the chair. "What's it to you anyway? Are you the law?"

"Nope."

A flicker of a smile crossed Lothry's lips. "Then, fuck off."

"You can walk with me to the law or you can die where you sit. It's up to you. Either way, I mean to make you pay for killin' Jody."

Lothry sneered. "Was that his name?"

"Yes, he was called Jody," blurted Jim. "And he was a decent kid," he said, aiming for Lothry's chest. "Jody . . . Taylor."

"He drew on me!"

"Liar! His gun was in his holster."

"You put it there."

"You *are* a snake. You know what I do with snakes? This!" He fired once.

Lothry pitched back.

"Jody Taylor," whispered Jim, stepping forward. "His name was Jody, snake!"

Lothry was writhing on the floor.

"Jody," said Jim coldly, straddling Lothry with his boots and firing again. "Jody was his name," he yelled as Lothry died twisting, snakelike. "Remember it in hell."

There was nothing to do now but skedaddle.

That was the unanimous judgment and advice of the men

and sportin' women of the Horse Blanket Saloon. As justified as the killing of Lothry may have been, to the law it was murder. Stick around Tascosa, and he'd hang for sure.

Unless the rest of the Lothry gang got him, Cibola suggested grimly. Recognizing that there was no way to get at Jim when he was surrounded by his friends at the Horse Blanket, they'd lit out of town fast, he reported. "No doubt to bide their time before coming back to track you down and exact their vengeance."

Best to get out of Texas altogether, advised Moonlight Rose. "You was allus talkin' about hookin' up with that friend of yours."

"Lou Garrard." Jim smiled. "He's out in the Arizona Territory. Tombstone. I just wrote him a letter! I was goin' to give it to you, Rosie, to give to the mail hack next time it comes through."

"The hell with the mail hack, honey," said Rose, hugging him tightly and kissing his cheek the way Jim remembered his mother kissing him. "Deliver the damn thing in person!"

Part Two:
Trail Talk

Chapter Eight
Tales of Bad Men

Unobstructed by any mountain ridges and straight as an arrow over an elevated plain stretching treeless to the horizons, the trail baked in the sun and radiated heat back into the air to form shimmering waves that looked like rippling water and formed mirages like distant lakes. To a thirsty man, Jim thought, the sights might be maddening. But he had plenty of sweet water in four hard canteens hanging from the saddle and a supply for soaking his wipe in a leather pouch cinched to the saddle horn.

Except for himself and Midnight, the only animation was an assortment of sand-colored lizards and other ugly, bug-eyed and flicking-tongued reptiles darting out of the way of the horse's hooves or poised motionless on rocks, staring blankly as he rode past.

Midnight's pace was slow and gently rocking, mindful of the relentless sun.

Squinting from beneath a broad-brimmed hat, Jim found beauty to be appreciated: desert blooms in a vast variety of colors, the dark green thumbs of cactus, the dry brown earth slashed and streaked with a rainbow of hues in jutting ledges of rock, dark blotches where boulders rose above the flatland and, overall, the clear blue sky.

He listened to the strange natural music everywhere: the cries of unseen birds, odd clucking noises of the creeping creatures, the creaking of saddle leather, the plodding of Midnight's hooves upon the Spanish Trail and the occasional shaking tail of the hated, lurking rattlesnake.

As he rode into Las Vegas, a steady but uncooling breeze had come up to twirl the spoked wheel of a windmill that squealed like a stuck pig with each turn and served to remind him of how parched he was.

A crudely printed sign nailed to the mill attracted his attention.

NOTICE TO THIEVES, THUGS, FAKIRS AND BUNKO STEERERS AMONG WHO ARE J.J. HARLIN ALIAS "OFF WHEELER," SAW DUST CHARLIE, BILLY THE KID, BILLY MULLIN, LITTLE JACK THE CUTTER, POCK-MARKED KID AND ABOUT TWENTY OTHERS: IF FOUND WITHIN THE LIMITS OF THIS CITY YOU WILL BE INVITED TO ATTEND A GRAND NECKTIE PARTY, THE EXPENSE OF WHICH WILL BE BORNE BY 100 SUBSTANTIAL CITIZENS.

"What a lovely place, eh, Midnight?" he muttered, riding on to a broad central plaza, abandoned and silent in the noontime glare as the locals sought shade and siesta inside their adobe-walled, slat-roofed structures.

Another sign marked the town's saloon, the Buffalo Bar, on the ground floor of the two-story Amigos Hotel. Inside, faro was in play opposite a short bar, and a six-handed game of poker was under way at an eight-sided, green-covered table at the far end of the cool square room. Strangers being commonplace in a town that seemed to have nothing to offer except a pause on the way farther west, only the bartender looked up at him. As excess in girth as Charlie Carew had been in height, he waddled behind the bar and appeared to be out of breath from exertion, puffing his words. "What'll it be?"

"When you're dry as I am," Jim said, bellying up to the bar, "anything'll do."

"Rotgut rye," grunted the bartender, pouring a tall glass halfway.

"You can top it off," said Jim, slapping down a dollar coin.

"You must hanker to die young."

"How far to the next town?" asked Jim, sipping the tepid whiskey.

"Depends which way you're headin'," wheezed the fat man.

"Southwest."

"That way, it'd be Piños Wells, about a two days' ride, mebbe less if you push yourself, past the Rio Grande River."

"The Rio Grande?" said Jim, wiping his lips with the back of his hand. "I thought that was over in Texas."

"It starts here."

"I'm headin' for Tombstone in the Arizona Territory. Any other rivers to cross?"

"You'll ford the Pecos afore you get to Piños Wells," the bartender answered breathily. "Can't say about Arizona. Never been there myself, though quite a few folks have passed through here goin' that way. They say there's silver and gold there."

"I'm hopin' to join up with a friend, name of Lou Garrard. He prob'ly passed this way couple of years back. Maybe you recall him?"

"I don't ask nobody's name or business."

"How's the Indian situation in these parts?"

"Apaches mostly. The Jicarilla, Mescalero, Chiricahua, Mimbrenos, Coyoteros and some other tribes. Real savages. But the army rounded up most of 'em last year and moved 'em onto reservations. There are a few renegades. So keep your eyes peeled." A grunted laugh turned into a hacking cough. "Better to have peeled eyes," he gasped, "than a scalped noggin!"

Jim surveyed the room. "Can I get a meal here?"

"There's a dinin' room across the hotel lobby. Last eatin' place you'll be seein' for a while, the direction you're goin'. No hotels down that way that I know of, though I heard there was a boardin'house down in Nutt."

"How far's that?"

"Long, long way."

"Who do I see about a room?"

"We got two. The one in back's taken. Yours is the one in the

69

front at the top of the stairs."

"What about a bath?"

"There's a tub and a pump in a shack out back."

Cramped by a large four-poster bed, the room caught the sun, making for a sweaty, sleepless rest, and soon the noises of the street drifted through the open window as the town roused from its slumber. But the bath shack was quiet, and drifting to sleep was easy in the cooling water.

The smells of cooking beef and boiling onions in the cook house woke him.

The dining room was small, affording only four tables, but when he entered it at sundown, there was only one other patron. Seated at a table that had been set for two, he had on a black frock coat and purple vest that reminded Jim of Reverend Dilbert. Beside his plate lay an open book. Black and thick, it appeared to be the Holy Bible.

"Howdy." said Jim respectfully, drawing out his chair.

"Good evening. John Ringo is my name," replied the man in the soft tones of a Southern gentleman as he looked up from his book.

"Jim Hardin's mine."

Ringo raised a long and delicate hand and stroked neatly combed auburn hair. "Any relation to the notorious gunman John Wesley Hardin?"

Odd that a man of the cloth would ask that, thought Jim as he sat. "Everybody asks me that," he said with a shrug. "I was told by my pop that we were kin. But I never met him."

"Well, I have," said Ringo. "This was a while back when I was living in Missouri. I can see where you might find it irksome to be asked about him all the time, Mr. Hardin."

"Folks call me Tascosa."

"That's the name of the town in the Texas panhandle?"

"I grew up there."

"You must be in the cattle business?"

"I was. But I gave it up."

70

"I tried that line of work for a time. After the war, I drifted down to Texas and was signed on for a while with the John Slaughter outfit. But I quickly discovered that the drover's life wasn't for me. Now I'm on my way to Arizona."

"Say, so am I," exclaimed Jim. "There's a place called Tombstone. Ever hear of it?"

Finishing his beefsteak and folding a large red napkin onto the table, Ringo nodded "It also happens to be my destination."

"I've got a pal out there, name of Lou Garrard," said Jim excitedly. "He struck out for Tombstone a few years ago, hopin' to strike it rich in silver. Is that your intention, Mr. Ringo?"

"I've got no objections to striking it rich, but digging in the dirt is about as appealing to me as droving. Gambling is my intention."

"Gambling?" gasped Jim. "And here I was thinkin' that you were a preacher!"

Ringo snorted a laugh. "Just goes to show how looks can be deceiving."

"You must be pretty good if you think you can make gambling a way of living!"

"The secret of success in gambling is in not making as many mistakes as the people you're playing against," said Ringo, lifting his hands and studying them admiringly. "If you're careful, you come out ahead. Like everything else in life, winning at gambling is a matter of applying your intelligence. You appear to be intelligent. You would probably do very well."

Jim shook his head. "Nah. I doubt I'd have the nerve."

"Yes, you do have to have nerve," said Ringo, closing the black book, "but, as William Shakespeare put it in the second act of *King John*, 'courage mounteth with occasion.' "

Jim's eyes turned to Ringo's book. It was not the Bible but *The Metamorphoses* by Ovid. "Even though you're not a preacher, you're obviously a well-educated man, Mr. Ringo."

"Please call me Johnny. Yes, thanks to my family, I have had the benefit of a college education and can now tell a man to go fuck himself in Latin and Greek. But I have discovered that it's life that's the best tutor. And in that school of hard knocks, I've also picked up a few lessons. As have you, I expect."

"Some," said Jim, looking up as the cook brought his meal. "But prob'ly nothing compared to you."

"Yes, you would have been too young to be in the war."

"You fought in it?"

"Yes, I took arms for the cause of the Confederacy."

"Where was that?"

"Up in Missouri. I rode with Quantrill's Raiders. I was about your age. Nineteen."

"I'm twenty, goin' on twenty-one."

"Are you tarrying in Las Vegas or will you be leaving for Tombstone right away?"

"Sun's up and I'm gone," said Jim, chewing the stringy beef. "How 'bout you?"

"There's blessed little to keep me here another day. May I suggest that we travel together?"

"It's fine with me, Mr. Ringo —"

"Johnny!"

"I'd be honored to have your company, but a man of your learning might find an unschooled clod like me kind of boring."

"Never mind that, Tascosa," Ringo laughed. "If you run out of things to say, you may rest assured that I'll never run out of words!"

Spearing a boiled onion with his fork, Jim chuckled. "You can quote some more Shakespeare!"

" 'If a man be gracious and courteous to strangers, it shows he is a citizen of the world, and that his heart is no island cut off from other lands, but a continent that joins to them.' "

"Shakespeare sure had a knack for words."

"I've misled you, Tascosa. That wasn't Shakespeare. It was Francis Bacon. He was a contemporary of the Bard of Avon. There are some scholars who say it was actually Bacon who wrote Shakespeare's plays."

"And what do you say?"

"I say it doesn't matter! It's not who wrote them. It's the words that matter."

Dawn broke cool, but the heat was mounting fiercely as they climbed southward out of the shallow valley of the slow, lazy Pecos. With little goading by Jim, Ringo had been talking since they'd ridden out of Las Vegas, sketching a portrait of a man who now reminded Jim of Lou Garrard: homeless, the footloose wanderer with his eye toward the horizon, the drifter. In keeping with his fine education, he'd started out to be a teacher, but no classroom could contain him. Then came the war and adventuring raids with Quantrill. "That's where I made the acquaintance of Jesse James," he said as they left the Pecos Valley.

"You knew Jesse James?" exclaimed Jim.

"Yep! The little terror himself, though when I first laid eyes on him, he looked mighty puny. He was such a weedy kid that Quantrill didn't want to take him on. But Bloody Bill Anderson took him under his wing, and pretty soon Dingus was showing us all that he could cut the mustard. Jesse was called Dingus at the time. Don't know why. Maybe because it sounded funny. It was easy to make fun of him then. But after the raid on Centralia in '61, nobody poked fun at Jesse anymore, believe me. And since he and his gang took up train robbing as a profession, he's made quite a name for himself. Of course, I haven't seen him for a few years. By the time he was sticking up trains, I was sewing wild oats in Texas and getting arrested for the first time. That was in '76 in what they're now calling the Mason County War. I wound up in the hoosegow. But I escaped and lit out for the Texas Panhandle and the Slaughter outfit. That's when I changed my name to Ringo."

"Your name's not Ringo?"

"It's Ringgold."

"Johnny," sighed Jim. "You're plumb full of surprises."

Proceeding southward, they passed through Piños Wells the next afternoon, pausing only for quenching whiskeys. Next came the crossing of the Rio Grande flowing slowly on the start of its long journey toward Texas and then to the sea. At night they came to Nutt where they indulged in blazing-hot Mexican food in a cantina washed down with mescal — and the same at

Rincon a day later.

Ringo's tales did not diminish as they swung westward through a broad pass flanked by the San Andreas Mountains on their right and the Sacramentos on the left.

That night as he squatted Indian-fashion by the campfire, the yellow and red of the flames flickered in Ringo's deep blue eyes. "The one thing that appealed to me about pushing cattle up the trail to Kansas," he said on a plume of after-supper cigar smoke, "is that a man was accepted with no questions asked. It was a good way for me to disappear for a time. I kind of liked the idea that nobody knew who I was. John Ringgold was left behind. The man in the saddle was Johnny Ringo. Now I've put John Ringgold away forever."

In the cool before sunup as they saddled their horses, Ringo was quiet. "Somethin' wrong, Johnny?" asked Jim.

"Just thinking," said Ringo.

"About what?"

"I was thinking about what I said last night. Just mulling over the strange twists that life can take and the choices a man has to make. He comes to a fork in the road and has to pick the one to follow. The choice he makes is what he has to live with. But what if he'd chosen the other trail?"

"You sound as if you regret the one you took. Do you?"

Suddenly Ringo smiled. "Look at it this way. Tascosa. If I'd taken some other trail, I wouldn't've had the distinct pleasure of making your acquaintance. You're a likeable kid. It's a privilege to ride with you."

Climbing into the saddle, Jim felt a blush rising in his face. "That's mighty kind of you, Johnny."

"Know what I like best about you, Tascosa?"

Jim's face was on fire with embarrassment now. "What would that be?"

"Even though I know your ears must be aching from all the jawing I've been doing, you don't tell me to shut up."

"I like listenin' to you. Johnny." said Jim. "You're mighty entertainin'. This'd be a damn lonely journey without you."

Ringo's eyes fixed on the deep distance. "We'll soon be in Arizona," he said. "Chiricahua Apache country. That's Cochise's territory." The cold blue eyes turned watery. "For a dozen years that tall, straight-as-a-rush, crafty redskin rampaged against the white eyes. But in the end he lost, cooped up by the white man in a reservation until he died, probably of a broken heart." The teary eyes flicked toward Jim. "As for me, when my time comes, I'd prefer a quick bullet than a slow dying surrounded by shattered dreams."

Feeling uneasy, Jim joked. "I hope to die an old man in a woman's arms, shot by the outraged husband."

Ringo's laugh rolled across the bleak landscape and came back at them, echoing.

Three days later with Ringo's well of tales as deep as ever and with the sun dipping low, they splashed through the shallow San Simeon River and into Arizona. "About a dozen miles till we reach Galeyville," said Ringo, "where they've got a fairly decent hotel and several accommodating Mexican women." Turning his head slowly, he had a wide, leering grin. "Ever had a Mexican whore, Tascosa?"

Jim thought of Moonlight Rose. Was she a Mexican? With her black hair and brown eyes, she might have been. But what did it matter? "A woman's a woman," he answered.

"And none is to be trusted." Ringo laughed. "Not the best of them."

Stretched on the south bank of Turkey Creek, Galeyville was deep in dusky shadows. A man who seemed to have a bottomless well of facts, Ringo expounded the town's brief but booming history. It was founded by John H. Galey, an oil man from Pennsylvania, who'd bought a silver claim in 1880, opened the Texas Mine, built a smelter and organized the Texas Mining and Smelting Company. In its shadow sprouted the town which now boasted six merchandise stores, a pair of hotels, two restaurants, two butcher shops, three lumberyards, two blacksmith and wagon shops, a dairy, a jeweler, several lawyers, a justice of the peace, a shoemaker, Wells Fargo office, three doctors and eleven saloons.

They tied up their horses in front of the Dragoon. Looking up at them as they entered, a reedy bartender bellowed, "Well, look who's back!"

"Glad to know I was missed," said Ringo, bellying up to the bar. "Is Curly Bill around?"

"Ain't seen him in a month of Sundays," said the bartender, setting up drinks. "But Ike Clanton passed through 'bout a week ago."

Ringo carried his glass to a table.

"Who's Curly Bill?" asked Jim, following him.

"Curly Bill Brocius. A friend from up in Dodge. I was hoping to run into him. He usually hangs around Galeyville," said Ringo, tilting back in his chair. "I have to admit" — he smiled — "that I didn't cotton to him at first. He was too familiar for my taste. He was all for practical jokes, which never appealed to me. Fact is, it was one of those harebrained deeds that brought us together. I was just stepping out of a barber shop and paused a moment to light up a cigar. The crazy galoot shoots it right out of my mouth. He could have killed me. But did that count? Not to Curly! He stands there laughing and yelling 'What's the matter, cowboy? Can't you stand a little funnin'?' I was mighty angry, but I could see that he didn't mean any harm; so I settled for him buying me a fresh cigar, and we've been friends ever since. He's the one who started talking-up the attractions of Arizona. He's been here awhile, linked-up with Old Man Clanton and his sons. There's Ike, who's somewhat of a loudmouth and does a lot of running around carrying out tasks for the old man. There's Finn, who's a little slow upstairs in my opinion and not much of a man. And there's Billy Clanton, the apple of his old man's eye. But it's Old Man Clanton who's the backbone of the clan. He's got a spread over by the San Pedro a little ways west of Tombstone. And take it from me, Tascosa, there's nothing illegal in these parts that Old Man Clanton doesn't get part of."

"You mean the Clantons are bandits?"

"Tascosa, when it comes to lawlessness—" Ringo laughed — "the Clantons wrote the book!"

Chapter Nine
Tombstone

Hemmed in by the ragged Whetstone, Burro, Mule, Huachuca and Dragoon mountains, the low mesa called Tombstone onto which the kid from Tascosa rode in the company of Ringo on a late afternoon of June 1881 looked like a scar rising above sun-baked, rolling and relentlessly dreary desert carpeted with cactus, scrub brush, yucca, rocky outcroppings and sear unyielding earth — unyielding, that is, save for the precious silver ore that was being gouged out by willful men who proved harder than the ground.

By no means the first, dauntless Ed Schieffelin had turned out to be the luckiest prospector to scour Arizona, sojourning out from Fort Huachuca in 1877 looking for stones. Ignoring warnings about the danger from Apaches and the derisive laughter of the horse soldier who'd predicted that the only stone he'd find would be his tombstone, Ed had scraped and scraped until he'd come across some rich-looking ore. Staking it out, he'd gleefully muttered, "Here is my tombstone." A second find he called the Graveyard. And, in company with his brother Al and an assayer named Richard Gird, he'd opened a rich third dig, dubbed the Lucky Cuss, followed by the plentiful Tough Nut.

Immediately, fearless and foolhardy men with fortunes in their eyes rushed in.

The town that resulted was laid out on a grid pattern around the mines and incorporated with the name Tombstone. By the end of the year, it boasted more than forty houses, cabins and tents and a population of a hundred permanent residents while thousands more built camps roundabout in which the only thing permanent was a hunger for striking it rich.

To slake their other more attainable thirsts, businesses opened and boomed. Of every three, two were saloons or gambling houses. Beyond the assay office and the O.K. Corral on the main drag of Allen Street, east of Third Street, grew Hop Town, the Chinese district.

Because these men were rough in spirit as well as body, a burial ground was also laid out based on the not unreasonable expectation that a number of these reckless men would die with their boots on.

So freshly turned that no marker had yet been placed upon it, a mound of the cemetery's earth caught Jim's eye. "Wonder who that poor soul is," he muttered, gazing sidelong at the nameless grave.

"Never send to know for whom the bell tolls," answered Ringo in the pleasing voice that Jim had grown accustomed to and that suited the teacher Ringo had started out to be until his fortunes directed him otherwise. "Sooner or later, it tolls for all of us and we get our own little patch on Boot Hill, just like that poor cuss, whoever he was."

Wrenching his eyes forward as they neared the leveling off of the climbing trail and the beginning of a broad, straight road that was Tombstone's main drag, Jim grunted, "Make mine later."

"The place has grown even more since I was last here about a year ago," said Ringo as they progressed along Allen Street. "And things look a damn sight more permanent. This might become a genuine town yet."

Twisting from side to side to take in both sides of the street as they picked and dodged their way through a steady flow of other riders, rumbling freighters loaded with the offal of the diggings of eastside shafts, rattling empty wagons going the opposite direction and daring pedestrians in every sort of raiment braving the traffic to reach the other side of the bustling, dangerous street, Jim said, "Looks like Dodge without the herds."

"There's cattle from time to time," said Ringo, signalling Jim to make a righthand turn onto Fourth Street. "We'll wet our whistle at the Capitol Saloon. It's not the fanciest in town — the Oriental claims that title — but it's where I do my imbibing."

"Whiskey's whiskey," said Jim with a shrug, studying the facades along Fourth Street: gun shop, furniture store, tinsmith and the Can Can restaurant on the left and Brown's Hotel on the right, looking little better than the Amigos in Las Vegas.

A one-story wooden rectangle, the Capitol Saloon occupied the southeast corner of Fourth and Fremont. The same as every drinking emporium he'd been in, its long bar on the left was sparsely manned. Behind it, short and thick-chested with slicked-down black hair, droopy walrus mustache and a stub of a black cigar stuck in the right side of his mouth, its keeper looked up with the barest flicker of interest at the new customers stepping through the permanently opened doors, squinted a moment and then exploded with a roar. "Well, I'll be a son of a redskin if it ain't Johnny Ringo!"

"G'day, Moe," said Ringo, shaking hands across the bar.

"Thought you was gone forever," said Moe, chuckling heartily. "The town ain't been the same since you left."

"Quieter, perhaps?" joked Ringo.

"Things *was* a little hot at the time of your departure," guffawed Moe.

"I remember it well." Ringo laughed, taking off his broadbrimmed hat and laying it on the bar. "But the word I got up in New Mexico is that Town Marshal Behan's been given the boot, tossed out of office on the wave of John Clum's civic reform movement, according to reports."

"That's right. The upright editor of the *Epitaph* got himself elected mayor. Then no sooner than Clum took the oath of office, he handed Behan his walkin' papers."

"Don't expect me to shed any tears into my beer!"

"You drinkin' your usual? Double rye, beer chaser?"

"I am indeed. And a double shot of rye for my friend Tascosa," said Ringo, clapping a hand on Jim's shoulder. "Moe, if you ever have the need for a first-class trail companion, you'll find none more pleasing than this young man who's accompanied me without a single complaint about my long-windedness all the way from Las Vegas." He paused to gulp the rye and sip the beer. "There's no better man to ride the trail with, believe you me!"

"Any friend of Johnny's is a friend of mine," said Moe, reaching over the bar and clasping Jim's hand. "And to prove it, your first drink's on the house."

"Much obliged," said Jim with an appreciative nod.

"Since you heard about Behan, Johnny," said Moe, pouring the drinks, "I guess you also got word on who's been appointed in his place."

"None other than Virgil Earp," answered Ringo confidently.

"But did you hear that Virg has appointed his brothers, Morgan and Wyatt, as deputies?"

"That I hadn't heard," answered Ringo solemnly.

"Well, he has," declared Moe, punctuating his words with a slap on the bar.

With a cough that splashed his whiskey, Jim gasped, "Wyatt Earp? Is that the same Wyatt Earp who marshaled in Dodge City?"

"God made only one Wyatt Earp," said Moe.

"Hell and damnation," grumbled Jim, setting down the glass.

"What's the trouble with you?" asked Ringo, his face twisted with concern. "You run afoul of Wyatt Earp somewhere?"

"Sure did." Jim gulped. "He kicked me out of Dodge a few years back."

Ringo grinned. "Tascosa, you once said I was a man of surprises. Well, you've got a few of your own up your sleeve. Have another drink and tell me all about it!"

"It was nothin', really," said Jim, launching a recounting of the events of Lou Garrard's gun duel with Mickey Ludlum. "It was a case of self-defense on Lou's part! But that wasn't goin' to cut no ice with the rest of the Ludlum gang, so Lou lit out. I'd've come with him if Earp hadn't locked me up. For my own good, accordin' to him."

"Which it was, as I see it," said Ringo. "I'm familiar with the Ludlum bunch, and a nastier gang you never will find. But if that's all that happened, I wouldn't worry about Wyatt. I doubt he'll even remember the event."

"Besides that," chimed Moe, "the Earps have bigger fish to fry." He paused, rubbing his jaw, and when he spoke, his voice was low and mysterious. "They've got the Clanton family on their minds."

"The Clantons?" said Jim, turning abruptly to Ringo. "Would that be the Clantons you claim as friends?"

"There's only one set of Clantons," said Ringo, grinning broadly and stroking his mustache. "Moe, this is a fine kettle of fish, indeed! With Clum's reformers to back them up, the Earp brothers are bound to bring things to a head with Old Man Clanton, that's for sure. They've been feuding for as long as I can remember. Golly gee, things aren't going to be as dull in Tombstone as I'd expected!"

"It's even more interestin'," said Moe, his voice rising almost cheerily. "The Earps are also teamed up with someone else you've crossed paths with, Ringo. Doc Holliday."

Ringo jerked his head up and laughed bitterly. "Holliday? That consumptive old fart of a drunk? He'll prove as useful to the Earps as tits on a man. He should stick to being a dentist!" Glancing at Jim, he found a face crinkled with confusion. "All this must have your head swimming, Tascosa."

"A mite," said Jim.

"Then, come sit with me at that table in the back and I'll give you the whole story. Moe, give us a bottle. This story will take some time in the telling!"

He spun the yarn with all the relish of voice and gesture he'd exhibited reciting Shakespeare on the long ride from Las Vegas.

Wyatt had appeared in the raw and bustling boom camp of Tombstone in '79, he began, taking a job as shotgun messenger for Wells Fargo. "He was thirty-one years old and a man with a reputation as a lawman that preceded him from Dodge. Packed a hogleg of a gun some eastern writer of dime novels named Ned Buntline had gifted him with."

81

Jim remembered the gun, an eighteen-inch barrel that seemed the size of a cannon.

"But it wasn't until October 1880 that Pima County Sheriff Charles Shibell appointed Wyatt as deputy," continued Ringo. "The editor of the *Epitaph* had welcomed the choice with exalted praise for Wyatt as a man with bravery and determination." He paused to sip his beer. "Mr. Clum was always a man for superlatives."

"The shotgun job with Wells Fargo," he continued, "went to Wyatt's brother Morgan, a real hothead. Then there's Virgil Earp, who is cool and deliberate like Wyatt."

"Entering the picture now," Ringo went on, growing even more enthusiastic about the tale he was spinning, "is John Henry Behan, who wangled himself an appointment as a deputy sheriff. Well, that didn't sit well with Wyatt, who quit and promptly threw his backing to deputy U.S. Marshal Bob Paul from Tucson, who was challenging Sheriff Shibell in the forthcoming election for sheriff. Behan won. And Wyatt landed the job of deputy U.S. Marshal. That was at a time when I'd run afoul of the law, and since Wyatt and I had had differences in the past, I took off for New Mexico. Now Behan is county sheriff, and the Earps are the law in Tombstone with the wind of reform at their backs."

"But if you and Earp don't get along and you skipped town once to getaway from him, why come back now?"

"Because of the Clantons," said Ringo. "You'll recall me saying that when it comes to matters illegal in these parts Old Man Clanton takes a keen interest?"

"Ah, and since you don't cotton to the Earps, you want to assist the Clantons."

"Don't get me wrong. I've no abiding love for the Clantons either." Ringo chuckled. "There's been bad blood between them and me, too. But if it looks like things between them and the Earps will be coming to a boil, my place is with the Clantons. Those Earps for all their cocky righteousness as they sport lawmen's badges aren't above breaking the law themselves if there's a profit to be made. That's another reason why, if anything happens, I'll be on the side of the Clantons, who are at least honest enough to admit they're crooked. The truth is, if I had my druthers, the Clantons and the Earps would kill each other."

Darkening with worry, Jim muttered, "Do you think gun-play's in the cards?"

Ringo shrugged. "The Good Lord blessed me with many skills when it comes to cards, my friend, but not the ability to tell the future by them. But what's all this to you, anyway, eh? What goes on between the Earps and the Clantons doesn't concern you. You've come to Tombstone looking for your friend Lou. I hope you find him safe and sound. As for me, I've got to be getting along. It's turning dark, and there's another ten miles to the Clanton ranch over on the San Pedro."

"It's only so long, though," said Jim. "Not good-bye."

"Hell no, Tascosa! We'll be seeing one another for sure."

"You made that long ride from Las Vegas a real pleasure, Johnny. Without you, I might never even have found my way to Tombstone."

"There's a boardinghouse just down Fremont, run by Camillus Fly. I recommend it," said Ringo, clapping on his hat. "It's a decent house, affordable. And as to that handsome black horse of yours that I've been admiring since we left Las Vegas, you can stable him right in back of Fly's in the O.K. Corral."

Chapter Ten
Doin' the Town

From the window of his room at the rear of Camillus Fly's Lodginghouse, Jim peered down at the pens, stables and sheds of the O.K. Livery and Corral. "It's a convenience to have that livery so near to your boardinghouse, Mrs. Fly," he said, turning from the window. "Is it reliable?"

"Oh, my yes," said the landlady.

"My horse and I've come a long way together," said Jim. All the way from the Palo Duro. A long time ago. How long had it been, he wondered, since Lou Garrard had cut out the pretty black from Colonel Goodnight's remuda?

Aglow with dwindling daylight, his room on the second floor was plain but as comfortable as the stout and motherly Mrs. Fly could make it. "I'm afraid you've missed supper," she said as she fussily smoothed the yellow cover of the big brass bed. "But there is some hearty soup I could warm up for you," she added, placing a pile of thick white towels on the washstand.

"Don't bother, Mrs. Fly, I'll find me a cafe."

"Restaurant food!" said Mrs. Fly with a shudder and a look of disgust. "It can never be as good as home cooking. After this, you must make sure you have your meals with me!"

"That's a promise," said Jim.

The O.K. could be reached simply by walking out the back door of Fly's or through vacant lots on all sides of the block formed by Third, Fourth, Fremont and Allen streets, but the free-standing wooden square with a flat roof slanted from front to rear that was its office was entered from Allen. Pleased by this convenience, Jim led Midnight through the corral to the street, tethered the horse to the rail in front and went in declaring, "Glad to find you're still open!"

"The O.K. never closes" came the reply from a boy with his feet propped upon an open drawer of a rolltop desk. Standing, he was lanky, gap-toothed and freckle-faced with long hair as yellow as straw and wide, bony, sun-tanned bare shoulders extending from blue bib overalls that years of hard washing had turned almost white.

"I've got a horse to be stabled," said Jim, looking around. "When will the man in charge be back?"

"I'm in charge," said the boy proudly, hooking his thumbs on the overall straps and studying his customer. With a glance, he took in everything: the black hat that had suffered a beating from the elements, the red neckerchief dangling across a sun-weathered shirt, blue hard-worn jeans that fit like a glove and were tucked into Texas boots and the Colt Paterson strapped to his hips. Adding up all that he saw, he said, "How long will you be leavin' the hoss, cowboy?"

"Hard to say," said Jim.

The boy lowered calloused hands. "We got day rates," he said, flicking out a thumb. "We got night rates, week rates, rates by the month," he went on, popping up fingers. "We even got a rate for the year."

There was no telling how long it would be before he located Lou, thought Jim. "Let's say a week to start with," he said. "But it could be more."

From a pigeon hole, the boy drew a sheet of paper. "You want feed?"

"Sure I'll want feed!"

"Some don't," said the boy, picking up a pen and writing. "They figure they come out cheaper if they buy feed from the general store, which they don't."

"You handle the feedin'," said Jim. "But only the best."

"You must love this hoss of yours."

"We've come a long way together."

85

"You want to corral this hoss," asked the boy without looking up, "or do you want a stable?"

"Stable! Nothin' but the finest for Midnight."

"If you really want the finest, you'll want me to tend 'im" said the boy boastfully, rearing back and tapping a thumb against his swelling chest. "But that'll cost extra."

Thoughtfully, Jim chewed his lip. "And what do I get for the extra?"

"Best feed at best price, bathin', curryin', the works. And I exercise 'im every day. Even tend to your saddlin'. You can't go wrong, believe me. I'm the best in Tombstone."

"Whats your name?"

"David Stone but called Chip."

"Well, Chip, I guess you're the man for me. Midnight's tethered out front."

"That'll be a dollar a day."

Jim slid back his hat and grinned. "Includin' the extra?"

"Yep. In advance."

From his shirt pocket Jim drew seven coins and dropped them onto the desk. "Now maybe you can recommend a good place to eat."

"Top of the hog is the fancy place with a Frenchy name, Maison Doree, in the Cosmopolitan Hotel, couple a blocks west on Allen. There's cheap Chinee chow, chop suey and stuff, at Sam Chung's in Hop Town, west on Allen."

"Where would you go?"

The boy made a face. "I'd go home."

"But if wanted to take some of that extra you're chargin' me" — grinned Jim — "where'd you spend it?"

"The Can Can on Fourth."

"And what's the best saloon in Tombstone?"

"If it's beer you want, then it's the Eagle Brew'ry. They got it by the bucket. Ten cents for a big 'un. Five for a small 'un. If you want hard liquor, the best is at the bar at the Oriental."

"And what's a fella do for entertainment in Tombstone?"

"If it's a musical show you want, there's the Schieffelin Concert Hall." Mischievous blue eyes again assayed Jim from head to toe. "But seein' as how you say you been on the trail awhile, and figurin' you're lookin' to get laid, the cribs and whore houses are on the other side of Sixth. Try Diamond Annie's. Mention my name to Annie."

Wide-eyed, Jim gasped, "How the hell old are you, Chip?"

"Sixteen. But I been goin' to Annie's since I was fourteen."

Remembering himself at fourteen, Jim gulped in amazement. "Hell and damnation! When I was that age I didn't even know what a whore was!"

The boy beamed. "I tried gettin' into Annie's house when I was twelve, but she tossed me out."

"What's your ma say about you takin' to whores?"

Like the sun going behind a cloud, the boy's smile faded. "I ain't had a ma since I was six and no old man since ten."

"Sorry."

"What's to be sorry about? I'm doin' fine."

"Apparently!"

"I'm assistant manager of the O.K., and I got money in the bank. So don't fret about that hoss of yours. He'll be in very capable hands. And if there's anythin' else I can help you out with here in Tombstone, just let me know."

"As to that, I'm lookin' for a friend of mine. He came here a couple of years ago. Name of Lou Garrard. Ever run into him?"

The boy shook his head. "The name don't ring no bells. But that don't mean he ain't here. There's plenty of folks in Tombstone I don't know."

"Well, if you should run into Lou," said Jim hopefully, "pass on to him that I'm stayin' at Fly's Lodginghouse."

"That's a decent place. Mr. Fly's a good man. Did you know he's a photographer? He has a pitcher studio in a shack behind the house. He lets me watch him workin' sometimes. I'm interested in pitcher-takin', and Mr. Fly promises to teach me all about it. Maybe if you hang around Tombstone long enough, I'll be able to take a pitcher of you and your friend!"

"That'd be swell, Chip," said Jim, turning to leave the office, "but I gotta find him first."

"You could ask about him from Mr. Clum over at the *Epitaph*. That's the town's newspaper. Mr. Clum's the editor and knows everybody."

"Much obliged, Chip," said Jim with a wave of his hand as he opened the door.

"No extra charge, amigo!"

The last glimmer of twilight had painted the Huachuca Mountains purple as Jim gently stroked Midnight's nose, and said, "I'm leavin' you in good hands, fella," and then walked east on Allen Street examining every figure and face for Lou's. He turned left at the corner and north on Fourth Street to the Can Can, where the food was plentiful, the service amenable and the cost reasonable.

Night had settled when he made his way to the Oriental Saloon. Its windows blazed with lights from twenty-eight burners suspended from the ceiling and affording an ample brilliancy with the bright lights reflecting from the many colored crystals decorating a long hand-sculpted walnut bar whose brass rail supported the muddy heels of dozens of hard drinkers from the mines, brush-scuffed boots of leathery men in sun-bleached trail gear and the polished shoes of smooth-looking and elegantly dressed gambling men. The sawdust-sprinkled floor was wood. Arranged upon it for convenience of those who chewed plugs of tobacco or simply had the habit of spitting were shiny spitoons, cuspidors and gaboons. Knotted to equally handy rings hung towels for wiping mustaches and beards. Picking sparkling bottles of every sort of whiskey from three rows of shelves backed by three gilt-framed, glittering diamond-dust mirrors was a lanky man with long blond hair and drooping mustache, dressed in a fringed buckskin shirt.

Behind him were two nearly life-size oil paintings of voluptuous naked women cavorting in lush settings of Oriental gardens as the laughter of a dozen of their fleshy counterparts cut through the twang of a piano and the baritone rumble of a hundred men with staring, hungry faces. These were wayfaring men but none of them was the wayfarer Jim was looking for as he bellied up to the bar and asked for a rye.

"New in town, eh?" said the bartender.

"Fresher than a daisy!"

"Welcome to the Oriental. Best spot in town" came the reply.

"Since you're new, this first one's on the house."

"That's very kind. Thank you."

"Name's Frank Leslie. Commonly called Buckskin."

Poker players drew Jim's attention, and he ambled to the back of the room to watch, settling on a spirited four-handed game. Propping a foot against the wall, he nursed his whiskey until one of the players was cleaned out. Raking in the cards to deal, a lean and leathery trail-dressed player looked up and asked, "Care to join the game? We could use some fresh blood."

"Happy to," said Jim, sliding into the empty chair.

"Johnny Deuce is my name," said the dealer. He tilted his head to the left. "This is Seamus Dolan, newspaperman."

"Howdy," said Jim, smiling at a small red-faced man in a gray suit.

"You mean *ex-newspaperman*, don'tcha, Deuce?" said the third man at the table, a tall, thin, rangy figure with a mousey-brown, tobacco-stained mustache. Slouching in his chair, he peered out from under the narrow brim of a gray hat.

"It may be a fact that the *Nugget* has no further need for my talents, so I am unemployed at the moment," answered Seamus, turning on the third man with a defiant and yet friendly air. "But once a newspaperman, always a newspaperman. I have several enticing offers, however they would involve leaving Tombstone, which I do not care to do at this time."

"In that case," said the third man, "why not ask John Clum for a job at the *Epitaph?*"

"My dear Frank," exclaimed Seamus, "I would never stoop to work for a Republican!"

"This is Frank McLaury," said the dealer with a rightward tilt toward the jibing third man. "Frank's a rancher with his brother Tom, who's the sore loser that just quit the game when it was getting good."

"I'm Jim Hardin," said Jim. "No relation that I can prove to John Wesley of the same name," he added quickly. "I say that cause everybody seems to ask," he explained.

"Yes, that could be nettlesome." The newspaperman winced. "I shudder to contemplate the possibilities for a case of

89

mistaken identity! Why don't you simply avoid that unpleasant prospect by changing your name?"

"I sometimes answer to Tascosa. That's a handle hung on me by a pal of mine. His name's Lou Garrard. I've come to Tombstone lookin' for him. Perhaps one of you gents is familiar with him?"

"Oh, my," sighed the newspaperman, darting anxious looks at the others.

Jim frowned. "Somethin' wrong?"

"I'm afraid so," sighed Seamus Dolan.

Jim searched the three somber faces. "What is it?"

"I'm sorry to have to tell you, Tascosa," said Seamus, "but, you see, there was an incident. . . ."

White-faced and dry-tongued, Jim muttered, "What incident?"

"A shootin'," blurted Frank McLaury.

Slapping down the deck of cards, Johnny Deuce said, "Look, there's no easy way to put this, kid. Your pal Lou is dead."

Chapter Eleven
Obituary

"It happened just a week ago," said Seamus Dolan.

Grim faced, Jim asked, "How'd it come about?"

"He was gunned down," said Johnny Deuce.

"Right out front of this very saloon," said Seamus.

"Lou did have himself a temper," said Jim, shaking his head. "What did he do, call somebody out?"

"The reason for it is sketchy," said Seamus. "Marshal Earp is still hoping to make an arrest, but he's having difficulty finding witnesses who are willing to speak up about it."

"Why in hell wouldn't witnesses want to say what they saw?"

"Scared to," said Deuce.

"Scared of what?"

Frank McLaury spoke up. "Prob'ly 'cause they're scared of bein' shot themselves by the one that killed your friend."

"Why should they be scared if it was a fair fight?"

"On account of it wasn't a fair fight."

"What's that mean?"

"It wasn't a duel," said Deuce. "Your pal never knew what hit him. It was murder, pure and simple. Your pal was blasted as he stepped outside. Hall was layin' for him."

"So the name of this killer is known?"

"Oh sure," said Seamus. "His name is Frank Hall."

"I don't get this! Everybody knows who it was that killed Lou. There were witnesses who know. It was a case of outright

91

murder, But this Frank Hall ain't locked up?"

"Hall took off right after," answered Deuce.

"Why in blazes didn't the law go after him?"

"As I said, no witness was willin' to swear that it was Hall that did it," said Deuce. "The law's hands was tied."

"Smells mighty fishy to me," thundered Jim, jumping to his feet. "Where's the marshal's office?"

"Over on Fremont. Why?"

"I'm goin' over there and get a proper explanation."

"I wouldn't do that," declared Deuce. "Virgil Earp don't take kindly to folks walkin' in and takin' him to task for the way he does his job."

"Ain't that just too damn bad," grunted Jim, wheeling angrily toward the door.

"Seamus, you'd best go with that kid," said Deuce quietly.

"Good idea," answered the newspaperman. Catching Jim at the door, he fell in step with long and purposeful strides. "You're on the wrong track thinkin' that somehow Marshal Earp didn't want to slap Frank Hall into jail for what he did," he said, breathing hard. "Virgil Earp's not a fella to let anybody get away with murder."

"Seems to me that's just what he's done, else Hall would be locked up." He pulled up short. "Better'n that, hanged."

"I think you'd better get a hold of that anger of yours," pleaded Seamus. "You don't want to go flying off the handle with the Earp brothers."

"Lawmen don't scare me!"

"They're more than lawmen, kid. They're the Earps. And the plain fact is, you don't mess with the Earps."

"All I know is, my pal Lou is dead. Gunned down like a dog in the street. And nobody's doin' anythin' about it, least of all the Earps. Well, I can't let somethin' like that slide by, can I?"

Pushing open the door of the marshal's office, immediately Jim's gaze fell on the Wyatt Earp of his vivid memory of Dodge City. Chewing a toothpick and stroking his leonine mustache, he was cocked back in a barrel chair to the right of the door with the tail of his black frock coat hanging down and knee-high, shiny, black leather boots resting against the cold potbelly stove against the wall. A nearly spitting image of Wyatt, though perhaps a few years younger, slouched in an opposite corner. Ringo had said that there were several Earp brothers, Jim recalled. Here were three of them—maybe even a quartet—though a fourth person seated just inside the door of the small office bore them no resemblance, being younger, less keen of eye, sickly looking and in the thrall of a coughing spell as Jim came in. Except for him, they all had badges pinned to their coats. Jim decided the one he was looking for was likely to be the one seated before a large and colorful map of the Arizona Territory on the wall behind the only desk in the room. Striding toward it, he declared, "I take it you're Marshal Virgil Earp?"

"I am," answered Virgil calmly, talking around a half-smoked cheroot dangling from the left side of his mouth. "What can I do for you?"

Jim leaned forward, the balls of his fists pressing the hard wood of the desk, "You can explain to me why you've done nothin' to bring about the arrest and hangin' of a cold-blooded killer name of Frank Hall," said Jim, resting a hand on the butt of his Colt.

Easing back in his tiltable chair, Virgil Earp shrugged. "No evidence! No idea where in hell the son of a bitch might be." He dragged on the cheroot. "Now permit me a couple of questions," he said, easing forward. "Who the devil are you and what's the alleged crimes of Frank Hall got to do with you?"

"His name's Hardin," came the soft, forbearing voice of Wyatt Earp, talking around a toothpick in his mouth as he eased his feet from the stove and came down flat on his chair.

"So you remember me and my name!" said Jim, flicking an angry glance at the man who'd run him out of Dodge City.

"Hardin's a name not easy to forget." Wyatt smiled. "There's John Wesley, and there's you. Each a troublemaker."

"You know this kid, eh, Wyatt?" asked Virgil, amused.

"I know him. He's a bit taller and a bit older since I saw him last. But apparently just as big a pain in the ass. He's a friend from way back of that fella that Hall gunned down. I had to boot both of 'em out of Dodge a few years ago."

Anger flooded bright red into Jim's face and worked the bones of his jaw, like an animal chewing a bone. "You've got quite a memory for—"

"For faces," cut in Wyatt, smiling as he arose to his feet and placed his hands on his hips in a fluid motion that drew back the black coat and revealed the Buntline Special. "And for fools."

"I don't see nothin' foolish about askin' how come nothin's been done to bring this Frank Hall to the bar of justice so's he can be promptly hanged!" thundered Jim.

Also rising, parting his coat and revealing a sidearm which Jim judged to be a Smith and Wesson Schofield .45 revolver, the Earp in the corner stated flatly, "My brother gave you the answer."

"Easy, Morgan," said Virgil. "I'll handle this youngster's complaint." Removing the cheroot from his mouth and grinding it out against the edge of the desk, he spoke patiently. "It took you a long time to come in here to lodge this opinion of the way I conduct myself. Why's that?"

Jim's tone softened. "I just got into town today and heard about Lou's killin' a few minutes ago."

Virgil lifted his eyes, directing them to the newspaperman. "Evenin', Seamus." He smiled.

Seamus tipped his gray hat. "Evenin', Virg."

"You're not by chance tryin' to stir up this youngster so as to have yourself—what do you call it in the newspaper game—a scoop?" asked Virgil.

"You forget that I'm on temporary leave from newspapering," said Seamus. "My only interest in this is that of a concerned citizen who feels there's been enough violence in Tombstone."

"You expect us to believe that's what you're doing here?" snapped Morgan from his corner. "You got some angle you're workin'."

Seamus removed his hat, holding it in front of his chest and twirling it nervously. "I had the unhappy chore of telling this young man that his friend was dead—and of the circumstances of that unfortunate event. When he stated he was coming over here, I felt the wise thing for me was to accompany him. Perhaps to calm him down."

"That's very public spirited of you, Seamus" came the raspy voice of the ash-blond, cadaverous-looking man by the door, who'd remained silent except for the occasional gurgle of his cough.

"Thank you, Doc," said Seamus with a little bow.

"There's no evidence to prove that Frank Hall killed anybody," said Morgan.

"It *does* take evidence to arrest a man and convict him," said Virgil. "Unfortunately, I don't have that evidence. Oh, I know!" His blue eyes flitted to Seamus. "People have told you that there were witnesses. Indeed there were. A man doesn't get shot down in broad daylight in the street and nobody sees it happen. But the plain fact is, young man, that none of the witnesses to this killing is willing to come into this office and give me a sworn statement that would give me the authority I need to justify a warrant to arrest Frank Hall. And without such reasonable cause to charge Hall, I have no right to go dipping into the treasury of the taxpayers of Tombstone and Cochise County scouring the country for him. That's the law."

"Then, the law's an ass," sneered Jim.

"See that map?" said Virgil, tilting his head rearward. "It is a rendering of the vast territory known as Arizona. On it you see the names of lots of towns ranging in size from a pimple on the desert like Douglas and Bisbee down on the Mexican border to much larger spots such as Prescott, Tucson and Phoenix. By now, Frank Hall could be in any one of them."

"Much more likely," continued Wyatt, edging behind his brother's desk and studying the map, "is Hall going to ground in the mountains." He slapped the lower right corner of the map with the flat of his right hand. "Cochise County abounds in mountains. Tombstone's ringed by them." A long finger drew a circle, then stabbed down. "The Huachucas, southwest." The finger edged upward. "The Whetstones." Continuing the movement of his hand, he tapped the map again and again. "The Galuro. Pinaleno. Chircahua. Lots of mountains, riddled with caves and canyons that Frank Hall knows — he shot his hand up as if swearing an oath in court — "like the back of his hand."

"If he's out there," said Jim defiantly, "he can be found."

Morgan Earp laughed scornfully. "Not by you!"

Fuming, Jim glared down at the marshal. "Yeah? We'll see about that."

Virgil allowed a small smile. "And what's that supposed to mean?"

"It means if you can't or won't bring Frank Hall to justice for the killin' of Lou Garrard, then I will," seethed Jim.

"Leave the enforcing of the law to me, Mr. Tascosa, or Hardin, or whatever the hell your name is," growled Virgil, rising slowly behind the desk. "That's a warning, kid. An *official* warning."

Chapter Twelve
Midnight Supper

"Now just calm down," pleaded Seamus catching up with Jim.

"Don't they just take the cake?" groaned Jim, angrily stomping the hard ground. "A man's been killed, and they sit there and tell me they can't do a damn thing about it. And then that tinhorn marshal has the balls to warn me. Well, Seamus Dolan, I swear to you, to the world and to God Almighty that Frank Hall ain't gettin' away with it. If it takes as long as I live, I'm goin' to get that son of a bitch."

"You're not going to get him tonight," said Seamus soothingly, tugging at Jim's sleeve, "so you might as well calm yourself down and come with me and have a grand supper at the Occidental."

"Ain't hungry," said Jim, wrenching his arm away.

Insistently, Seamus seized it again. "The grub's on me!"

"It ain't a matter of money," said Jim, loping away.

Catching up, Seamus said, "Did I ever tell you the three main rules that a reporter lives by?"

"Not that I recall," said Jim, slowing his pace. "Besides, I ain't known you but a couple of hours at most!"

"Rule one: never stand when you can sit. Rule two: never pass a privy without relieving yourself. Rule three: never turn down a free meal!"

Jim was stopped now with his hands on his hips, head tilted like a puppy dog's and showing a lopsided grin. "You are a hoot," he said, looping an arm across Seamus's shoulders. "And I'll wager a dollar that you think I'm a first-class jackass."

"Haven't known you long enough to judge" — laughed Seamus — "but any man who'd stand up to Virgil Earp like you did is a man worth buying a first-class supper for."

Even more opulent than the Oriental, the Occidental seemed tamer and its customers a cut above — by far better-dressed and quieter-spoken — as Jim stood at the front of the large room with its glittering crystal chandeliers while Seamus spoke to an elegant woman with golden hair piled up like thick ropes and dotted with glinting jeweled combs. Strands of pearls cascaded down the ample bosom of her high-necked, tight-fitting scarlet gown. White gloves sheathed her arms. In her right hand she held a Japanese fan, in her left, a bundle of leather-bound menus that seemed as big as barn doors. Her name, said Seamus, introducing her, was Cassandra Buford. "She is the grandest lady west of the Mississippi" — he beamed — "and manager of this most delightful of eating emporiums." With a squeeze of the arm holding the fan and a wink at Jim, he added, "If we play our cards right, Tascosa, Cass might be persuaded to join us in some champagne afterwards."

"Don't know if I care for champagne, never having tasted the stuff," said Jim, "but it'd be a pleasure to sit with this lady anytime."

"You're as sweet as you are good-looking." Cass laughed. She spoke in a throaty voice that hinted of too many years of too much whiskey. Folding the colorful fan with a click, she tickled Jim's chin with the edge of it. "You never tasted champagne?" Frowning, she clucked her tongue teasingly. "We'll certainly have to correct that deficiency!"

"We'll be wanting only the best tonight," said Seamus. "I'm treating this young man to the top of the line."

"Don't tell me," whispered Cass. "He's struck a lode bigger than the Lucky Cuss!"

"Better'n that," exclaimed Seamus. "He gave what-for and a dandy piece of his mind to none other than Marshal Virgil Earp with Wyatt and Morgan looking on. And Doc Holliday as witness. And lived to tell about it."

"What a remarkable young man," cried Cass, taking Jim's

arm. "I shall want to hear all about it."

"Your best table, Cass, darling," coo'd Seamus.

"All the tables at the Occidental are the best," said she, leading them across the room to a large round one with a white cover and a commanding view of the room. "How's this?" she asked.

"Perfect," said Seamus, raising fingers to his lips and blowing Cass a kiss.

With delicate grace, she placed a pair of the giant menus before them on the crisp white tablecloth. "Enjoy!"

"You will join us after?" pleaded Jim.

"Wild horses couldn't keep me away," she said, brushing his cheek with the fan. "What a face," she sighed, gliding away.

Opening the bill of fare, Jim gulped. "This is amazin'!"

SOUPS
Chicken Giblet and Consomme, with Egg

FISH
Columbia River Salmon, au Beurre Noir

RELIEVES
Filet a Boeuf, a la Financier
Leg of Lamb, Sauce, Oysters

COLD MEATS
Loin of Beef Loin of Ham Loin of Pork

BOILED MEATS
Corned Beef and Cabbage, Ribs of Beef, Russian River Bacon

ENTREES
Pinions a Poulett, aux Champignons
Cream Fricassee of Chicken, Asparagus Points
Lapine Domestique, a la Maître d'Hôtel
Casserole d' Ritz aux Oeufs, a la Chinoise
Ducks of Mutton, braze, with Chipoluta Ragout

ROASTS
Loin of Beef Loin of Mutton Stuffed Veal Leg of Pork
Apple Sauce Suckling Pig, with Jelly Chicken

PASTRY
Peach, Apple, Plum, and Custard Pies
English Plum Pudding, Hard Sauce, Lemon Flavor
And we shall have it or perish.
This dinner will be served for 50 cents.

"Cripes, I don't even know what most of this stuff is," whispered Jim. "How'm I supposed to pick? Why don't I just order a steak and a potato?"

"Leave the selection to me," said Seamus.

"Never had anything like this back in Tascosa." Jim sighed, setting aside the menu and gazing down at the gleaming plates flanked by knives and forks and spoons in shiny array. From the corner of his eye he watched and then emulated Seamus unfolding a napkin and placing it in his lap, then listened quietly as Seamus addressed a waiter, tall and elegant with a stiff white apron. "And we'll begin with a white wine," Seamus concluded. "You do have a taste for the grape, I trust, Tascosa?"

There'd been plenty of red Mexican wine in the camps of the Palo Duro. And he'd drunk finer wines from time to time when conferring with Colonel Goodnight about ranch matters. But he'd never had wine in a public dining room as spiffy as this one, he thought; in fact, he'd never seen a place like this! Had Lou ever taken a meal here? he wondered. Poor Lou! Now he would never know the sweetnesses that life might have held for him. Cut down in the prime of his years. Gunned down in the street like a dog. Had anyone mourned for him? Was there a man of the cloth like the Reverend Dilbert in Tombstone to see about the burying of Lou Garrard? Footloose no more! Were words said over him? Did anybody put flowers on his grave? Where had he been laid to rest? Thinking these things, Jim remembered the fresh grave that had caught his eye as he'd ridden past Boot Hill in the company of Johnny Ringo. Could that mound have been Lou's grave? Looking up as Seamus bent over the soup the waiter had laid before them, he blurted, "I'd like to find the spot where my pal was buried. Would you know where?"

Seamus nodded. "I'll go with you to Boot Hill tomorrow."

"Much obliged," muttered Jim, picking up a spoon.

"Well, well," boomed a voice from behind. "You're living mighty high on the hog, Seamus, for a man who's out of work!"

Tall and thin, wearing a black frock coat, white shirt, string bow tie and gray striped trousers, this was John Clum, editor of the Tombstone *Epitaph*, "Mr. Clum is one of the leading lights of Tombstone," he went on. "If not *the* leading light explained Seamus."

"Sorry to hear about your falling out at the *Nugget*," said Clum, drawing up a chair. "The door's always open for you at the *Epitaph*."

"Thank you very much, John," said Seamus with an exaggerated bow of his head, "but I'm taking advantage of my leisure to mull over several promising options."

"Nothing to take you away from our town, I hope." Clum smiled. "Tombstone wouldn't be the same without Seamus Dolan."

"Time will tell," said Seamus, laying down his soup spoon.

"Well, as I said, the door's open at the *Epitaph*," said Clum. "You're a fine writer and reporter, and I can always use a man who knows how to dig out a story."

"As a matter of fact," said Seamus, "there's a damn good story sitting right here at this table. Meet Mr. Jim Hardin, also called Tascosa, who's just had a dandy run-in with your friends the Earps."

Clum turned to Jim. "Is that so? Concerning what, may I ask?"

"Jim's a friend of that fella that Frank Hall gunned down the other night," answered Seamus, "and he was considerably miffed to find out that Hall had escaped. He just took Virgil Earp to task about it. Quite effectively, I thought. It was a pleasure to behold!"

"Perhaps I should explain, Mr. Hardin," said Clum, glancing sidelong at Seamus, "that Mr. Dolan takes some delight in giving me a hard time about my newspaper's support for Marshal Earp. The paper that Seamus worked for was opposed to the appointment of Virgil Earp as city marshal."

"It all sounds like politics to me," said Jim, abandoning the chicken soup and rubbing his nose as if he'd caught a whiff of a bad odor. "Politics bores me silly. All I care about is the bringin' to justice of the dirty bastard that killed Lou. And if the law won't do it, then I s'pose I'll have to take the matter into my own hands."

"I don't advise that," said Clum sternly.

"I don't believe I solicited your advice, Mr. Clum," snapped Jim as the waiter cleared away the soup bowls.

With a howl of derision, Seamus slapped the table, rattling the silverware. "I guess that'll hold you for a while, John." He turned to Jim and patted his back. "You've had quite an evening for yourself, telling off the Earps *and* the chief of the *Epitaph* in the space of a few minutes."

"I fully understand this young man's feelings," answered Clum placidly. "And were I in his boots, I'd probably feel the same way. But taking the law into one's own hands is never the answer. Lawlessness only begets more lawlessness. Revenge wreaks revenge. An eye for an eye, a tooth for a tooth. There is too much lawlessness in Tombstone already."

"And you and the others who make up the Law and Order party honestly believe the Earps are going to tame this town?" said Seamus incredulously as the waiter brought the fish course.

"I do," replied Clum emphatically.

"Their record is hardly one to hold up as an example of virtue," scoffed Seamus, studying the salmon before him. "They've been on the other side of the law quite a bit. And if you and your righteous associates would open your eyes, you'd see that the Earps are using those badges of theirs to shake down the saloons, gaming parlors and brothels."

"Nonetheless," said Clum, his voice rising angrily, "I and others in this town and county feel that Virgil Earp with the help of his able brothers Wyatt and Morgan are just the ones to put an end to the depredations of Old Man Clanton and his gang of cattle rustlers, horse thieves and hold-up men."

"The hell with these Clantons and the Earps," interjected Jim impatiently as he speared his fish with a fork. "All I care about is gettin' the cowardly snake that killed my friend."

"Then, it should interest you to know that Frank Hall is in very tight with the Clantons," said Clum disgustedly, "and in all probability is being afforded sanctuary by them in their many hideouts over on the San Pedro at this very moment. The Clantons are well known for their hospitality to the worst elements in the West. That is why they and all like them must be rooted out ruthlessly, so that the decent people of Tombstone, Cochise County and Arizona may get on with the work of building a decent society. Now, I must bid you good evening. It was a pleasure meeting you, Mr. Hardin. But I do advise you to take Marshal Earp's advice and leave this Frank Hall matter to the law."

"Tascosa, my friend" chuckled Seamus as Clum strode away, "I believe we've just been given a preview of the editorial in the next edition of the *Epitaph*."

"It all seems mighty bewilderin' to me," said Jim, shaking his head.

"Clum doesn't realize it," said Seamus, "but he's probably done more harm than good. He's only making the situation worse, splitting the town into factions. By his backing the Earps, he's goading those like Sheriff Behan and others who are making quite a nice living off what Clum calls 'the cowboy element,' meaning the Clantons and others who want to keep their meat business thriving."

"So what's stoppin' 'em?"

"Well, you see, the meat they're trading isn't always theirs to peddle. The Clantons are fast and loose, if you get my drift. And very able when it comes to changing the brands on any cattle they run across."

"Ah! That's what Clum meant about the Clantons bein' cattle rustlers."

"With the Earps waxing strong on the wave of Clum's law and order crusade, there's bound to be trouble."

The next course had arrived—a filet of beef. "I wonder if this meat's legal?" joked Jim, grinning as he sliced into it. "Legit or not," he went on, chewing, "it sure is tender."

"With Cass in charge, nothing but the finest will do," said Seamus.

Jim's eyes searched the room for her. "She's somethin', that's for sure," he said, finding her speaking to customers across the dining room. "A real lady, seems to me."

"Heart of gold, too," said Seamus.

His tone seemed wistful to Jim. "Might you be stuck on her, Seamus?" he asked.

"A worn-out newspaperman who's been fired for getting drunk on papers from New York to Tombstone isn't worthy of a classy woman like that," said Seamus.

"Did she tell you that?"

"She doesn't have to tell me. I know it."

"That seems mighty presumptive to me," asserted Jim.

He would have said more, but the woman in question had made her way to their table, taking the chair Clum had vacated. "Is everything satisfactory with you two?" she asked, folding her gloved hands under her chin.

"Just great." Jim grinned.

"How long will you be staying in Tombstone, Tascosa?" she asked. "Awhile, I hope."

"Can't say for sure," said Jim. "I came here to hook up with my friend only to find he's dead, murdered by that snake in the grass name of Frank Hall. So I guess I'll be around for as long as it takes to settle my account with Hall."

Cass frowned. "That could be quite a spell. Hall's not likely to breeze back into town anytime soon — if he comes back at all. What will you do while you wait?"

"Get me a job, I guess."

"I might be able to help you there," she said. "That is, if you don't mind my butting into your business!"

Jim cracked a smile. "Need somebody to wash the dishes?"

"The Occidental's well supplied with hired help," she said, "but I could put in a word with Josh Durkee. He runs a freighting company. He's always looking for reliable men. Can you handle wagons?"

"I've driven my share."

"Durkee's a good man," declared Seamus. "Square! That's a good idea, Cass."

"Tomorrow's my day for taking care of business around town," she said, gently touching Jim's cheek with her soft, white glove.

"I'll pay a call on Josh in the morning and put in a good word for you. Then you go by in the afternoon and see him."

"Will do." Jim beamed as she rose. "Thanks!"

"I think she fancies you," whispered Seamus as she left them to drift through the room speaking to other customers.

"Bull! She's just being kind and helpful."

"Oh, is that what it is? You think that because she's quite a bit older than you that she wouldn't take a fancy to a youngster like you? Well, think again, boy." With that, their waiter served their entrees. "Ah, the Lapine Domestique!" cried Seamus, gleefully clapping his hands.

Peering down at something drenched in sauce, Jim made a face. "What is it?"

"Rabbit!" Seamus cackled. "Good old Arizona rabbit!"

Part Three:
Tombstone Epitaphs

Chapter Thirteen
View from Boot Hill

Like a new silver dollar on a purple cloth, a full moon was riding low over the black silhouette of the Huachuca Mountains as Jim parted from Seamus Dolan in front of the Occidental to walk slowly west on Allen Street, as lively long after midnight as it was at high noon, though perhaps drunker. Light-headed himself from the two bottles of champagne he'd polished off with Seamus and Cass Buford and with a food-stuffed belly that forced him to loosen his belt a notch, he longed for nothing more than sleep as he proceeded unsteadily and untempted past noisy saloon after noisy saloon sandwiched between the closed and darkened shops of purveyors of goods.

Suddenly feeling queasy, he paused, leaning his shoulder against the front of the Boot and Shoe Store, his bleary eyes working hard to focus on the price of a pair of brogans in the window. "Dollar seventy-five," he muttered, gulping for air as his stomach turned, belching up a bubble of champagne-flavored bile. Lurching from the boardwalk into the street, he vomited. Heaving and gasping, he shook his head. "So much for that fifty-cent supper," he groaned, swaying back onto the sidewalk toward the yellow light blazing in the window of the O.K. Livery and Corral office.

With his feet up on the desk, tilted back in his chair, his hands forming a cradle for the back of his head and a long thin cigar smoldering between his lips, Chip snorted a laugh. "Jesus, you look like you got the worst of it."

"Ate too much, drank too much," sighed Jim, leaning against the door. "How's my horse?"

"In a hell of a lot better shape than you are." Chip laughed, sitting upright.

"Good," said Jim, turning and pulling open the door. "I'll be needin' him in the mornin'. Presumin' I survive to see the sunrise."

"Whether you're dead or alive," cackled Chip as the door banged shut behind Jim, "the hoss'll be here."

Quiet encompassed Jim as he staggered around and behind the office, through the wide open, scrubby, manure-dotted expanse of the corral and along the side of Fly's Lodginghouse, then onto its porch facing Fremont Street. A chimney lamp was glowing in the foyer as he dropped heavily onto a bench to remove his boots before tiptoeing up the stairs to his second-floor room, where he pitched facedown onto the big bed, moaned once and plunged into a deep, dreamless sleep.

The sun woke him to the smells of Mrs. Fly's breakfast being cooked directly below his room. Rolling onto his back, he sniffed the bacon, eggs, biscuits and coffee-laced air and remembered the same aromas drifting from his mother's tiny kitchen in the house beside Blue Creek as he and his father had handled early morning chores. Then his memory skipped to the enticing odors of Frank Raphael's dirt-floor cookhouse. As his stomach growled, he ran his tongue over his sticky teeth, stale with the tastes of last night's thrown-up supper and champagne. Sitting up, he felt the stabbing ache of a hangover behind his eyeballs. Easing to the window, he muttered, "Good God Almighty," then pulled up the sash, gulping for air. Peering down, he found Midnight waiting for him. Saddled and tethered to a rail, the animal stood with its black coat glinting in a pool of sunlight. A fine horse. Lou's gift to him, so long ago.

"You were late coming in last night," said Mrs. Fly, sounding like his mother as he entered her kitchen.

"Yes, ma'am," he said sheepishly.

"Well, sit down and have your breakfast," she said, gesturing toward the table. "Nothing clears a man's head or settles his stomach like a good meal in the morning," she went on, placing a plate before him.

"Is Mr. Fly not having any?"

"He ate hours ago. Up and at 'em early, that's my husband. He's over at the Tough Nut mine taking photographs, though God knows he's got plenty of pictures already."

"I guess he just likes takin' pictures," said Jim, dipping a hot biscuit into the yolk of a sunnyside-up egg.

"He says he takes them for posterity," she replied, filling a china mug with steaming black coffee. "It's Mr. Fly's settled belief that men won't have to write history because everything will be recorded in photographs. He'll be wanting to take one of you, by the way. He takes pictures of all our lodgers. It's nice. Sometimes I spend a whole evening looking through his collection, recalling the folks who've been our guests." She sat opposite him, smiling. A pleasant, motherly smile, Jim thought. "Maybe you'll get yours taken with that friend of yours you've come to Tombstone to find," she said. "Have you located him? Was that what kept you out late? Catching up for old-times' sake?"

"No, ma'am, I haven't found him yet," he answered, deciding not to tell her the truth — that Lou was dead. "I hope to find him today, though," he added, thinking ahead to the moment when he would be standing over Lou's grave. "A man I met last night is takin' me to him this mornin'."

Finishing his breakfast in the dining room of the Hotel Cosmopolitan, Seamus Dolan greeted Jim with a beckoning wave of his hand. "Have you had your morning vittles?" he asked as Jim drew up a chair. "Or are you still stuffed with that sumptuous supper we had at the Occidental?"

"No, I woke up famished," said Jim, electing not to inform Seamus that he'd thrown up the meal and the champagne somewhere along Allen Street. "Mrs. Fly cooked up a real fine breakfast for me."

"Had your picture taken by her husband yet?"

"Nope."

"You will. Camillus Fly's everywhere with that camera of his. He even took a photograph of —"

As Seamus cut himself off, Jim grasped what he might have

111

said. His stomach turned, and for a moment he feared he was going to be sick again. "Fly took a picture of Lou lyin' dead in the street? Is that it, Seamus?"

"Afraid so, Tascosa. I know it must sound hideous to you, but it happened."

Jim cracked a smile. "Well, I hope one day soon to give Mr. Fly the opportunity of photographin' Frank Hall's dead body. Either danglin' from a gallows or lyin' where I dropped in the dirt with a bullet from my shootin' iron. As to Lou, I'm still intent on findin' his grave and payin' my respects and would be pleased to have your company if you're still willin'."

"Course I am, Tascosa," declared Seamus, sounding offended. "You may not recognize it, but I'm just as interested in getting justice for your friend Lou as you are! I didn't know the young man, but I find his being shot down in the street offensive. I may not be as loud-mouthed about wanting law and order in Tombstone as John Clum, but that doesn't mean I'm not prepared to do what I can to drive the uncivilized elements out of town and out of the Arizona Territory." Fetching his hat from a rack, he clapped it on, peering into a gilt-edged mirror and adjusting it to a rakish slant. "Ready!"

As they neared Boot Hill, a smart, hot wind swirled dust into small cyclones which seemed to chase one another as they spun across the flat, scrubby desert stretching eastward to the rugged uplift of the Dragoon Mountains. Cutting through the unloveable landscape was the road he'd followed in the company of Ringo. The Barfoot Trail, Ringo had called it. Beginning in Galeyville, it cut through the Chiricahua Mountains by means of Morse's Canyon and ran in an almost straight line across Sulphur Springs Valley to reach and overcome the Dragoons to arrive at Tombstone and then continued westward to the ranches and mines of the San Pedro River Valley.

Swinging off the trail, they climbed a small knoll surrounded by a rail fence and passed through an opened, sagging wooden gate whose roughly hewn supports held up a weathered plank with "Boot Hill Cemetery" chiseled into it. "Never send to know for whom the bell tolls," muttered Jim as he ducked his head to clear the sign and turned his eyes to the unmarked mound of earth he'd first seen in the company of Johnny Ringo.

"What's that?" said Seamus.

"Nothin'," answered Jim, sliding down from Midnight at the foot of the grave. Taking off the misshapen and weather-beaten black hat Lou had given to him so long ago, he said, "You're sure this is Lou's grave?"

"Positive," said Seamus, dismounting. "I accompanied the undertaker."

"Was words said over him?"

"Yes indeed! The Twenty-third Psalm."

"Who said 'em?"

"The undertaker."

"That was decent of him. I'd like to thank him for it."

"His name's Goldstein. Sid Goldstein. His parlor's on Tough Nut Street, close by the Russ House Hotel."

"Did anybody pay him for services?"

"The town paid. There's a special fund for such things."

"That's also decent," said Jim, reaching under his shirt for his wallet. Drawing out the letter that he'd written months ago, intending to give it to Moonlight Rose for the mail hack, he knelt beside Lou's grave and scooped a hole. Folding the letter, he placed it tenderly at the bottom, then shoved the dirt onto it. "Message delivered," he said chokingly as he rose to his feet. So many graves, he thought. First had been his mother's. Then his father's. Aaron Place's eternal claim of his portion of the earth somewhere along Colonel Goodnight's cattle trail. The hole they'd put Mickey Ludlum into, sent there by Lou Garrard's bullet. Jody Taylor, gunned down unmercifully by Lothry. And Lothry himself, sent to face his maker by Jim Hardin in full payment for the untimely death of Jody. Now here was Lou's grave, so fresh it had no marker. "Who do I see about gettin' him a stone or somethin'?" he asked, turning to Seamus.

"The undertaker," said Seamus, looking as grim as Death himself.

Jim nodded, then gazed toward the valley and a cloud of dust rising from the Barfoot Trail, kicked up not by the wind but the hooves of hard-charging horses.

Moments later, they thundered past.

He counted nine riders, heads down, duster coats flapping behind them. "They're in a rush," he said, mounting Midnight. "That's the Clantons," said Seamus, climbing into his saddle.

Jim's head jerked sideways. "The Clantons?"

"The Old Man, Ike and Finn and the McLaury's, Tom and Frank. Billy Claiborne. Wes Fuller. Looked like Curly Bill Brocius, too. And Pony Deal, a real hard case. Didn't see Ringo, though."

"What about Frank Hall?" said Jim excitedly. "Is he ridin' with 'em?"

"No," said Seamus, spurring his horse. "Frank's not among them."

"Damn," grunted Jim, slapping his holster. "Ain't *that* too friggin' bad?"

Chapter Fourteen
Bob Hatch's Billiards Saloon

It was approaching noon when they plodded down Allen Street from the east, their slow-riding horses kicking up chalky dust in the middle of the nearly deserted thoroughfare as Tombstone's inhabitants sought refuge in siesta from the broiling June sun. "There's their mounts," said Jim, nodding to nine lathery horses baking in the sun at the long hitching rail in front of Bob Hatch's Billiards Saloon. "What kind of horse does Hall ride?"

"I told you Hall wasn't with 'em," grumbled Seamus, taking off his hat and wiping beads of sweat from his forehead with a red kerchief that seemed half the size of a blanket.

"They was movin' fast," said Jim, studying the hard-run horses. "Maybe you missed seein' Hall."

"I know Hall's horse," said Seamus gruffly, pulling rein and stuffing the kerchief into his coat pocket. "It's an Appaloosa mare. You see any Appaloosas?"

"Is this where the Clantons usually hang out?"

"They shoot pool here in the daytime while Old Man Clanton does his banking. They do their nighttime drinking at the Capitol Saloon. Then they bed down at the Grand Hotel. They trade their livestock at Bauer's Union Market on Fremont. Anything else you care to know?"

"I seen the meat market," said Jim. "Near to Fly's. It backs up against the O.K. Corral." He licked his dry lips and peered up at the sign running the width of the billiard saloon. "Is there drinks for sale in this establishment?"

Seamus shifted impatiently in his saddle. "You don't want to go in there."

"Why not? It's a public place, ain't it?"

"It's a *cowboy* joint."

"I *am* a cowboy," said Jim, swinging down to the ground.

Seamus remained mounted. "In the politics of Tombstone, the word cowboy takes on a different meaning."

"The hell with politics," said Jim, looping Midnight's reins around the end of the long rail. Seamus was a black paper cutout against the glare of the sun. To see him, Jim lifted a hand to shield his eyes. "You comin'?" he asked with a lopsided grin. "I'll buy the beer."

"That's Rule Four of the Reporter's Creed," cried Seamus, easing off his horse. "Never refuse the offer of free suds!"

Dim and dank, the pool hall smelled of men's sweat, smoke and beer and clicked with the collision of billiard balls. Those playing at a table in the back were Frank McLaury and a younger version of him—Frank's brother Tom, Jim presumed. The backs of six men presented themselves at the bar on the right. Seamus could name them all: Ike and Phineas Clanton, young spitting images of their father; Billy Caliborne, who could manage to swagger even when leaning on a bar; lanky Wes Fuller, notorious from the San Pedro to Galeyville for his hair-trigger temper; treacherous Pony Deal; and a tall, rugged, blue-eyed bear of man with twin forty-fours in gun belts criss crossing his chest—Curly Bill Brocius, so named because of his dark, kinky hair. The ninth man was seated alone at a corner table. A pile of folding money and a gray-covered ledger lay before him. Older than the rest, he had to be Old Man Clanton, Jim figured.

Looking up, the old man shouted, "Seamus Dolan! To what do we owe the dubious pleasure of your company?"

"Just seeking relief from the scorching sun," said Seamus light-heartedly, doffing his hat. "Been showing my friend around the town," he added, clapping Jim on the shoulder. "He arrived the other day in the company of your old pal Ringo. Maybe Johnny mentioned him? Name's Jim Hardin."

"Nope," grunted the old man.

"Ringo calls me Tascosa," said Jim, advancing to the old man's table.

"Still never heard of you," grunted the old man.

"I came here lookin' for a pal of mine. Name of Lou Garrard," said Jim.

"Fascinatin'," said Clanton, turning yellow eyes down to the pile of money.

"Only I found out Lou got himself killed the other night," said Jim. "The word I got is, Lou was gunned down by a pal of yours, Mr. Clanton," said Jim, looming above the old man and glaring down. "Folks who know what happened to Lou says he was shot in cold blood by a Clanton man named Frank Hall."

"News to me," said Old Man Clanton with a shrug. "Any of you boys know anythin' about Frank Hall shootin' somebody?" he yelled across the room.

"Far as I know, Frank's been down in Mexico for at least a month," answered Ike Clanton, stirring upright at the bar. "Ain't that right, Finn?"

"That's right," said his younger brother, twisting to gaze toward Jim at the rear of the room.

"Looks like whoever told you it was Frank Hall that killed your pal was wrong." The old man smiled as he opened the ledger book. "If it was Frank," he added, cackling a thin laugh, "I expect the marshal would have him locked up by now."

"That's fer sure," bellowed Ike, yanking his neckerchief upward like a hangman's noose. "If Frank Hall killed anybody, the Earps would 'a already jerked Frank to Jesus."

"And even if Frank did resort to his shootin' iron," chimed in Finn Clanton, gently stroking the holster of his Colt Army, "he would'a had to be provoked into it."

"It weren't no fair fight," declared Jim. "His six-gun was still in its leather."

"Oldest trick in the Earps' book," scoffed Ike. "Frame a man by puttin' a gun back in its holster and make it look like it wasn't an honest fight."

"How do you know what went on, anyways?" barked Finn, resting his hand on the grip of the Army. "Was you there to see it?"

"If I had been," snapped Jim, drumming fingers on his six-gun,

117

"Hall wouldn't 'a got away scot-free."

"These are matters for the law to settle, not us," said Seamus anxiously, stepping to Jim's side. "Especially on a hot day like this. All folks ought to avoid disputes in hot weather, eh, Mr. Clanton?"

"That's good advice." The old man nodded, peering coldly at Jim.

"Absolutely! Cool heads should prevail at all times," said Seamus, addressing everyone. "Especially in times of grief, as this young fellow is experiencing. After all, all you fellas can appreciate that it was quite a shock to Jim, here, coming all the way from Tascosa way over in Texas only to find his friend had met a tragic and untimely death." He looked down at the old man. "I'm sure you, Mr. Clanton, and all your men share the deepest sorrow and outrage at what happened."

"Well said, Seamus," boomed the voice of Frank McLaury from the billiard table as Seamus tightened a grip on Jim's gun arm and tugged him toward the door.

"Who the hell's side are you on, Seamus?" blurted Jim as they emerged into the stifling heat.

Face flushing, Seamus stamped the boardwalk. "I ought to kick your ass," he blared. "You lookin' to get yourself the same medicine as your pal? Those Clantons would as soon gun you down as look at you. Boy, you take the cake for craziness! What the devil got into you?"

"I just wanted them to know that I'm around and that I mean to settle accounts with Frank Hall. They're sure to get out the word to him. That's all I wanted."

"Yeah. And on account of this stupidity, you're likely to get it in the back."

"Bull. I can handle myself."

Seamus grasped Jim's shoulders, shaking him hard. "Boy, that's the Clanton gang." Letting go, he softened his tone. "They're the worst collection of owlhoots ever to set foot in Arizona Territory. And you breeze in on 'em tossin' around threats!"

"I made no threats."

Seamus backed into the street. "If I hadn't been in there with you, you'd be lying in a puddle of your own blood by now."

"Mebbe so," said Jim, vaulting into his saddle, "but there'd be

118

some Clanton blood mixin' in with it."

Angrily, Seamus climbed onto his horse. "You best heed my advice, kid, and leave this Frank Hall affair to Virgil Earp and his deputies."

"From what I seen of them," said Jim, riding toward the O.K. Corral, "they ain't worth a bucket of spit."

Chapter Fifteen
Contention

At Fifth and Tough Nut streets, J. Durkee Stagecoach and Transportation Company was a large flat yard for the parking of a fleet of well-used Studebaker freighters and a pair of handsome red-painted Concord stagecoaches, a corral full of horses and hinny mules and a shed that sufficed for an office. Jim found Joshua Durkee seated at a rolltop desk. He was a lean and lanky man of advanced years with the sinewy arms that were the mark of one who'd worked a lifetime running teams. From clenching reins, his hands were large and gnarled, one drumming the desk top and the other around a pipe with a bowl as big as his fist. Decades in the sun atop a wagon box had made his skin the texture and hue of saddle leather. Keen, blue, assaying eyes weighed the youth standing before him. "Cass Buford says you can cut the mustard as a mule skinner," he said on a cloud of gray, putrid-smelling tobacco smoke. "Though how she knows that to be a fact is beyond my ken, Cass having no experience whatever in the freight business save as a customer. But she's never failed when it comes to plumbing the character of people, so I'll take her word for it that you'll be a reliable and capable employee, Mr. Hardin."

"I handled wagons plenty for my pop on our farm," said Jim. "And I had lots of experience workin' for Colonel Goodnight up in the Texas Panhandle. So you needn't worry about me bein' up to whatever task you set before me, sir."

"You look capable enough," said Durkee, rising from his creaky chair. "C'mon, I'll show you around."

To the left of his office at the bottom of the long slope of a curving road gaped the Tough Nut, Contention and Grand Central mines with their distant buildings like brown smudges on the rough land. The criss crossed beams of towers above the shaftheads of the mines shot up looking like windmills above the gaping black maws of the shafts. To the right of the road was the Lucky Cuss. Nearest of all was the Million Dollar. "Naturally, most of our work is connected with these outfits," Durkee explained as he pointed them out. "We do a lively business cartin' the ore from these digs over to the mills in Charleston and Contention City along the San Pedro, about a nine-mile haul from here. It's on the Contention-Charleston run you'll be starting work. You'll be partnered with Felix Catlin. He's getting up in years now. When he was younger, none was any better than Felix at freighting. You'll be his helper, doing all the heavy work. He'll be your teacher. The pay's fifteen dollars a month. If that's acceptable. . . ."

Jim beamed. "It sure is!"

"Good." Durkee puffed , the pipe smoke swirling east toward the mines.

"I can start today," Jim exclaimed.

"I admire ambition, young man," said Durkee, ambling toward the officer "but Felix won't be around till tomorrow. That's five o'clock in the morning, by the way."

Elated, Jim rode directly to the Occidental. He wanted Cass to know first. And he had to thank her. Barging through the door, he found her at the back of the room full of lunch-eating patrons. "Hey, Cass," he blared, dodging their tables as he rushed to her. "I got the job! Mr. Durkee hired me just like that. I start workin' for Mr. Durkee's shippin' outfit first thing in the mornin'. I'll be team-sterin' on the run over to Charleston and Contention. I wanted to thank you right away. I'd never have been hired without a good word from you. Thanks a heap!" He was standing next to her table now and noticing for the first time that Doc Holliday was sharing her meal. "Excuse me," he said. "I didn't know you had somebody with you." He took off his hat. "Howdy, Mr. Holliday."

"You two know each other?" asked Cass.

"Only in passing," said Holliday. "I just happened to be present the other evening when this young man exchanged some robust words with Marshal Earp regarding the quality of law enforcement in Tombstone. But the name escapes me."

"Jim Hardin."

"Ah, yes. I remember now. You said you were fresh from Tascosa."

"That's right. Came here lookin' for a pal of mine only to find out he was dead—murdered—and the damned marshal wasn't doin' a friggin' thing about it." He glanced at Cass. "Pardon the language, please."

"But now, I'm glad to see"—smiled Holliday—"that you've obviously taken Virgil's advice and abandoned that fool idea of launching a vendetta and turning yourself into a one-man posse. No more vigilante stuff? You've gotten yourself a job! That's wise."

Jim stiffened. "Who says I gave up on trackin' down Frank Hall? I got a job because I have to have somethin' to live on till I locate the snake who killed Lou." Abruptly turning to Cass, he softened his tone. "I'm much obliged for your assistance. Again, excuse me for intrudin' on your meal." Clapping on his black hat, he bowed slightly. "I'll bid you good afternoon."

Cass reached up and caught his sleeve. "Sit down, cool off and have yourself something to eat."

"Well, I'm paid up in advance over at Fly's boardinghouse," said Jim, acutely aware of his dwindled wallet, "so I reckon I'll eat there."

"You'll have your meal right here," insisted Cass. "And don't worry about paying."

Jim stared at his toes as embarrassment flooded into his cheeks. "That's kind of you," he muttered, "but I really couldn't."

"It's my treat," declared Cass. "To celebrate your new job."

Jim's eyes lifted to Holliday's. "Well, if it's all right with Mr. Holliday?"

Holliday gave a nod. "Happy to have the company of a fella who told off Virgil Earp and didn't get himself brained for it. Or worse."

"You're lookin' well today, Mr. Holliday," said Jim, drawing out a chair. "I trust that your health's gettin' better."

"I've had worse days," said Holliday. "And call me Doc."

"I don't believe I ever met a physician before," said Jim.

"You still ain't," said Holliday. "My sheepskin says I'm a dentist, not a physician."

"Well, never met a dentist before, either." Jim laughed. "If my tooth ached, my ma treated it with oil of clove. One had to come out once, but the barber in Tascosa took care of that. It's nice to know that if I get the toothache while in Tombstone there's a genuine dentist at hand."

"I haven't practiced lately." Holliday chuckled. "So maybe you'd better just call the barber again. But if you ever get interested in a good game of poker or faro, then's the time to put out the call for Doc Holliday."

With that, he began coughing violently—worse than Jim remembered it earlier. Covering his mouth with a napkin, he leapt up and rushed hacking and coughing out the door. "What ails him?" asked Jim.

"Consumption," said Cass, grimly tapping her chest. "He's got it real bad. Dying from it, prob'ly."

"He's a young man," said Jim. "Can't be more'n forty, I'd reckon."

"Actually, he's not yet thirty," said Cass.

"Seems like a decent fella," said Jim, picking up one of the Occidental's giant menus. "Prob'ly stand up beside you in a pinch."

"Yeah, Doc's all right," said Cass. "But enough about him! I want to hear all about this new job you've got for yourself!"

"Thanks to you," said Jim, grinning. "And don't you worry none about me lettin' you down. I'll do real good!"

Jim went to bed early but slept little and was awake at the first glimmer of dawn, creeping down the stairs bootless so as not to wake the Flys, then walking from the boardinghouse to the freight yard in the dead quiet of Tombstone, arriving a full hour ahead of Felix Catlin.

Smoking a cigar, the tall, scrawny old man with a slouching straw sombrero, threadbare brown duster coat and a short gray beard, said, "I take it you'd be the new boy. Called what?"

"Jim Hardin."

"From out Texas way, I hear."

123

"Tascosa."

"Tascosa? I was there once. Not much of a spot."

"No, sir."

"Don't call me that. Reminds me that I'm old. Call me Felix."

"As you wish, Felix."

"We got a load of ore to pick up over at the Million Dollar," Felix said, striding toward a Studebaker wagon. He paused to draw a plug of chewing tobacco from his coat pocket. "It's a four-mule job," he said, biting off a chunk. "You fetch 'em and hitch 'em."

An hour later, loaded with the ore, the wagon lumbered along Allen Street. Passing through Hop Town, Felix said, "This is where the Chinee live. Not many of 'em, though." He spat tobacco juice in a long yellow arc. "Not nearly as many as they have in Frisco."

"Frisco?" said Jim. "Where's that?"

Felix lifted his sombrero and scratched his balding pate. "San Francisco! You never hear'd of San Francisco? That's a city out in Californy."

Snapping the reins on the rumps of the slow-moving mules, Jim looked sidewise at Felix. "You've been out in California?"

"Hell, son, I was a forty-niner. Don't tell me you never hear'd of the forty-niners!"

"Oh, I heard of them. That was the California gold rush. Long before I was born, of course."

Felix spat again. "No foolin'!" Placing fingers to his eyes, he made slits of them by drawing back the corners. "As Confucius say," he said in a sing-song voice, " 'All man need to be happy is loose boots, tight woman and warm place to crap.' "

"What's it like in California?" asked Jim.

"It was excitin' at the time of the rush. But then it got too crowded for my taste." He paused, chewing hard and thinking. "Nah, that ain't the truth at all. The crowdin' didn't bother me all that much. I just missed Arizony, is all. That's why I came back. But you? I reckon you'd take to Californy like a duck takes to water."

"Why's that?" said Jim, grinning.

"You're young. Californy's for the young."

"Maybe I'll go and have a look someday," said Jim, turning

124

to Felix.

"No time like the present!"

Jim looked forward again. "I got business to take care of here first. Somethin' to settle."

Ten miles west of town, the road forked.

"Which one's ours?" asked Jim.

"Keep to the right," said Felix, pointing. "Left cuts over to the Clanton ranch."

"I heard they're a contrary bunch," said Jim. "Cattle thieves and the like. Even stage stickups. Is that true?"

"I hear'd the same. But never seen no proof of it. Don't make no neverminds to me, long as they leaves me alone. But if I was drivin' a stage with a bank strongbox under the seat, like the Concord that got robbed on the way to Benson a few months back, I might be concerned. I expect you hear'd about it."

"Can't say that I have."

"Oh, it was somethin'! March fifteenth. The *Grand Central* coach of the Kinnear and Company stageline got stopped by four hard-cases wearin' false beards and wigs. Can you imagine such a thing? Eli Philpott was the driver—shot dead. Passenger named Peter Roerig was also killed. But thanks to the fella ridin' shotgun, Bob Paul, the bandits didn't get a cent."

"Did the law collar the bandits?"

"Marshal Earp grabbed one of 'em, a no-account by the name of Luther King. But the others escaped into Mexico. There was talk the gang was connected with Old Man Clanton but no proof of it. And for a time Sheriff Behan suspected the deed was pulled by the Earp brothers and their friend Doc Holliday. But nothin' came of that, neither."

"Have you ever been stuck up, Felix?"

"Never hauled anythin' worth stickin' me up for," said Felix with a laugh. "But if anybody ever did, I'd know exactly what to do."

"You'd fight 'em?"

"Hell no," said Felix with a spray of tobacco juice for punctuation. "I'd give em everythin' on board! There ain't a piece of goods in the *entire* world worth losin' your life over. Like the Good Book says. If a thief takes your cloak, give 'im your coat, also."

"What if somebody takes somethin' more precious than goods?"

125

"Such as what?"

"Such as the life of a friend of yours. What would you do about that, Felix?"

"So that's the business that brings you to Tombstone. The matter you say you have to settle involves killin' the one who killed your pal!"

"Wouldn't you do the same?"

"I can't recollect anytime in my life when there was anybody that precious to me."

"You must've had at least one close friend!"

"Nope."

"What about women?"

"What about 'em?"

"You never been in love with a woman?"

"Nope," said Felix, loosing a wad of spit.

"Excuse me for sayin' it, Felix, but I don't believe you never had a woman."

"I didn't say I never had a woman," said Felix, wiping his lips on his sleeve. "And that ain't what you ast. You ast if I ever been in love with a woman. That ain't the same as havin' a woman. Had plenty. Loved none."

"But you never had a friend?" asked Jim incredulously as the wagon rattled onward. "Not one single friend?"

"I moved around a lot. Born with itchy feet, that was me. Sired by the wind. Some people are like that. Tumbleweeds."

"That's true," said Jim, thinking of Lou.

The fork to the Clanton ranch was well behind them now as the road pushed through the rolling hills, arroyos and washes of the San Pedro, the river flanked by cottonwood trees providing roosts for the eagles that soared overhead, wheeling on huge wings against the pale blue sky.

"Contention's just acrost the river," said Felix. Abruptly, he grabbed the reins. "I'll take us acrost," he said. "This ford's a bit tricky for anyone's first time out." Silent as he guided the mules into the river, across and up the opposite slope where he returned the reins to Jim's hands, he reverted to his previous subject. "You mind ya'self in Contention, boy," he said sternly. "Contention didn't get its name for nothin'. It's seen many a man planted afore his time. You just bear that in mind, Tascosa, and you'll live to make the trip back to Tombstone!"

"The place is that rough, hunh?"

"Yep," said Felix, spitting. "Meaner'n a gunnysack full a bobcats."

Doing business in a mixture of wooden and adobe buildings and canvas tents were Mason's Western Hotel, a mercantile house, blacksmith shop, dairy and meat markets, a Chinese laundry and John McDermott's saloon.

Three mills operated in the town reducing the ore hauled from the Tombstone mines—Grand Central, Head Center and the Contention. At a barn that was the Durkee Stagecoach and Transportation Company's office and receiving depot at the Contention mill, the unloading of the ore took Jim and two burly helpers only an hour.

Shirtless, Jim propped his hands on his hips and squinted through the sun at Felix lounging in the shade of a porch. "The work's done. How soon do you think we'll be headin' back to town?" he asked.

Stirring in his loafer's chair, Felix tilted against the wall. "First thing in the mornin'."

"Plenty of sun left today," said Jim, putting on his shirt as he stepped onto the shaded porch.

"No arguin' about that." Felix sighed. "But I don't fancy bringin' no wagon down no steep trail from no mill in the dark, and I sure ain't plannin on beddin' down up at the Mason's Hotel neither. We'll wait here till sunup."

Twilight was brief. The sun simply disappeared behind the steep hills on the west bank of the San Pedro, plunging the mining camp that called itself a city into instant darkness, like blowing out a lamp. But there were lamps glowing in the sprawl of ramshackle buildings and tents that were Contention's version of the saloons and gambling houses of Dodge City, Tascosa, Las Vegas and Tombstone.

The men were the same as those he'd encountered in those towns, Jim decided as he stepped into McDermott's saloon and to the bar for a rye.

"Howdy," he said to the lanky figure beside him.

Unanswered, Jim shrugged and gulped his whiskey. "Another," he said to the bartender, who poured the rye wordlessly.

This was different, he thought. Though the saloon was as noisy as any he'd ever visited, there appeared to be none of the easy openness to strangers that he'd found in men fresh off the cattle trail. These were tight-lipped men, talking only to themselves. Closed up and secretive. Clanish. Unwilling to open up to one they didn't already know, and as unyielding as the mines they worked. Which was what made them that way, he reckoned. When you looked for riches in the earth, he supposed, you soon learned to keep things to yourself.

He was startled, therefore, to hear his name bellowed from the back of the crowded saloon. "Tascosa! Hey, Tascosa."

Turning, he searched the room until he found a face he knew. "Well cripes, if it ain't Ringo," he muttered, pushing away from the bar. Ringo was leaning against the back wall, alone as best Jim could make out as he approached. "Never figured on seein' you in Contention." Jim grinned as they shook hands.

"Same here." Ringo laughed. "Don't tell me you're taking up working in the mills?"

"A man's gotta work," said Jim, going on to explain the circumstances that had brought about their unexpected reunion. "Remember us passin' the graveyard as we rode into Tombstone," he said grimly, "and the fresh grave we saw? You said somethin' about never sendin' to know who the funeral bell tolled for? Well, it was Lou's grave we saw."

"Hell and damnation," groaned Ringo, stomping the floor. "That's awful about your friend being killed. And I certainly understand and sympathize with your feelings. But it seems to me that the chances of your finding the man who murdered Lou range from slim to none. He's probably down in Mexico. That's a spot where lots of outlaws hide out. Or he could be lying low someplace up north in Colorado."

"Don't matter where that snake Frank Hall is," growled Jim. "When I get a lead on him, I'll be there." He paused to slap his Colt. "But enough about my woes," he said, brightening his tone. "What the devil brings you to Contention?"

"Business! I own a piece of one of the mills."

"You? Mixed up in minin'? I'd a never thought it."

"Why not? Business is a gamble. Gambling's what I do."

"Well, I wish you luck."

"And I wish you the same in tracking down Frank Hall. But you'd better be careful. That's a dangerous undertaking. Hall's a nasty character."

Jim's eyes widened with puzzlement. "You know him?"

"Well, I don't exactly *know* him. I've *heard* of him. He's got a pretty sour reputation. Why not just leave all this to the law?"

"I seen the law in Tombstone, and I ain't impressed a bit with Marshal Virgil Earp. Don't care much for his brother Wyatt, either."

"I'll drink to that." Ringo laughed. "C'mon. Step up to the bar with me and I'll stand you to another rye!"

"Much obliged," said Jim, following Ringo through the crowd of tight-lipped men and thinking again what a surprise it was to have found Ringo, and what a small world it was, really, full of the unexpected.

Chapter Sixteen
Dead Men for Breakfast

Working six days a week and with seemingly countless trips to Contention and Charleston listening to Felix Catlin's weak jokes and windy reminiscences, Jim passed the remainder of June without a clue as to the whereabouts of Frank Hall. It was as if he had vanished from the face of the earth. But at no time in the routines of the strenuous, passing days did he give up on his belief that the day would come when he would encounter Hall and make him pay for murdering Lou Garrard.

He had Sundays off and spent them exercising Midnight with rides into the countryside, picking him up early at the O.K. and giving Chip the money for the horse's upkeep for the coming week. "For all the use you make of that pretty black hoss," said Chip as he noted the latest payment in his ledger book, for the second week of July, "you might as well sell 'im."

"Couldn't do that," said Jim. "Midnight was a gift from a friend."

Chip put Jim's payment money into a tin box. "The one who got killed?"

"That's right," said Jim.

"You're sure a sentimental cuss," said Chip, writing out a receipt. Handing it to Jim, he cocked back in his chair, feet up and head cradled in his hands. "Where you ridin' to today? You must've seen everything there is to look at round here by now."

"I thought I'd head east, maybe go over to Galeyville."

"If I had a Sunday off" — Chip leered, — "I'd spend the whole day rollin' around with a whore in one of them big beds upstairs over at Diamond Annie's. Not ridin' around the damned desert."

"The desert's pretty," said Jim.

Chip's leer became a sneer. "Well, I say, you seen one cactus, you seen 'em all!"

There *was* a fierce, lonely beauty to the desert, thought Jim as he rode slowly past Boot Hill, glancing momentarily at the stone that now marked Lou's grave. Paid for out of his first earnings from Mr. Durkee, it had been raised a week ago—a slab of light-gray polished marble with plain engraving:

LOU GARRARD
1881
"Good night, sweet prince."

Johnny Ringo had suggested the words from Shakespeare and had stood with Jim as the undertaker, Goldstein, supervised its placing. Cass Buford also stood with him, holding his hand as a preacher by the name of Loewenwarter, who'd been hired for the occasion, spoke briefly about the "Better world that lay ahead for all of us." Seamus Dolan had also come, emitting a cough at the close of the preacher's speech, though whether it was really a cough or an expression of doubt as to the sentiment, Jim could only guess.

Now, proceeding at a trot down the sloping road, Jim rode east on Barfoot Trail toward the closer Dragoons and the more distant, rugged Chiricahuas with the desolate beauties of the desert unfolding all around him. A rebuke to Chip's wisecrack about when you've seen one cactus you've seen them all, here was a vast array of them, a miriad of plants tough enough to survive in their bleak surroundings: the prickly pear, maguey, yucca, ocotillo and the immense saguaro. The land, too, was a wonder to behold, so different from the flat and featureless plain around Tascosa. Here were buttes, mesas, arroyos, washes, canyons and the abrupt, sheer climb of mountain ranges. Places where a man could lose himself, he thought, squinting through the sun glare toward the Dragoons. Frank Hall could be hiding out anywhere in those mountains, he thought. Or in the Chiricahuas to the east, the

131

Huachucas west of the San Pedro, or up north in the Winchester, Galiuro or Pinaleno. South, in the caves of the Mule Mountains around Bisbee? Holed up in the outlaw-cradling expanses of Mexico, as Ringo believed? Maybe he'd fled to the anonymity of Phoenix or Tucson. Or even to California. Was Frank Hall at that moment in San Francisco, or, as Felix always called it, Frisco? Was the notion that Frank Hall would come back to Tombstone a pipe dream? Was Jim Hardin, the sentimental kid from Tascosa, a plain fool?

Noontime saw him through the Dragoons and into Sulphur Springs Valley, and approaching the cut-off to the wagon trail that came up from the town of Douglas on the Mexican border. Drawing rein on Midnight, he paused to gaze southward to a cloud of yellow dust. "Somethin's movin' up that road, Midnight," he said, lifting his hat and wiping the sweat from his brow. "Goin' slow, too." Probably a wagon train, he thought, replacing his hat, pocketing his wipe and gently nudging his boot heels into Midnight's ribs.

Half an hour later they reached the juncture of the Barfoot Trail and the Douglas road, pausing again to watch a long train of mule-pulled wagons driven by Mexicans — at least two dozen, he figured. He knew little of their language but enough to greet the one at the head of the mule train with *"Buenos dias"* and a friendly tip of his hat as the heavy, creaking wagons lumbered onto the Galeyville road.

Surging ahead, Jim soon left them behind, but in the middle of the afternoon as he was drinking beer and playing poker in the Dos Pesos Saloon, the train rumbled slowly through town on its apparently implacable drive to the east. The short runs he was making to Contention and Charleston were hard enough work, he thought as he watched the passing of the last of the wagons; how much harder must it be on a long journey such as theirs?

Back in Tombstone at six o'clock, Jim returned Midnight to Chip's keeping at the O.K., bathed in a deep wooden tub that was the pride of Fly's Lodginghouse, put on a powder-blue suit and starched white shirt and headed on foot to the Occidental for another of his new Sunday rituals — supper with Cass Buford.

Two men were seated with her at her usual table. "Gentlemen, this is my friend Jim Hardin," she said. "Jim, meet the Honorable

John Gosper, acting as Governor of the Arizona Territory in the absence of John C. Fremont." A handsome man with gray muttonchop whiskers, a fine gray suit and a long black after-dinner cigar which he switched from his right hand, to shake Jim's hand firmly.

"How do, sir," said Jim with a self-conscious half bow. "This is a thrill for me. I never met a governor before."

"Mr. Gosper's in Tombstone to see what can be done about the lawlessness," said Cass. "And you know John Clum, I believe," she said, turning and tapping Clum's shoulder with her fan.

The editor of the *Epitaph* rose halfway. "How goes the job with Josh Durkee, Mr. Hardin?"

"Well, he ain't fired me yet." Jim grinned, sliding into the chair Cass pointed out for him. "So I s'pose it's goin' fine."

"Jim has had a personal taste of the lawlessness of the cowboy element," said Clum, addressing Gosper. "He came to Tombstone a few weeks ago all the way from Tascosa in the Texas panhandle expecting to join up with an old friend, only to learn that the friend had been shot to death, unprovoked, by one of that cowboy element — Frank Hall, a hanger-on with the Clanton gang."

"May I express my sincerest condolences," said Gosper. "It must have been a terrible shock for you." He drew on the cigar a moment. "And what of this Hall? Has he paid the penalty for his foul deed?"

"Not yet," said Jim gravely. "So far the lawmen around here have failed to do their duty."

"Now, that remark interests me," said Gosper, leaning forward with a frown. "I've spoken to the constituted authorities and found that they seem to be either unable or unwilling to deal effectively with these outlaws. I find it distressing to have to report that neither the county sheriff, Mr. Behan, nor the town marshal, Virgil Earp, nor his brother Wyatt, has demonstrated any noticeable effect. I conferred with Sheriff John Behan, and he represented to me that Deputy U.S. Marshal Wyatt Earp and City Marshal Virgil Earp are unwilling to cooperate with him in capturing and bringing these outlaws to justice. But when I conversed with the Earps, I was informed that Sheriff Behan is in cahoots with the cowboy element." He threw up his hands. "Whom to believe?"

"Believe the Earps," said Clum emphatically.

"Do you mean to say, John, that Sheriff Behan has defiled his oath of office and is actively collaborating with the outlaw element?"

"To be precise," said Clum, "Behan is lock, stock and barrel on the side of the Clantons."

"Unconscionable," exclaimed Gosper, flicking a long cigar ash into a silver ashtray. "Something must be done about this! Decent people simply must insist on genuine law and order. The criminal must be dealt with."

"I couldn't agree more, sir," said Jim, "so let me promise you that once I cross paths with Frank Hall, there'll be one less outlaw runnin' loose in the Arizona Territory."

"That's the idea!" exclaimed Gosper, tapping the table for emphasis. "Capture these outlaws and put them on trial for their crimes!"

"Oh, I ain't turnin' Frank Hall over to no one for trial," said Jim, studying the sumptuous offerings of the supper menu. "I intend to kill 'im myself."

Pleasantly full and drowsy after his meal, Jim sank into a loafer's chair on the porch of the Occidental and tilted back with his feet crossed at the ankles and propped against a post as a gentle, cooling breeze caressed him. Piano music floated out from the Occidental to serenade him, and all of Tombstone seemed to be greeting him like an old friend as church-goers paraded past the Occidental in performance of their own rituals on the day God had set aside for rest, even in Tombstone where, it was said, there was a dead man for breakfast every day.

Fifty miles away, there was no rest for the Mexicans Jim had encountered on the road to Galeyville. Having lumbered out of the San Luis Pass, their mule train was deep in the narrow confines of Guadalupe Canyon in the Chiricahua Mountains when, suddenly, they were fighting for their lives.

Ambushed.

* * *

"I guess you already hear'd what happened last night over in the Guadalupe," said Felix Catlin on Monday morning as he waited for Jim to hitch a mule team to their freighter for the first run of the new week to Contention.

Fitting the rigging to the lead mules, Jim braced for another of Felix's jokes. "No," he said. "What happened?"

"It was nothin' less than a bloody mass-a-cree," said Felix, chewing a wad of tobacco. "Nineteen Mexicans shot to pieces. Some of 'em tortured to death."

Frozen with horror, Jim thought back to his Sunday ride and the Mexicans he'd run into. Were they the ones Felix was talking about? A massacre? "Apaches?" he asked.

"Bandits," said Felix, spitting for emphasis. "Word of it came through late last night, and Wyatt Earp, his brothers and Doc Holliday headed out right away to investigate."

Jim stared eastward across the lightening desert with a look of disbelief. He'd seen those Mexicans. Dirt poor, he'd thought when he'd crossed their path. He'd supposed they were making their way north in hopes of finding a new start in life. "What in hell would a bunch of Mexican mule skinners have that somebody'd kill 'em all for?"

"Bullion," said Felix. "The word is, they was haulin' seventy-five thousand in silver bullion."

Chapter Seventeen
Divided Trail

It was two days later before the Earps and Doc Holliday rode back into Tombstone — alone. "The carnage in that canyon was the worst thing I ever saw in my entire life," said Holliday to Jim and Cass that evening at the Occidental. "The feeling I had was that whoever did it wanted it to look as if Indians were guilty." He was drinking hard and leaving his supper go cold before him. "But it was worse than anything the Apaches might have done," he went on bitterly. "It was clear that the job was well planned. You could see where the gang lay in ambush. This was white men's work!" He gulped more whiskey. "Wyatt's convinced it was the Clantons who pulled it off."

"Is that conviction based on evidence?" asked Cass. "Or is this another case of Wyatt's animosity toward Clantons clouding his view of things?"

"It's the kind of outrage you expect from Old Man Clanton," said Holliday. "In running his criminal empire, he's got spies everywhere to keep their eyes open for herds to be rustled. They dress up like peons, hang around in the cantinas along the border and keep a watch on all the watering holes. One of them must have heard about this mule train carrying bullion. That's just the sort of news that'd have Old Man Clanton licking his chops."

"Suspicion's one thing," said Cass. "Provin' it is another."

"True, my darling," replied Holliday, raising his whiskey glass as if to toast her. "However, there is some evidence, though not enough to hang anybody on."

"Such as?" asked Jim eagerly.

"A rancher who's got a small spread on the other side of Galeyville saw the Clanton gang earlier that day — Sunday — riding hell bent for leather toward Guadalupe Canyon. This rancher's had a few run-ins with the old man and a scrape or two with Ike, so he knows a Clanton when he sees one. In this instance, he says, he saw Old Man Clanton, Ike and Billy. And he *thinks* but isn't sure that Curly Bill Brocius was one of them. And Johnny Ringo appeared to be there as well."

"Ringo?" protested Jim. "I'll never believe that Ringo would take part in a massacre."

"Believe what you like," said Holliday, cracking a smile and shrugging. "I'm only relating what the rancher said." He paused and peered at the forgotten meal. Pushing his plate aside, he lit a cigarette. "There was another rider about Billy Clanton's age, possibly Billy Claiborne." He interrupted himself again, puffing on his cigarette and then holding it out and studying it as he mulled over his next words. "And there was a seventh rider," he said, shifting his eyes to Jim. "Frank Hall."

"That son of a bitch?" yelled Jim, leaping to his feet. "He was there?" Instinctively, his hand enclosed the grip of his Colt. "Are you sure about that, Doc?"

"I'm not sure of anything," answered Holliday, smoking again. "I only know what the rancher said. But the Earps feel confident that all he told us was true."

Jim's eyes narrowed to angry slits. "Then, why the devil ain't the Earps arrested nobody?"

Holliday raised a hand and counted the fingers. "P-R-O-O-F."

"This rancher you talked about," said Jim excitedly. "The one who says he saw Frank Hall. Was he sure it was Hall? There was no mistake?"

"He seemed pretty certain of himself to me," said Holliday.

Grimacing, Jim slapped his holster. "So the bastard *is* still in the vicinity!"

"Maybe not."

Jim's eyes opened wide. "Whatcha mean by that?"

"From examining the ground in Guadalupe Canyon, we could

137

see that there were, indeed, seven men who staged that ambush. The prints of their horses' hooves were evident. We followed those tracks out of the canyon as far as Turkey Creek where six of the riders swung west. The seventh turned south toward the Mexican border. Since all the others were heading back into Clanton country, it appears that trail heading south was likely to be Hall's. Wyatt figures Hall's probably been hiding out down around the border, maybe in Douglas or Bisbee, and was the one who found out that this bullion train would be moving north."

"So Hall's headin' south!" Jim's eyes were ablaze now. He licked his lips. His fingers drummed his holster. "If I'm to find him, that's the likeliest spot. How far to Bisbee? To Douglas?"

"Twenty miles to Bisbee," answered Holliday, crushing the last of his cigarette on the heel of his shiny black boot. It's another thirty or so to Douglas. But I suggest you just put any ideas of going after Hall straight out of your head. That's not a part of this country where a man ought to be venturing on his own. That's a wide, open border, Tascosa! It's infested with cutthroats who are a lot worse than Frank Hall, believe me. Not to mention the bands of renegade Apaches that frequent the area, dodging back and forth across the border."

"Frank Hall seems to have no trouble gettin' around safely," said Jim sarcastically.

Cass tugged at his sleeve. "Doc's talkin' sense, Tascosa! You'd be a fool to go ridin' down there lookin' for Hall all by yourself. Why, if he got wind that someone was trailin' him, he'd. . . . Well, you've heard what he did in Guadalupe Canyon!"

"He was with a gang then," grunted Jim. "This'd be just the two of us. Him and me."

"Listen to me, honey," beseeched Cass. "Frank Hall knows that territory." She directed blue, pleading eyes to Holliday. "Right, Doc?"

Holliday held out his hand. "Like I know the lines in my palm."

"It's no use debatin' this," cried Jim, pulling away from the table. "I'm goin' after that rattlesnake."

"Wait a minute," shouted Holliday, following him.

Jim halted. "It's settled, Doc! I'm goin'."

Holliday nodded. "I can see there's no talking you out of this.

But you're a damned fool if you think you can go it alone." He paused again, thinking. "You're pretty tight with Johnny Deuce, am I right?"

Jim nodded slowly. "You could say that."

"The Deuce is no friend of Frank Hall," said Holliday. "He might fancy the notion of settling some old accounts. And Deuce knows that territory down there as well as Hall."

Jim gripped Holliday's hand appreciatively. "Thanks for the advice, Doc. I'll see if Deuce is around."

"Don't mention that I suggested it," said Holliday. "Deuce doesn't exactly count me among his closest friends! You'll probably find him —"

"I know, Doc," said Jim, spinning toward the door. "Playin' cards over at the Oriental!"

Also a creature of habit, Seamus Dolan was as impeccably dressed as ever at Johnny Deuce's poker table and holding nothing better than two eights. Folding, he greeted Jim jovially. "You're just in time to bring me a change of luck!"

Raking in his earnings, Deuce shot Jim a studious glance. "You got the look of a man with business on his mind, Tascosa." A knowing grin appeared. "Might it be named Frank Hall?"

"You guessed it," said Jim.

"Wasn't no guess at all," objected Deuce. "I was expectin' you to show up sooner or later, all worked up by what happened over in Guadalupe Canyon. I heard the story that Hall was one of those who participated in the raid on those Mexicans."

"There is no proof of Hall's being there," interjected Seamus.

Deuce snorted. "What happened over there in the Chiricahuas has Frank Hall written all over it, and you know it, Seamus! And Old Man Clanton's bloody handprints are on it, too!"

"The facts point to Hall headin' down Mexico way," said Jim urgently. "I mean to go after him, Deuce. Question is, are you comin' with me?"

Deuce reared back in his chair. "What makes you think I'd be interested in helpin' you settle your account with Hall?"

"Because you've got some outstandin' affairs with Hall yourself."

"That's the trouble with Tombstone," said Deuce sourly. "A man's business is everybody's business!"

Jim leaned across the poker table. "You told me on your own that you'd like to square matters with Hall." He pulled up straight, fingering the grip of his Colt. "So, you comin'?"

"Dunno," teased Deuce, studying the deck of cards before him. "I've got me a pretty little winnin' streak goin' for me in this here game."

"There's always poker," whispered Jim, leaning close again. "But there may be only one golden opportunity like this to nail Frank Hall." He bolted upright, hand resting on the butt of his Colt once more. "Well? In or out?"

Deuce ruminated, shuffling the deck, flipping out five cards: a full house. He winced. "See what I mean?"

"Time's awastin'."

Deuce gathered the cards, straightened the edges of the deck and slapped them into the middle of the table. "Sorry to quit on you while you're in a hole, Seamus," he said, rising. "But deal me out."

"Hold on," declared Seamus as he leapt to his feet. "If you think I'm going to let this story pass me by, think again! I'm coming along!"

"Seamus, this might get a little dangerous," replied Jim. "If we do find Hall, there's goin' to be shootin'."

"For your information, young man," Seamus huffed, "I was with Sherman on the march through Georgia." He retrieved his gray hat from a rack. "Now *that*," he said, carefully donning it, "was a real shootin' party!"

140

Chapter Eighteen
Discoveries

The following morning with an unforgiving sun directly over the Huachuca Mountains, Johnny Deuce led Jim and Seamus wendingly and painstakingly slowly southward on a single-file trail that snaked up through a rocky corridor of a narrow canyon whose steep eroded walls soared to peaks that were red and raggedy against a pale blue, cloudless sky.

Already, Jim was feeling parched, but he knew he'd be even thirstier in the afternoon. There'd be no water until they came to Bisbee which was still almost twenty miles farther, Deuce had warned them, so Jim fought the urge to drink from the canteens that hung heavily from the saddle horn.

Ahead of them a flock of screeching hawks and a pair of silent eagles wheeled and soared on the hot updrafts, their keen eyes searching for carrion in the wasteland that Jim, Seamus and Deuce would be reaching soon. "Looks like those birds have found something big to feed on up ahead," said Deuce. "There's so many of 'em. Some cattle must've died up."

"Or some renegade Chiricahua Apaches did a little of their dirty work recently," said Seamus grimly. "Raided one of those little ranches, maybe. Or hit a wagon train, perhaps." He paused with eyes narrowed and mouth hard-set. "The Clantons don't hold the patent on attacking wagoneers, you know. The Apaches wrote the book on ambushes." He squinted upward. "Just look at these cliffs! They could be concealing a war party right now, watching down

141

on us, waiting for their chance to attack."

Twisting in his saddle and looking back, Deuce grunted a laugh. "Seamus, are you tryin' to put a scare into our friend Tascosa?"

"Injuns don't scare me," snapped Jim bravely.

"Well, they scare the blazes out of me," cried Seamus. "I've seen their handiwork! I've seen the hell raised by the Commanches and the Kiowas up in the northern plains and in Texas. I was a witness to the carnage left behind by a war party of Kwahadi allies of the Commanche chief Quanah Parker seven years ago. I saw what was left of two white men taken alive by Apaches and then strung up, head down over fires that slowly cooked their brains while those savages danced around gleefully. And I wrote many a newspaper story of the depredations of Cochise as he waged his merciless war on the white eyes all across the Apacheria."

"That may be," answered Deuce, "but all the bad ain't been on the Indians' side. I was present up in Tucson in seventy-one when a lynch mob marched on Camp Grant and butchered eighty-five of the Aravaipa Apache bein' held prisoner by the army."

"In seventy-six I laid eyes on what some Chiricahuas did when they attacked Sonora," answered Seamus, his voice rising angrily and echoing from the surrounding cliffs. "So don't give me any bullshit about the ill-used red skin. Nor any of that sentimental malarkey that John Clum writes about ever since he was the Indian agent in the Territory. I don't want to hear none of that crap about Cochise, Victorio and Geronimo being heroes. And nothing of this old man they call Nana who's been leading renegade Chiricahuas on the warpath!"

"Seamus obviously has strong feelings." Deuce chuckled, addressing Jim. "And what are your views on the murderous red man, Tascosa?"

"The only killer I care about," said Jim passionately, "is Frank Hall." They'd cleared the canyon now and faced a vast, scrubby, cactus-dotted, rock-strewn and rolling desert stretching several miles to the Mule Mountains and the settlement of Bisbee where, Johnny Deuce expected, they'd find someone who could put them onto Hall's trail. "I just pray we find him in Bisbee," Jim went on, "so I can settle up with him right away."

"Then what?" asked Seamus, riding beside Jim now. "What do you do with your life after you're done with Frank Hall?"

Pulling a wipe from his sweat-soaked shirt pocket, Jim dabbed beads of perspiration from his face. "I'll think about that after."

"You seem to have fit in nicely in Tombstone," said Deuce. "Why not settle permanently?"

"I don't exactly fancy bein' a mule skinner the rest of my life," said Jim. "And I can't say that I care much for the Earps. Or them for me. Old Felix Catlin says California's nice. Maybe I'll move out there." He fixed his gaze on the distant mountains. "But first things first."

A mile south of the canyon the land roughened considerably, laced with cuts and washes and deep ravines. Above one of these swarmed the hawks and eagles they'd seen earlier, drifting down and duelling in the air with black buzzards.

Fighting among themselves on the ground with flapping wings, hideous squawks and shrill cries, they were picking at the dead, bloating bodies of six Mexicans.

"This is Apaches' doing for sure," shouted Seamus furiously. "And not so long ago; two days, maybe. Three at most."

"They had wagons," said Deuce, pointing to wheel tracks in the sandy earth. "Looks like they were camped. Ambushed. The red skins took the wagons and whatever they were carryin'."

"It couldn't have been much," said Seamus, dismounting to study the tracks. "Two wagons, lightly loaded. They couldn't have been hauling anything of real value. No ore. No silver bullion. They probably had nothing more than personal goods. Looks to me like this was a family on the move."

"Couldn't've been a family," declared Jim, shifting uneasily in his saddle to draw his wipe again and cover his mouth and nose with it as the sickly sweet smell of the dead drifted up from the ravine. "Where's the women and kids?"

Seamus looked up wordlessly.

"The Apaches took 'em," said Deuce.

"Aw, Jesus," moaned Jim, feeling as if he had to throw up, "that's horrible."

Seamus stood, hands on hips. "I reckon we ought to ride over to Fort Huachuca and report this to the army. Maybe they'll be able to track down this party of savages."

Jim frowned. "How far's the fort?"

Deuce answered. "About twenty miles due west."

Jim's mind raced southward to Bisbee. Was Frank Hall there? If so, how long would he hang around? Perhaps he'd already moved on. If so, how long ago? Bisbee was still a few hours distant. Time was passing, the day progressing. Divert from their goal now and it would be time lost and distance widened between him and Frank Hall. "That's a pretty long detour," he said sourly. "What about just one ridin' over to the fort? Or the two of you head there whilst I proceed to Bisbee."

"The hell with that," bellowed Seamus.

"Why not?" demanded Jim.

"With this band of Apaches on the loose, this is no time or place for a man to be on his own," said Seamus, his narrow eyes drilling into Jim's. "So get any notion out of that head of yours about us splitting up. Either we all go over to Fort Huachuca or we don't." Eyes shifted to Deuce, then back to Jim. "What's it going to be?"

"We're closer to Bisbee," answered Deuce. "They've got a town marshal. We can report this to him. He can then send over to Huachuca for the army."

"Yeah, that sounds like a good idea to me," exclaimed Jim.

"Very well," said Seamus with a nod as he reached for his horse. "That's what we'll do."

"Keep your eyes peeled," muttered Deuce as they rode off. "There's always the possibility those Apaches ain't so far away."

Minutes later, the words proved prophetic.

Seamus saw them first—five Apaches in war paint appearing from behind a large shelf of rock and pounding toward them from the east with bloodcurdling whoops. "Hostiles!" he shouted.

As Jim looked up sharply, he saw the flash of a muzzle and heard the bang of the gun and then a bullet whizzing past an ear.

"Run for it!" cried Seamus.

They were less than a quarter of a mile distant, Deuce estimated. And closing fast. "We'll never outrun 'em," he yelled.

"There's cover up ahead," shouted Seamus.

Riding furiously, they plunged toward and into a shallow dry wash. Flinging themselves from their horses, they slammed against the hard wall of the gulley, their pistols blazing.

Deuce screamed, "Shoot their mounts!"

A fussilade downed three, the animals letting out tortured sounds as they were hit, cartwheeling and throwing their wildly yelping riders.

As two Apaches staggered to their feet, Jim fired twice at the closer and gaped with satisfaction as the tiny, nearly naked figure spun like a top, whereas a shot from Deuce's pistol simply dropped a second Apache like a sack of grain.

Drawing rein on their painted ponies, the remaining pair whirled back as bullets from Seamus and Deuce missed them.

The third, whose horse had been shot from under him, was stirring from unconsciousness. Moving, slithering snakelike, he edged toward the cover of his fallen pony, which was writhing and wailing in the throes of dying. Three guns roared at once, the bullets kicking up dust as they fell short, then fired again, riddling the struggling Apache. Reloading his Colt .45, Seamus muttered, "There's a brave and a horse that can ride into the Happy Hunting Ground together!"

"Looks like the other two's decided to skeedaddle," declared Jim, nodding toward the remaining pair, who were now retreating rapidly.

"Don't count on it," grunted Deuce. "There's prob'ly a lot more than just these five. Those two will be back. With help."

Moments later, these words, too, proved prophetic as the two Apaches reappeared, accompanied by at least a dozen more, as best Jim could reckon. "Sweet Jesus," he sighed, as much in amazement as in fear or prayer.

"Hold fire till they're closer," whispered Deuce. "Then make every shot count. We'll take as many of 'em with us as we can."

So this is how it ends for me, thought Jim as he waited. "I'm too damned young to die like this," he muttered as the Apaches thundered at him. Feeling the beat of their hooves under his belly as they raced toward the wash, he whispered, "I've got unfinished business!" *Frank Hall must pay for the killing of Lou Garrard,* he thought, cocking his Colt and squinting down the barrel to sight an Apache on a big brown horse.

They were a hundred yards away now, yelps and whoops growing louder, a huge cloud of dust trailing them. Would they scalp him when they were done killing him? Suppose they didn't kill him outright? What kind of torturing might they inflict? Seamus's story about Apaches hanging men head down over a roasting fire came back to send a shiver down his back.

"Save one bullet," he muttered, checking the chambers of his Colt.

Would God count it a sin if he killed himself under such a circumstance? Wasn't it better to commit suicide than be cooked alive upside down? Was it a sin to kill Indians? Did "Thou shalt not kill" apply to Apaches? Expecting to die, he prayed, "Lord God Almighty, have mercy on my soul. But let me take a few with me. And may Frank Hall burn in hell."

Steadying his Colt, he had a flash of memory of Lou Garrard instructing him how to shoot—so long ago in the Palo Duro—and accusing him of holding back.

"I'm not holdin' back anymore Lou!" he shouted, firing at the Apache on the big brown pony and dropping him.

The Apaches were shooting now, bullets gouging up dirt from the lip of the wash and raining it down on his back.

As they raced toward him, he emptied the Colt's chambers, save one, and prepared to die, but exploding behind him, far to the rear of the wash, he heard another volley. "Cripes, they've got us surrounded," he gasped.

Spinning around, he gaped in astonishment at hard-charging cavalry racing toward him. Blinking his eyes, he thought this had to be the imagining of his frightened mind. But they were blessedly real. "Horse soldiers," he shouted exultantly as he tugged at Johnny Deuce's shirt sleeve while the miraculous, amazing, lifesaving, yelling, blue-uniformed riders surged forward with the Stars and Stripes flapping above their vanguard.

Flooding past the wash with blazing Colts and Winchesters, they turned the Apaches into a bloody retreat.

With the firing ended, gunsmoke drifting away and the land lying silent and strewn with white-painted, brown-skinned corpses, the officer in command of the soldiers rode back, saluted, stepped down from a winded, broad-shouldered bay mare and introduced himself as Second Lieutenant Mike Lee. Tall and ramrod-stiff with a bushy black mustache that seemed out of keeping with his baby face and soft-spoken tones, he explained that he was posted at nearby Fort Huachuca and that he and his troop of twenty dusty horse soldiers had been on patrol searching for perhaps fifty rampaging Apaches. "We'd bivouacked overnight at Bisbee," he continued. "Then this morning we received a report of a massacre of some Mexicans up this way."

"Afraid it's true," said Seamus. "We found 'em a few miles north of here and were going to make a report when we reached Bisbee."

"A prospector discovered the bodies late yesterday," said the lieutenant, stroking his luxuriant mustache, "but it was nearly high noon today before he could reach Bisbee. We rode out right away. Lucky we did, eh?"

"From our viewpoint, the timing couldn't've been better." Seamus grinned. "Of course, this can't be all of them. You said there may be as many as fifty? I'm sure that's right because there's still got to be those who have the Mexican women. And children, if any."

Grim-faced, the lieutenant muttered, "I understand that there were two families. They passed through Bisbee a couple of days ago moving up from Sonora, Mexico, and hoping for a fresh start up in Colorado. There were five children, I was told."

The silence of imagined horrors gripped them for a long moment.

"Then, you'll be wanting to go after them promptly," said Seamus. "We shan't detain you further."

"I won't hear of it, sir," insisted the officer. "I'm detaching two of my troopers to accompany the three of you into Bisbee. No telling how many of these hostiles remain in this vicinity."

"Much obliged," said Johnny Deuce.

As the lieutenant mounted his horse, Jim stepped forward. "When you were in Bisbee, did you happen to come across anyone by the name of Frank Hall?"

The lieutenant stiffened. "What's your business with him?"

"Personal matter," said Jim, taken aback by the unexpected brusqueness.

"Hall's a friend of yours?" demanded Lee.

"Far from it," snapped Jim. "He gunned down a friend of mine in Tombstone, and I mean to bring him to justice. One way or the other."

"Well, you won't find Hall in Bisbee," said Lieutenant Lee sharply. "Last I heard he'd hightailed it across the border into Mexico."

"When was that?"

"Just ahead of our arrival in Bisbee. We missed him by a day, apparently." He adjusted his weathered hat. "Much to my chagrin."

"So you are familiar with Hall?"

"I've been wanting to nab that owlhoot for months," said the lieutenant, pulling on his gloves. "I have sought that son of a bitch ever since he and a pal of his stuck up a stagecoach on the Iron Springs-to-Tucson road a couple of months ago. They killed the driver, the fella who was ridin' shotgun and two passengers, one of which was the supply sergeant from Fort Huachuca on his way to Tucson on business for the army. From that day to this I've had my sights set on Hall and the cold-blooded killer who assisted him in that stage robbery — a lowlife gunman who was going by the name of Lou Garrard!"

Jim lunged at the officer, grabbing his shirt in his fists. "That's a damned lie!"

Deuce dragged him away. "Calm down, Tascosa."

Struggling against Deuce's restraining arms, Jim yelled, "Not till he retracts that scurrilous lie about Lou!"

The officer calmly mounted his horse. "I assure you it's the gospel truth. There was another passenger on that stage who lived long enough to tell about it. And it happens that he recognized both Hall and Garrard."

"Then, he's also a damned liar!"

"Don't be a fool," said the officer, riding away. "Why would a dying man lie?"

Chapter Nineteen
Burying the Dead

That night in Bisbee while a Mexican band and a pretty girl singer with a white dress and a flowered sarape provided lively entertainment beneath the latticed roof of the small garden of the Los Tres Amigos Cantina, Jim sipped mescal and sulked. He'd kept this sullen silence since hearing the stunning assertion by Lieutenant Lee that Lou Garrard had been nothing more than a cold-blooded killer.

During their cavalry-escorted, peaceful ride into Bisbee, it had seemed appropriate to Seamus and Deuce to leave Jim with his thoughts, but now Seamus turned to him chastisingly. "Look, Tascosa, there's no use fretting about what was. Cheer up, amigo! Let bygones be bygones. Bury the dead!"

Head down, Jim peered from the tops of his eyes. "You two knew all about Lou, didn't you? You both knew what the truth was. Cass Buford must've known, too."

"Of course we knew," snapped Deuce.

Jim's head jerked up, the piercing blue eyes narrowing accusingly. "And what the hell is the truth?"

"It is," said Seamus calmly, "that Garrard was a gunslinger and outlaw, just as the lieutenant told you. He'd been in cahoots with Frank Hall almost since the day he rode into Tombstone. The two of them met at Hatch's billiard parlor. Hall was already tied in with the Clanton gang. Soon, Lou Garrard was taking orders from the old man, as well."

"So what led to Hall gunnin' Lou down?" demanded Jim. "Or was that tale a lie, also?"

"No lie," said Deuce. "Hall gunned Lou down, just as you've been told."

"I was told it was a case of Lou bein' shot while he was just mindin' his business," said Jim. "Now it turns out that he was gunned by an outlaw partner of his. And instead of tellin' me this straight away, people who said they were friends of mine kept the facts from me." The Mexican girl was bending beside him now, singing her song into his ear and running fingers through his long hair. "Leave me be," he grunted, shoving her away. "How come you never told me, Johnny? Seamus?"

"What would have been the point?" said Seamus. Digging a coin from his vest pocket and placing it in the pouting girl's palm, he muttered, "*Gracias, señorita.*" Turning to Jim, he said, "You never would have believed us. We could've sworn on a stack of Bibles, and you wouldn't've accepted the truth."

Jim gulped his mescal. "Didn't you think I'd ever find out?"

"We knew you'd learn all this, of course," said Seamus. "But Cass thought it would be best if you learned about your pal on your own."

Drying his mustache on his sleeve, Jim grunted a bitter laugh. "So Cass Buford was the brain behind all this!"

"Cass likes you quite a bit," answered Deuce. "She didn't want to see you hurt. She didn't want the bad news coming to you from your friends. Besides, she said, you'd never have believed it coming from one of us. 'Let him find out from Marshal Earp,' she told us. So that's why we kept our mouths shut. We figured the Earps or somebody else would break it to you. We were amazed it took so long for you to find out. Finally, that lieutenant did it. So now you know the truth. Let it be forgotten. Put this revenge crap aside. Nobody wants to see you hurt. Or killed. You can make a place for yourself in Tombstone. Get on with your own life."

Jim cracked a smile. "It don't change a thing! It's still a fact that Frank Hall gunned Lou down like a dog. And he's goin' to pay for it. I don't care what Lou might've been. No matter what his sins were lately, when I knew him, he was decent and my friend. He didn't deserve to die that way. As God's my witness,

Hall's goin' to answer to me."

"I doubt that you'll ever find him," asserted Seamus. "He may have run into the same band of Apaches we did. Or he's holed up in Mexico. He could've taken his share of that bullion robbery up in Guadalupe Canyon and headed for God-knows-where. Denver, maybe. Or back east someplace."

Slowly, Jim shook his head. "Hall's still in these parts. I'm sure of it." He tapped a thumb against his chest. "I feel it right here."

Part Four:
The Clanton Bunch

Chapter Twenty
Retribution

For the first time since he'd arrived in Tombstone and been treated to a drink on the house at the Oriental by Frank Leslie, Jim found Leslie tending bar without his fringed buckskin shirt. A white one with rolled-up sleeves had replaced it. "Too blamed hot," explained Frank, pouring Jim a glass of rye. "Hell can't boast heat like that of Arizona in August!"

Jim sipped the tepid whiskey. "Is it August already?" Three weeks had flown by since the army had ridden to his rescue. "Time sure flies," he muttered, swiveling against the bar to survey the sweltering room. Three weeks and not a whisper had been heard as to the whereabouts of Frank Hall.

August! Almost two months since he'd arrived in Tombstone. All that time passed since Lou Garrard had been gunned down, and still, Frank Hall had not been called upon to pay the price for it. Maybe he *was* dead. Perhaps the band of Apaches that nearly massacred him, Seamus and Deuce *did* come across Hall and butchered him, leaving his body to be picked clean by scavenging eagles, hawks and buzzards. Or had he slipped across the border into Mexico? Was it possible, as Seamus and Deuce had suggested, that Hall had taken his booty from the pack train atrocity in Guadalupe Canyon and was now living high off the hog in Denver, someplace back east or in Felix Catlin's idolized Frisco? All of these were possible — even likely — but they did not keep Jim's eyes from searching the faces of the sweating customers in the Oriental for

155

the one that might be Frank Hall's, at last.

"He ain't here, Tascosa," said Leslie sympathetically as he topped off Jim's glass. "If he was, I'd've told you right away."

"Who's not here?" said Jim, cracking a grin. "Am I that obvious?"

"Hell, kid, there's nobody in Tombstone that doesn't know by now that you've been on the lookout for Frank Hall since the day you blew into town. Hall's got to know it, too, the way I see it. In my book, Hall's layin' low somewhere since his pals passed him the word about you."

"Just like a back-shootin' coward not to have the guts to come forward and face up to his deed," said Jim disgustedly.

"You're right. Hall is a coward. He's never demonstrated the gumption needed for facin' a man. That's why he ambushed your friend. Not enough guts to do it face to face. No doubt he's heard about your reputation with a gun. He'd be loco to show his face while you're around. He probably figures that time's on his side. He's thinkin' that sooner or later you'll tire of all this waitin' and leave. His friends in the Clanton outfit are keepin' their eyes on you, y'know." His gaze settled on a slender trail-dressed figure playing poker with the McLaury brothers at the back of the saloon. "Such as Billy Claiborne, back there."

"That pipsqueak," grunted Jim. "Don't know why Old Man Clanton tolerates that little whelp."

"The old man puts up with him because he's a saddle buddy of the youngest of the Clanton boys."

"That must lend some confusion to their friendship, each of em bein' named Billy,.' Jim chuckled.

"Claiborne calls himself Billy the Kid now," whispered Leslie. "Since the genuine article was sent to his just reward by a bullet from Pat Garrett's gun over in Fort Sumner a few days ago, this prairie dog pup has taken to referrin' to *himself* as Billy the Kid. Ain't that a hoot? And demandin' that he be called it by others to boot."

The news of the killing of Billy the Kid had greeted Jim on his return from Bisbee, the July 14 issue of John Clum's *Epitaph* devoting a large portion of the front page to recounting the criminal escapades of the diminutive young gunman who had been born

Henry McCarty but used the names Kid Antrim and Billy the Kid as he terrorized New Mexico. "Sheriff Pat Garrett brought this puny pistoleer's career to an end with a bullet to the heart," Clum had written gleefully. "The demise of this hoodlum ought to be a warning to the lawless element here in Tombstone," he continued, leaving no doubt that his reference to "the lawless element" meant the Clantons and their allies. Eyes fixed now on Billy Claiborne, Jim shook his head. *So this is the new Billy the Kid,* he thought, smiling. "Thinks he's that tough, huh?" he said to Leslie.

"He's just plumb gun crazy. Like all the Clanton cowboys," muttered Leslie as he mopped the bar. "They're all headin' for trouble. You mark my words, Tascosa! There's goin' to be a real explosion round here one of these days, between them and the Earps."

"Can't say that I have any use for either side," said Jim, gulping the last of his rye.

"There's nothin' worse than a clan feud for the sparkin' of gunplay," said Leslie. "And this one simmerin' between the Clantons on one side and the Earps on the other is about the worst I've ever run across."

"If they do go at it," said Jim, smiling behind his sleeve as he wiped his damp mustache, "it'll be somethin' to behold."

Frank McLaury shouted from the back. "Tascosa! C'mon over and join us. Make it a foursome."

Jim sauntered to their table. "Thanks for the invite," he said, "but I'm headin' to the Occidental for supper. Been so long since I ate, my belly thinks my throat's been cut."

"It ain't," said Claiborne, sneering up. "Yet."

"Somethin' tells me it ain't the chow at the Occidental that draws you," cut in Frank McLaury as Claiborne gathered the cards. "The talk around town is that you and Cass Buford is pretty thick these days."

"You oughtn't to give credence to talk, Frank," said Jim. "Talk is cheap, 'specially in Tombstone."

"So is life," said Claiborne goadingly as he shuffled the deck.

"See what I mean?" said Jim, clapping one hand on his Colt and the other on Claiborne's skinny shoulder. "Cheap talk. Big mouth."

"Seems to *me* you got a pretty big mouth," rumbled Claiborne, stirring ominously. "For a low-down mule skinner."

"Speakin' of mules," said Jim, pushing down on Claiborne's bony shoulder, "the talk I've been hearin', Billy, is that you were mixed up in the ambush of those Mexicans over in the Guadalupe a while back."

"Lissen," hissed Claiborne, flinging down the deck of cards. "What I do," he said, starting to rise, "or what I don't do ain't none of your business."

Grabbing Claiborne's gun hand and flattening it on the table, Frank McLaury barked, "Stay put and deal, Billy! Tascosa, you have a pleasant supper!"

"Thanks, Frank," said Jim with a grin and a tip of his black hat. "I will." Sauntering away, he kept watchful eyes turned to the big mirrors behind the bar that reflected the entire saloon. Seeing Billy Claiborne with his hands in plain view atop the table, he waved good-bye to Frank Leslie and stepped out into the undiminished heat.

"You look wrung out," said Cass Buford, looking cool as a cucumber as Jim slid into a chair between her and an equally comfortable-looking and spiffy Doc Holliday. "You'd best be careful," she said. "You can get heat stroke out in that street."

"Or shot in the back," answered Jim, glowering.

"You're in a sour mood," said Holliday, fighting a cough. "What burr have you got under your saddle?"

"Billy Claiborne! Excuse me! Billy *the Kid* Claiborne."

"Where'd you run into him?"

"Over at the Oriental. Snide little bastard. Full of empty threats."

"So the Clantons are in town," said Holliday. "Maybe I'd better hike over to the marshal's office and let Virgil know."

"The McLaury's were with Claiborne," said Jim, "but I didn't see any of the Clantons."

"Nonetheless," said Holliday, lifting from his chair. "I should let Virgil know."

"Doc, sit still and have your supper," snapped Cass Buford, slapping him gently on the arm with her Japanese fan. "It's too damned warm to be worrying about the Clantons. If you ask me, you're all too jumpy. It's gettin' so that a Clanton can't even spit in the street without the Earps seein' somethin' dark behind it. And vice versa. Men! All you're ever lookin' for is an excuse to start a fight. You've all got some score to settle!" She shot a scolding glance sideways at Jim. "And, yes, that goes for you, kid! Since you hit this town all you've been thinkin' about is trackin' down Frank Hall and killin' him."

"The snake deserves it!"

"Maybe so. But in the meantime, what's the carryin' of this grudge doin' to you? It's ruinin' you. That's what hate does to you. Ruins you."

"I appreciate your worryin' about me," said Jim sweetly, hugging her, "but I still mean to bring Frank Hall to justice, one way or another. And don't hand me any of your well-meanin' lectures about Lou Garrard not bein' a saint. I've heard all that from Seamus and Johnny Deuce. And from Doc. Maybe Lou wasn't an angel here in Tombstone. Maybe he wasn't an angel when I knew him back in the Palo Duro. Maybe he was Satan's child. But he didn't deserve to die the way he did. He was my friend, and I mean to avenge his death, no matter how long it takes. When a man's friend is shot down like a dog, a man's got to do somethin' about it. That's what friends are for. An eye for an eye, a tooth for a tooth."

"Thus endeth the scripture reading for today," said Doc Holliday, clasping his hands prayerlike.

"The Good Book also says, 'Vengeance is mine, saith the Lord,' " said Cass, snapping open her fan.

"Touché," said Holliday with a laugh that turned into a hacking cough. When it subsided, he gasped, "Now, what does the lady of the house suggest for supper?"

"Somethin' cold, I hope." Jim sighed. Using his napkin to blot the sweat from his brow, he moaned, "Blessed Lord, ain't this heat wave *ever* goin' to break?"

In the following scorching days, relief seemed at hand as black clouds accumulated over the mountains ringing Tombstone. Vivid lightning was seen. Thunder rolled and rumbled. But no rain came. No cooling downpours. No refreshing breezes. Nor did the nights afford a break. Daytime temperatures barely dipped after dark, leaving Jim sweltering naked in his bed at Fly's Lodginghouse. Because sleep was nearly impossible, he felt more tired when he woke up atop the soaked sheets than he'd been when he went to bed. Making daily runs over the baking road to Charleston and Contention, he felt sorry for Felix Catlin as he seemed to be struggling for breath in the stifling heat and trail dust. And he pitied the laboring mules, permitting them to stand and drink in the water of the San Pedro ford.

But as bad as these torments of the weather became, worse were the plaguing thoughts that stabbed into his head of Frank Hall being someplace distant where the air was fresh and bracing, where there was cold water for a bath and to drink and where they had ice to put in whiskey. At these times he allowed himself to ponder the possibility that Frank Hall was dead and already condemned and suffering the burning without end that was the Bible's hell.

But no such likelihood presented itself. To Tombstone had come no reports of Frank Hall's bleached, buzzard-picked bones being discovered in the desert. No dispatches came to John Clum's editorial office at the *Epitaph* of Hall being gunned down in a barroom shootout in some far-off spot, as the news of the demise of Billy the Kid had been received.

It was as if Frank Hall had vanished, like the disappearing woman in the magic show at Schieffelin Hall that had entertained the sweating people of Tombstone.

That someone in the Clanton gang was likely to know Frank Hall's whereabouts, as Doc Holliday and Johnny Deuce suggested, was easy for Jim to believe. That anyone would let that information slip was unlikely. For such a sin, Johnny Ringo pointed out to Jim on a sultry evening of drinking at the Capitol Saloon, the retribution of Old Man Clanton would be swift and terrible. "He's like a biblical patriarch," declared Ringo in his teacher's voice. "Full of fire and brimstone! Believe me, you don't cross Old Man Clanton. And if he gets it into his head that you're disloyal, that you can't be trusted to keep your mouth shut . . ." He let the thought hang in the hot, heavy air. "That could be the explanation for the fact that nobody's seen Frank Hall all this time," he continued grimly. "The old man may have turned against him." Slowly he drew a finger across his neck. "That'd spell the end of Frank Hall."

During the unrelenting heat, Jim had seen little of the Clantons and nothing of the old man; but in mid-August the heat broke, shattered by raging storms that lasted for three days, and on the first clear, cool day, the patriarch of the Clanton clan rode through Tombstone accompanied by four hardcases, three of whom neither Jim nor Doc Holliday recognized as they watched from the porch of the Occidental. Galloping east, the old man had on a brown duster coat, a slouch-brimmed hat and an expression on his face that even glimpsed, seemed like venomous hate incarnate. "They're bound to be up to no good," muttered Holliday.

"Wonder where the sons are?" said Jim, rocking easily on the back legs of his chair. "Didn't see any of his regular gang with 'im. Curly Bill Brocius. Ringo. Pony Deal. None of them. Did you, Doc?"

"Nary a one," answered Holliday. "I did recognize one of this gang, though. A gunnie from up Tucson way, named Earnshaw, whose specialty is appropriating other people's cattle."

"Well that's right down Old Man Clanton's alley." Jim chuckled.

"Tomorrow we'll probably hear of some rancher over by Galeyville being rustled," said Holliday, coughing as he dipped into his coat pocket for a silver cheroot case. Popping it open, he offered one to Jim.

"You know, if you'd cut out smokin'," said Jim, taking the cigar and rolling it between his fingers, "that cough of yours might improve a whole lot, and you might delay your arrival at the Pearly Gates."

"Tascosa, my friend," said Holliday, lighting up, "if these things kill me, I doubt very much if I'll wind up at the Pearly Portal. But if I do and I discover they don't allow smoking in Heaven, I'll turn round and head to the other place. Which is where my friends will be. Like the man said: 'Heaven for the atmosphere, hell for companionship.' " Inhaling deeply, he broke into a long, hacking cough. When it subsided, he chewed on the cheroot then flipped it toward the distance where Old Man Clanton had long-since ridden out of sight. "Maybe I'd better hoof it over to the marshal's office and let Virgil and Wyatt know that the old man's up to something."

At supper with Cass Buford the following evening, Jim looked

161

up abruptly as Holliday barged into the Occidental and rushed to their table. Gasping for breath, he blared: "Old Man Clanton's dead!"

As astonished patrons of the Occidental abandoned their meals and gathered around, the story came out in fits and gasps, the result of the combination of Holliday's excitement and his struggling consumptive lungs. There had been another ambush in the Guadalupe Canyon. But this time Old Man Clanton and his gang of four local owlhoots were driving hard a small herd of cattle they'd rustled from the Gordon ranch near Portal by the New Mexico border. Only that hardcase named Earnshaw survived to tell about it. Old Man Clanton was riddled with bullets and buckshot. "It was a trap. Glorious retribution," huffed Holliday. "It was carried out by the kin folk of those Mexican muleteers Old Man Clanton butchered back in July for their bullion." He paused, fighting for air. "You got to hand it to those Mexicans! They bided their time and got their revenge."

If retribution for the Guadalupe Canyon massacre had been visited on Old Man Clanton, thought Jim, might those avengers also have tracked down another participant in that outrage? Had Frank Hall, someplace, somewhere, also felt the fury of their vengeance? Or was Hall still alive and breathing astride his Appaloosa at that moment? "God, don't let him be dead," he whispered. "Dear God, let Frank Hall still be alive. And, Blessed Lord, let him come back to Tombstone!"

Chapter Twenty-one
Billy the Kid

August passed slowly and hot with September proving little better as Jim's life settled into the uneventful routines of freighting, but now, in late October, he relished the bright and comfortable autumn sunlight and crisp, cool evenings that always ended with late supper with Cass Buford at the Occidental but began with unlimbering and restful drinks at the Oriental Saloon.

As he greeted Buckskin Frank Leslie on the busy night of Saturday, October 22, 1881, six Cornish miners lined the bar. Small men, neatly dressed and chattering with Frank in their curious English accents, they and their kind were known in the Territory as "Cousin Jacks" because they were immigrants from the coal fields of the land of the Union Jack who'd flocked to work beside their American cousins in the search for the gold in California and silver in Colorado and Arizona. Jim had met scores of them, hardworking and amusing men, laboring in the mines and drinking in the ramshackle saloons of the ore milling towns of Charleston and Contention City. These six, he soon learned as the nearest to him struck up a conversation, were from a dig near Bisbee. The miner next to Jim was of middle age with thinning, wispy, reddish hair and so short that Jim had to look down at him while he spoke. "The boss's daughter has just presented him with a grandson," the miner explained, "and in celebration of the happy event, he's given us two lovely days off." Behind his bushy mustache, a smooth round face was flushed from drink. Green eyes were slightly glazed and unfocused. "That was bloody kind, weren't it?"

"Very generous," said Jim as Frank Leslie brought him a rye, unasked and out of habit.

"So my mates and me decided to come up to Tombstone where the feminine attractions are much greater in number than down in Bisbee," said the Cousin Jack with a leer, another stroke of his mustache, a wink and a nod. "I presume you are a resident of this town, sir, and obviously a young man of worldly experience, so if you have any suggestions for us along that line . . ."

"I recommend Diamond Annie's," said Jim, sipping the rye. "It's just past Sixth Street. You can't miss it."

"An honest establishment, I trust?"

"As square as the day is long."

"My name is John Thomas, sir," declared the miner, "and I would be honored if you'd permit me to pay for your drink. My father of blessed memory taught me to always reciprocate a kindness."

"Well, I ain't done anything to deserve it," said Jim, "but a friend of mine taught me never to turn down a free drink, so, I will not decline your generosity."

"Mr. Barman," Thomas said, wiggling a finger above Jim's empty glass, "another of the same here, please."

"I've only been to Bisbee once," said Jim, "but I have a friend down that way. Maybe you know him? Name of Frank Hall?"

"Alas no," said the miner.

Presently, he and four of the miners sat down to play poker, the sixth standing aside as Thomas insisted that the last chair at the table be taken by Jim — "Our new-found friend!"

As the game proceeded safely with small wagers and guarded hands, the cards rewarded them evenly. "This is what I like. A nice, easy, friendly game," exclaimed Jim, recalling tense nights of poker or faro played with Johnny Ringo or Doc Holliday when the stakes often soared beyond his reach and the games went on silently, save for the clipped words and phrases needed to keep the game going. Ringo and Doc had been deadly serious, so unlike these happy Cornishmen for whom talking and laughing were as much a part of the playing as winning.

Presently, a shadow fell across Jim's hand, and a familiar voice rose from behind. "Is this an open game?"

"Next opening belongs to me," answered the standing miner.

As Jim looked up from his cards, Billy Claiborne moved into view. Lean and lithe and with slits for eyes, he reminded Jim of a cat. But this feline's claws took the form of a brace of Colt .45's worn on a low-slung buscadero. "Well, well, if it ain't Two-gun Billy Claiborne," said Jim.

"That's Billy the Kid to you," snapped Claiborne.

"Billy the Kid?" interjected Thomas nervously.

"That's right," said Claiborne, resting his hands on the grips of the twin pistols.

Thomas fidgeted. "Well, bless my soul."

"How can that be?" said the standing miner. "I heard that Billy the Kid was gunned down and killed by Sheriff Pat Garret over at Fort Sumner quite a few weeks back."

"The name's passed to me," said Claiborne coldly. "And rightly so."

Thomas sneered. "Don't make me larf! You've got as bloody much in common with Billy the Kid as Johnny Thomas has with his royal highness, the prince of Wales."

"Is that right?" said Claiborne, stiffening.

"Right as rain!" scoffed the miner.

In a blinding instant, Claiborne's brace of pistols blasted the miner, spinning him backward to sprawl dead on his back with blood gushing from two bullet holes in his chest. "Is there anybody wants to do anythin' about it?" growled Billy Claiborne, wiggling the smoking guns and easing toward the back door. "If'n anybody tries to follow me," he shouted, ducking out, "he gets the same."

A posse formed within minutes. Sworn-in by Virgil Earp in his capacity as Deputy U.S. Marshal, Jim counted seven men in addition to him and Wyatt Earp, who was wordless as he sat astride a big-chested gray. Morgan Earp stood aloof, staying behind to represent law and order in Tombstone. "According to witnesses," said Virgil from the back of a tall, eager bay, "Billy Claiborne hightailed it west, prob'ly makin' his tracks for the Clanton ranch." His eyes settled on Jim. "Now, I appreciate that some of you have your hackles up over this, taking the killing of Mr. Thomas personally. But I want this clearly understood. Billy's to be taken alive to stand trial. There's to be nobody shootin' without my say-so unless provoked."

"I want Billy Claiborne alive as much as you do," retorted Jim, blushing and bristling at being singled out. "Only I don't want to see him get away, either—as Frank Hall managed to do after he killed Lou Garrard."

"That was different," snapped the marshal. "There weren't any witnesses in that case. This time there are, includin' you, which is the only reason I'm lettin' you come along—to put the finger on Billy Claiborne on the spot."

A nearly full moon riding high in a crystal clear sky lit the chilly flat desert and made tracking Claiborne easy, but rather than cutting south toward the Clanton spread as Virgil Earp had expected, his trail abruptly swung due west, possibly heading for Iron Springs fifteen miles beyond the river, Jim figured. Or even as far as the town of San Pedro.

Fall rains where the San Pedro River had risen in Mexico had the brown stream close to the tops of its banks, making picking up Claiborne's trail easy at the point where his horse had surged splashing and dripping up the other side. But soon the horse was dried, and the tracks were growing dimmer as the posse climbed toward the rugged Whetstone Mountains. "He's moving slower," observed Wyatt presently. "He's either got a tired horse or is confident he's not being trailed."

"Either one's to our advantage," answered Jim.

"Just so," said Wyatt grudgingly.

Jim snorted a laugh. "You still don't like me, do you?"

"The truth is, kid, I don't give you much thought."

"You hang on to the memory of our meetin' up in Abilene."

"The circumstances didn't exactly cast you in a very flattering light."

"It was years ago."

"Seems like only yesterday to me."

"Have I caused any trouble in Tombstone?"

"Because you haven't, don't mean you won't. You're like every cowboy I ever met. You've got a cowboy attitude, kid. A real *bad* attitude."

"Wantin' to see justice done in the cold-blooded killin' of an old friend is havin' a bad attitude?"

"Your old friend was nothin' but a troublemaker who was part and parcel of the Clanton gang. Just one more gunnie runnin' with the Clanton cowboy element. If Frank Hall hadn't killed Lou Garrard, somebody else would've."

"You?"

"Mebbe."

"Tell me, Marshal, what would you do if somebody gunned down one of your brothers?"

"What's that got to do with anything? Lou Garrard was not your brother."

"No, but he was the closest I ever got to havin' one."

With the raising of Virgil Earp's hand, the posse came to a halt at the lip of a deep, shadowed arroyo. "Check me, Wyatt," whispered Virgil. "Is that a light winkin' at us down there?"

Peering into the black chasm, Wyatt nodded. "A campfire for sure."

"Think it's Billy's?"

"I'd bet my bottom dollar on it."

"It's madness for him to hole up."

"My guess is, his horse tuckered out."

"Maybe he's built that fire so's to trick us into thinkin' he's bedded down for the night."

"Don't think so," said Wyatt Earp as he stroked his elegant mustache. "He was ridin' hard earlier. But since crossin' the Pedro he's been takin' it easy. My feelin' is, he's certain he's made a getaway and it's safe to get some rest. For himself and his horse."

"Take him now? Or wait till daybreak."

"We'll divide the men and slip down quietly now," said Wyatt. "But we'll wait for the first blush of daylight before we pounce."

In a stillness unknown to him in the vast stretch of the Palo Duro Canyon or in the hushed blackness of nightriding Colonel Goodnight's herds on the trail to Dodge City, Jim hunkered down behind a boulder to wait for daylight and fixed his eyes on the flare of red and yellow that was Billy Claiborne's dwindling fire. Was he there? Or had he cleverly concocted the fire as a ruse? Might he by now be miles distant? Laughing? Congratulating himself on his shrewdness? Would he soon be a long way off and out of reach of the Earps? Might he simply vanish, now, in the manner of Frank Hall? As though the earth had opened suddenly and swallowed him?

At last, when Jim was certain that his cold, strained and stiffened legs might never be straightened again, a sliver of yellowish light sifted across the rocky lip of the steep face of the canyon to reveal Billy Claiborne asleep and curled into a ball under a snug gray blanket. His head rested upon his saddle. Within easy reach of his uncovered right hand were the grips of his pistols protruding like a pair of deadly heads from the snakelike coil of the buscadero.

Leveling his Colt, Jim drew a bead on Billy Claiborne's head, then cocked the gun.

Like an unleashed spring, Claiborne unwound and reached for the pistols.

"Don't!" shouted Jim. "Touch them guns and you're dead. Just keep your hands where I can see 'em, Billy. Pardon me. I meant to say 'Billy the Kid!' "

"You bastard," moaned Claiborne, motionless as the Earps and the others raced down upon him, guns drawn.

"I don't fancy draggin' him all the way back to Tombstone at this time," said Virgil Earp as Wyatt snapped irons around their captive's wrists. "The entire Clanton mob could be layin' for us in hopes of snatchin' young William Claiborne from our clutches. We'll wait till things cool down and then fetch Billy at our convenience. In the meantime, we'll lock him up in the San Pedro jail."

Two evenings later, as Jim was finishing supper with Cass Buford and Doc Holliday at the Occidental, he looked up with startled eyes as Wyatt Earp stormed across the room and threw himself down at their table.

Laying down a forked slice of beef, Doc Holliday looked worried. "What the devil's gnawing at you?"

Slack-jawed, red-faced and with his ice-blue eyes scanning their faces, Wyatt declared, "The son of a bitch escaped!"

"Claiborne?" gasped Jim.

Wyatt nodded. "We just got word from the San Pedro jail! Billy's been busted out!"

168

"Lord in heaven, how?" cried Cass, clutching her fan to her ample bosom.

"Three hardcases did it," seethed Earp. "They rode in hell bent for leather yesterday, got the drop on the deputy, grabbed the keys to Billy's cell, sprang him and locked up the deputy. It was hours before anyone else knew what happened. All the deputy could say was that there'd been three of them. From descriptions he gave, it has to have been the work of Ike Clanton, Tom and Frank McLaury. They've always been tight with Claiborne. And so's Curly Bill Brocius, who undoubtedly planned it and ordered it."

"Virgil must be fit to be tied," said Holliday.

"That's puttin' it mildly," answered Wyatt. "But there isn't a damn thing he can do about it without a witness to swear that it was them, so we can get a warrant. There's no such witness."

"That sounds familiar," whispered Jim bitterly.

"You just button your lip, kid," snapped Wyatt.

Chapter Twenty-two
Room with a View

Nothing was more satisfying to Jim after a hard day's work teamstering and before having supper than to lounge on one of the white cane armchairs of the long, broad gallery that fronted Cass Buford's second-floor apartment above the Occidental and gaze out at the panoramic view of Tombstone. Directly over or through the gaps between the buildings, he could observe the bustling street and foot traffic from Russ House at Tough Nut Street and Fourth on the south to the Capitol Saloon and Schieffelin Hall at the corner of Fremont on the north. Between them along Fourth were Spangenberg the gunsmith, the furniture store, the California Tinsmith, the Can Can restaurant, Brown's Hotel and the barber shop. Along Fremont he saw the backs of the Papago Cash Store, Bauer's Meat Market, Fly's Lodginghouse and the Harwood residence next door and the wide space occupied by the O.K. Corral. Down Allen Street past the office of the O.K and the assay office, he could see as far as the rooftops of Hop Town and the road coming in from the San Pedro Valley.

Taking all this in on the cool Monday evening of October 24 as the sun sank toward the Huachucas and the sky began its long slow fade from the colors of fire to deep purple and then black, Jim was especially interested in watching the rapid approach of seven horsemen. Even from so far away, he recognized them; no one else rode quite that way, as if nothing could or should get in their way.

At their center was Curly Bill Brocius, who'd usurped the boss-

170

ing of the late Old Man Clanton's cowboy element that Wyatt Earp and John Clum so detested. To his left rode Johnny Ringo. Flanking them were Ike and Finn Clanton, inheritors of all their father's ruthlessness but none of his brains. A little behind them were the McLaury brothers, whose limited success as ranchers had led them to partake of the spoils of the gang's enterprises. And bringing up the rear rode Pony Deal and Wes Fuller, whose only notable characteristic was being quick on the draw. Absent was young Billy Clanton.

"Tascosa, darling," called Cass Buford from the room, "what do you see out there that's so fascinatin'?"

"Trouble, prob'ly," said Jim, turning and stepping through the gallery door. "The Clanton bunch."

Seated before her dressing table mirror, Cass was preparing for her evening's role as hostess of the dining room below by pinning up the long silken hair that during the hour that Jim had spent making love to her had flowed around her silk-smooth white shoulders and now cascaded down the back of a pink chemise. "I hope they confine their business elsewhere," she said, fixing her eyes on Jim's reflection. Naked to the waist with red braces hanging in loops, he was seated now on the edge of the bed and pulling on his boots. "That's sure a pleasant sight," said Cass, smiling.

Jim looked at her quizzically. "What is?"

"You, you handsome galoot," she exclaimed. "To me, there's nothin' as pleasin' as a good-lookin' man gettin' dressed."

"What about a man gettin' *undressed?*" cackled Jim, reaching for his shirt. "Seems to me that's even more pleasin' to you."

"What would please me most," she answered, pinning the last swirl of hair into place, "is you movin' out of Camillus Fly's roomin' house and movin' in here with me. You spend most of your nights here as it is. What's the sense of spendin' your wages on rent?"

"Pride," said Jim, standing and stuffing his shirt into his pants.

Now Cass turned quizzical. "Pride?"

"That's what I said. Pride," declared Jim. "How would it look if I was to do such a thing? A man keeps a woman, not the other way round." He strapped on his gunbelt. "Why, I'd be the laughin' stock of Tombstone."

"Not if we got married," Cass whispered.

Stunned silent, Jim gaped in amazement.

"Lord in heaven" laughed Cass, "you look like you just got kicked by a horse!"

"I feel like it," Jim muttered. "Cripes, Cass," he said urgently. "You and me hitched? You hooked up with a tumbleweed like me? Hell, I'm—"

She cut him off. "Half my age?"

Embarrassed, Jim looked down at an ornate Persian carpet and pawed it with his heel. "I was goin' to say," he said, looking up with pleading eyes, "that I'm not *good enough* for you."

Returning her attention to her mirror, Cass sighed. "Not good enough, huh? That's certainly the sweetest way of turnin' somebody down that I ever heard of."

Jim stood behind her and stroked her bared neck. "Happens to be true." He bent and kissed where his fingers had touched. "What have I got goin' for me? A job skinnin' mules! A past that's got nothin' to recommend its bein' mentioned. No future beyond the day I settle up things with Frank Hall. And no future at all if he proves better with a gun than me. What the hell am I except exactly what Wyatt Earp believes I am? A good-for-nothin' kid with a Colt sixgun for brains." Bending across her shoulder, he kissed her cheek. "I'm flattered as the dickens that you think I'm somethin' more."

"You are," she said, smiling at him in the mirror.

"Yeah, right," he scoffed.

"You just haven't realized it yet," Cass said, clutching his hand to her breast.

"See you downstairs," he said, drawing free.

Having pre-supper drinks at his customary table as Jim descended to the Occidental was Doc Holliday, joined by Seamus Dolan and John Clum. "Evening, Tascosa. You're looking rather chipper," said Holliday with a teasing glint in his eyes.

"Hi, Doc," said Jim with a nod as he slid into his usual chair at the large round table. "Is there somethin' big goin' on?" he asked, turning to the others. "The editor of the *Epitaph* and the former star scribbler for the *Nugget* bein' at the same table and lookin' so serious, somethin' must be up! Are you about to enlist your pen on behalf of Mr. Clum's paper, Seamus?"

"Should such a thing occur," replied Seamus haughtily, "you will read the details on page one of both papers, I assure you."

"And what will the *Epitaph* subscribers be readin' about in to-morrow's edition?" said Jim, turning to Clum.

"There are a few items of interest for which you, Mr. Hardin, may pay to read like everyone else. I haven't decided what my lead story will be. I don't put the paper to bed quite this early," answered Clum.

"That's probably a lucky thing," said Jim. "Seein' as how the Clanton gang just rode into town, you might get yourself a big story for the front page. The way I see it, one of them owlhoots is bound to kick up some kind of fuss."

"The day is coming when the lawless element will cease to be a factor in the everyday news of this town," said Clum pompously.

"Where'd you see the Clantons, Tascosa?" asked Doc Holliday.

"I watched 'em from the gallery upstairs. Didn't see 'em come into town, exactly, but they were headin' this way. They're probably at their usual haunts by now — at the Grand Hotel or in Hatch's billiard parlor. Ringo was with 'em, so maybe they're up at the Capitol Saloon. Cass is prayin' they won't show up here."

She appeared as Jim spoke, a dressy figure with upswept hair studded with sparkling rhinestone combs that drew all the eyes in the Occidental to her. "You're a lady who sure knows how to make an entrance, Cass." Seamus beamed as the men stood for her. "You should've been an actress."

"But I am." Cass laughed, unfurling her Japanese fan, a gesture that signalled the Occidental's waiters to begin serving supper.

It was a grand meal — seven courses — with coffee and brandy being poured well past eleven o'clock. "It's late," said Jim, yawning and patting his strained belly, "and I've got to be up early for a haul over to Contention. So, if y'all will excuse me, I'll say g'night to you." With a flick of his eyes toward Cass, he added, "And hello to my bed . . . at Fly's."

"I'll walk along with you if you don't mind the company," said Holliday.

"Pleasure's mine," said Jim.

It being Monday night, they found Tombstone relatively quiet as they strolled past shuttered stores on Fourth. At the corner of

173

Fremont, they found the Capitol in full blare. Glancing through the open double doors, Jim's eyes met Ike Clanton's icy stare.

"Hey Tascosa, I want a word with you," Ike shouted. Lurching back from the bar and onto the sidewalk, he blocked Jim's way. "Yeah, you an' me got us some old business to settle."

"What business?" said Jim.

Unsteady on his feet, Ike was obviously drunk. "The bishness of my frien' Billy Clai . . . Claiborne. I hear'd it was you that fingered him. Don't deny it!"

"Why should I deny it?" answered Jim, curling his hand around his Colt. "And what's more, nothin' could've given me greater pleasure."

"Yeah? Well, nothin'll give me greater pleasure than makin' you pay for it, so shtep into the shtreet."

"You're soused," snarled Jim. "I wouldn't want to take advantage of somebody in your pitiful condition. See me when you're sobered up!"

"You little snot," cried Ike, groping for his gun.

Jim drew.

But Doc Holliday was faster, whipping out his pistol and clubbing Ike's head with the barrel.

With a moan, Ike collapsed.

"Let's get the hell out of here," exclaimed Holliday, gripping Jim's gun hand and wrenching it downward. "All of Ike's friends'll be upon us in a second."

"Let 'em come," protested Jim. "You and me can handle the whole friggin' bunch."

"Look, kid, this is no time for a fight," said Holliday, twisting Jim's gun from his hand and jamming the muzzle into Jim's ribs. "Shut your mouth and move or I'll blast you myself!"

With surprising strength for a sick man, he dragged Jim into the street, past Schieffelin Hall and east on Fremont.

"This ain't the way to Fly's," yelled Jim.

"Damned, right it ain't! You're not goin' near your place tonight," bellowed Holliday. "Fly's is the first place Ike's pals will come lookin' for you!"

Struggling vainly, Jim demanded, "Where you takin' me?"

Holliday had him by the collar now. "To the jail."

"Jail? You got no right!" bellowed Jim, dragged along. "You're not the law in this town!"

Holliday coughed. "I'm makin' a citizen's arrest!"

Ahead of them, seated in a loafer's chair in a square of light pouring onto the sidewalk from the front window of the jail, Morgan Earp looked up, startled, as Holliday delivered Jim kicking and screaming. Breathing hard, Holliday flung Jim against the wall hard enough to rattle the window.

An instant later, the door flew open, and Wyatt Earp emerged with a gun in one hand and a half-chewed chunk of bread in the other. "What in blazes is goin' on out here?" he shouted. "Can't a man have a meal in peace?"

"Lock this kid up for safekeeping," huffed Holliday, handing Wyatt Jim's gun.

"Sure, Doc," said Wyatt, breaking into a puzzled grin, "but you'd best tell me what I'm keepin' him safe from."

"His own damned foolishness." Holliday coughed. "Stick him in the cell without a window, else Ike Clanton might shoot him in the back."

Chapter Twenty-three
Advice

It was Cass Buford's custom to wake up not a minute before two o'clock in the afternoon, but this Tuesday she startled Max, the daytime bartender, and early patrons by descending the stairs at ten dressed in the plain outfit she wore on days when she was conducting Occidental business with merchants around town. "Max, I want you to go down to the O.K. and fetch my buggy," she said, coming round behind the bar. "I'll take over here till you get back."

Drawing up in front of the marshal's office, the trim two seater pulled by a lively, sleek-coated chestnut mare caught Wyatt Earp's attention as he sat at his brother's desk. "You're up and out early, Cass," he said as Cass stepped into the office. Rising, he bowed slightly. "To what do I owe the pleasure of this visit?"

"Good morning, Wyatt. Doc Holliday informed me late last night that you've got a friend of mine locked up."

"If you're referrin' to the Tascosa kid. . . ."

"I am."

"We've got him here all right."

"What's he charged with?"

"There's no charge," said Wyatt, inviting Cass to sit in a chair before the desk. "He's locked up for his own protection," he continued, resuming his seat. "He ran afoul of Ike Clanton last night. Doc kept him from makin' a fool of himself and maybe gettin' himself killed."

"You can't keep the kid locked up forever!"

"No, I reckon not. But I can hold him till things in town cool down a little more. If he maintains the mood he was in last night, he's just askin' for trouble."

"I'll see that he minds himself."

Wyatt leaned forward urgently. "What the hell's goin' on, Cass? I don't ever recall your goin' on like this for anybody. You've always been a woman who minded her own business. Why the sudden change?" He reared back. "Are you stuck on this kid?"

"I don't believe that's any of your business, Wyatt. Now, are you going to let the kid go or not? You really have no right to detain him further. I could go over to Justice of the Peace Wallace's courtroom and get a writ that'll compel you to release him."

"No need to disturb Mr. Wallace." Wyatt chuckled. Pulling open a drawer, he fetched a ring of keys. "But I'm countin' on you to keep that kid out of trouble." He strode to the doorway leading to the jail cells. "By that I mean he should keep out of the way of the Clantons," he went on, jabbing the air with the cell keys.

Red-eyed and disheveled from sleeplessness on a rock-hard cot, Jim trailed Wyatt into the office. Sheepishly, he looked at Cass and muttered "Thought that was your voice I heard."

"You've got to rid yourself of this crazy obsession of findin' and killin' Frank Hall," lectured Wyatt as he removed Jim's gun from a cabinet. "Things are tense enough in this town as it is — a powder keg — without you stirrin' matters up."

Jim jerked the gun from Wyatt's hand. "If the law did its duty —"

"Listen to me, you cocky little whelp," seethed Wyatt. "One more remark like that and I'll knock you on your ass and heave you back into that cell. I'm sick of you goin' around this town badmouthin' me and my brothers. The only reason I'm turnin' you loose is out of my respect for Cass. But I'm warnin' you. If you so much as look cross-eyed at anyone in Tombstone from this moment on, I'm goin' to beat the tar out of you and then run you clean out of Arizona. Now git outta here and show your gratitude to this lady by showin' some sense for once."

Brittle with fury, Jim slammed out the door.

"The marshal's talking sense, Tascosa," pleaded Cass as she followed him outside. "You've got to quit all this nonsense about Frank Hall."

177

"I'm grateful for your concern," said Jim, helping Cass into the buggy. "But it isn't nonsense to me," he went on, climbing up beside her. Taking the reins, he said, "Now, where shall I drive you? Back to the Occidental?"

"I'll do the driving," she said, whisking the reins into her hands and giving them a smart snap to the rump of the horse. "There's something I want you to see," she said determinedly as the rig jolted forward. Moments later, they rattled past the town line and up the inclined road to Boot Hill, where she turned the rig into the cemetery.

"Lou's grave is over there," whispered Jim with a nod to his right.

"Didn't bring you here for that," snapped Cass. "There's another grave I want you to see."

Stepping from the carriage, Jim helped Cass down, then stood beside a neatly kept plot with pots of red and yellow desert flowers arranged before a black stone. He gaped at the engraving.

ETHAN SAMUEL BUFORD
1860-1879

As though reading Jim's mind, Cass whispered, "He was my brother."

Wordless, Jim removed his hat.

"As you can see, he was about your age." She bent over the flowers, straightening the pots. "Just as hot-headed, too." She sighed, coming up straight. "Quick to anger. Quick with a gun. But not quick enough. Old Man Clanton was faster."

Jim gasped. "The old man killed him?"

"The old man shot him all right. But Ethan really killed himself. With his blind anger. Over nothing! Just one of those crazy notions you men seem to get into your heads that makes you think you have to prove your manhood. Just like the hate that's been eating at you all these months. You've got to let go of that hate, Tascosa. Else there'll be a stone like this for you."

"If Clanton killed your brother, how'd he get away with it?"

Cass stroked the name etched in the cool black stone. "There was an inquest. The judge heard all the witnesses and ruled the old man acted justifiably."

178

"A rigged proceeding, no doubt," said Jim bitterly.

"No. The judge ruled right. The fault was Ethan's."

"Look, Cass, I'm sorry about your brother, but the situation with me is entirely different. My friend was gunned down with his gun still in its holster. Frank Hall murdered him. He's got to pay for it."

"That's a job for the law, Tascosa. I beg you to understand that. Leave it be! I don't want to have to be putting flowers on a second grave. So, as much as I care for you and enjoy having you around, I'm pleading with you to leave Tombstone. You've got Ike Clanton all riled up. That's a vicious man, Tascosa. He's got tons of hate in him, beaten into him by his father. Or maybe born into him. I don't know which. Possibly both. So get on your horse and get the hell out of Tombstone before. . . ."

Her words trailed off leaving the cemetery quiet save for the whisper of the wind coming up off the desert.

Chapter Twenty-four
Sleepy Tuesday

With balled fists jammed against her hips, Cass Buford affected an admonishing expression. "You look like a mess."

Jim unbuckled his gunbelt and draped it on the back of a chair. "Just yesterday it was your judgment that I was pleasant to look at."

"Today you're a wreck," answered Cass, drawing down the coverlet of her bed. "Your eyes are as red as a four-day drunk."

Jim plopped into the chair. "Marshal Earp's jail ain't exactly built for sleep," he grunted, pulling off his boots.

"The answer to that is, 'Stay out of Marshal Earp's jail.' "

"When Doc Holliday's got a forty-four jammed in your side," Jim said, yawning and shuffling to the bed, "you don't have much of a choice." Running a finger under Cass's chin, he broke into a lopsided grin. "You joinin' me?"

"It's sleep you need," she answered, shoving him back. "Not that."

"Yeah, you're right." He sighed, stretching out and closing his eyes.

"I'm sending a boy over to Fly's to fetch your belongings," she said quietly, though Jim was already asleep.

It was a cool, bright morning with Tombstone fully awake as Cass left him to go down to the Occidental. This was the quietest the saloon and dining room would be during the day as the working men of Tombstone labored in the mines and mills and the gamblers and drifters slept. It would be noon before business picked up again as the lunch crowd came in. Then the afternoon quiet would settle on the town as the heat built — the sleepy hours of siesta.

A boy who did the sweeping out and cleaning up was keeping out of the way of four broad-shouldered deliverymen wrestling beer kegs inside from an Eagle Brewery wagon parked in front of the door. "Leave the broom for now, Eddie," said Cass to the boy. "I have an errand for you, over to Fly's Lodginghouse. There are some belongings I want you to fetch back here. I will write you a note to give to Mrs. Fly. On your way back, you are to call at the O.K. Corral and tell that boy who works there that he is to saddle the horse belonging to Mr. Hardin and bring it here, round in back. Have you got all that?"

"Yes ma'am!"

"While you're doing all this," said Cass, writing the note to Mrs. Fly, "I want you to take particular notice whether Ike Clanton, or Finn or Billy Clanton, are in town. You know them, don't you?"

"Sure do, ma' am. Mean cusses, each and every one!"

"They surely are," said Cass, sliding the note to Mrs. Fly into the boy's shirt pocket. "So if you see them, just keep your distance and when you come back let me know where you saw them."

Mrs. Fly took her time collecting Jim's few belongings and going on and on about how disappointed she was at losing her tenant. "He's such a nice, polite young man," she said at last, placing the meager bundle in the boy's arms. "Do tell him that I will miss him so."

Leaving the back way, the boy dodged past Camillus Fly's adobe-walled photographic studio and cut through the O.K. Corral. In its office he found Chip and related the message concerning the horse. "Tell Miss Buford not to worry, Eddie. I'll have that kid's hoss out back of the Occidental right away," said Chip as he chewed the stub of a cold cheroot. "Of course, there'll be no refund!"

Turning to leave the office, the boy turned quizzically. "Chip, you seen Ike Clanton or any of his brothers around this mornin'?"

"Not so far," said Chip. "But I seen Ike late last night ridin' out of town, goin' hell for leather. Why? What's the Clantons to you?"

"They's nothin' to me," answered the boy with a shrug. "Miss Buford's interested in knowin' if they're around."

Now, ain't that curious, thought Chip. What could account for Cass Buford's sudden interest in the whereabouts of the Clanton brothers? In the more than two years since Old Man Clanton killed Ethan Buford, the Clantons had been like poison to her. Something must be going on, he thought. But what? Did it have something to do with her asking for the Tascosa Kid's horse saddled up and delivered to the Occidental? And why must the horse be taken to the back of the saloon? he wondered as he fetched Midnight from its stable. Saddling it, he asked himself why Cass Buford should be sending for Tascosa's horse and not Tascosa himself?

As he climbed into the saddle for the short ride to the saloon, the likely explanation came to him. Something must have happened between Ike and Tascosa! "Whoo-ee," he yelped as he turned Midnight east on Allen Street. "That's gotta be it," he muttered as his thoughts raced back to Ike Clanton thundering past the office as if the devil himself were nipping at his tail.

Part Five:
Choose Partners

Chapter Twenty-five
Unfinished Business

From the safety of an outlaw hideout in the hills west of Calabasas on the Santa Cruz River twenty-four miles southwest of Tombstone, Frank Hall had been riding hard since dusk. Night had been spent needling through canyons of the jagged inhospitable Santa Rita Mountains. But now, at daybreak, the sleeping town of Patagonia and Sonoita Creek were behind him, and he was looking forward to making good time across the rolling basin between the Huachucas and the Whetstone range. Watching for dust plumes that might signal the movement of a patrol of soldiers, he stayed well north of Fort Huachuca and skirted Elgin, where an unflattering picture of him was on a wanted poster put up by the town marshal.

His friends in the outlaw camp had advised against what he was doing. "You go back to Tombstone lookin' for that kid who's gunnin' for you and you'll run smack into the buzzsaw of the Earp brothers" was the gist of their counsel. He appreciated their concern for him, he'd replied, but this thing had gone too far not to do something about it, finally. "Folks will start to think I'm scared to face this kid," he declared. "Well, I'd rather be dead than shamed!"

Besides that, he did *not* say aloud, he was sick and tired of hiding out in two-bit towns where there was nothing to do for excitment. He missed Tombstone's saloons and gambling halls. The good restaurants! The stage shows at Ed Schieffelin's Hall. The women!

But most of all he missed riding with the Clanton gang. Three months had passed since Old Man Clanton took a volley of rifle bullets in the Guadalupe. But the cranky old geezer had gone down shooting. He'd have liked to have attended the old man's funeral, but things were too hot at the time. The army was looking for him. The Earps wanted him. And that kid from Tascosa seemed to be everywhere, scouting for the hated Frank Hall and making it seem as if Frank Hall hadn't the guts to show himself!

Well, now, he thought as he spurred his Appaloosa into the rising sun and toward Tombstone, he was going to settle things with that kid once and for all!

Since daybreak, Ike Clanton had occupied the chair that for so long had been the throne from which his father had ruled the family and the gang that bore his name. "The time's ripe," he roared. "I aims to settle all outstanding business!"

Grim-faced along the sides of the breakfast table sat his brothers Billy and Finn, Tom and Frank McLaury, Wes Fuller, Billy Claiborne and Frank Hall, dusty from his ride from Calabasas.

From the chair opposite Ike's, Johnny Ringo spoke quietly. "Let's not do anything rash, Ike. I say we wait till Curly Bill gets back from Galeyville."

"To hell with that," thundered Ike with a bang of a fist on the table. "I ain't waitin' for Bill to get back. This ain't gang business. This is a Clanton family matter. That bastard Holliday humiliated me, and I mean to settle up with him now."

"If you take on Holliday, you take on the Earps," said Ringo.

"Ringo talks sense, Ike," said Billy Clanton in the cool way that had always set him aside from his explosive older brothers. "If you go after Doc, the Earps come after you."

"Good! We'll finish them bastards, too!" bellowed Ike. "It's about time!" He turned to the McLaury's. "Tom and Frank, the two of you have had a share of shit dumped on you by the Earps. Are you in on this or not? The time's come to make up your minds! No way of wormin' outta this. You sucked at the tit of the Clantons long enough."

"It's a dangerous thing, takin' on the Earps," replied Frank

186

McLaury as he toyed with a fork.

Ike reared back. "What are you, yellow?" he blared.

Unprovoked, McLaury laid down the fork and answered quietly. "Take on the Earps and the whole town of Tombstone comes down on us. Maybe the entire county."

"Johnny Behan represents the law in the county," snapped Ike. "And Sheriff Johnny Behan's in our pocket! I say 'jump,' and he asks how high?"

"John Clum might ask Governor Fremont to call in the army from Fort Huachuca," interjected Ringo.

"The hell with Clum and all the rest of those do-gooders," said Ike. Seething, he fixed his blazing eyes on Frank Hall. "You got an interest in this, you know! I refer to this kid who's been lookin' for you for months, vowin' to even things up in the name of that friend of his you gunned down."

"Why do you think I came back? I've been hearin' about that damned kid all the way to Mexico and back. What's his name?"

"Jim Hardin," answered Ringo with a tight smile. "Said to be a cousin of John Wesley Hardin. But folks who know him usually call him Tascosa. He's a friend of mine and a nice kid." The smile stretched into a mocking grin. "Quite single-minded."

"I'd've squared him away *permanent* last night," said Ike, "but for Holliday interferin'."

"If you're set on this," said Ringo, "then you'd better have a plan. You go ridin' hellfire into Tombstone without a plan and the Earps will make mincemeat out of you."

"Okay, Ringo," said Ike. "You're the brainy one! You got all that book learnin'. How would you do it?"

Ringo paused, thinking. "First off," he said at last, "you can't do anything unless you're all in it together."

"That's what I've been sayin' " said Ike.

"But you mustn't come ridin' into town all at once," said Ringo, warming to the problem. "That would attract too much attention."

"Yeah, it should look like everything's normal," declared Frank Hall.

"You drift into Tombstone a few at a time," Ringo went on. "Make everything appear to be business as usual." He turned to the McLaury's. "Tom and Frank, you made a big sale of cattle to

Bauer's Market the other day. Collected your payment yet?"

"Bauer said to come in some day this week," replied Tom.

"Excellent. That's your reason for going to town. You could go in tonight. Ike can go with you. You two are pals, so nobody will think twice about the two of you being together. Frank can come in tomorrow morning, early. Fuller, Claiborne and I, along with Frank Hall, arrive later."

"That's a good plan," said Ike, rattling the dishes by banging the table again.

Ringo turned to the youngest Clanton. "What about you, Billy? In or out?"

"If it's for the good of the Clanton family, I have to be in."

Worry lines etched Ringo's brow. "Now, the difficulty comes in getting the Earps where you want 'em to be, when you want 'em to be."

Ike tugged at his lower lip. "How do we manage that?"

"That's where you come in," said Ringo. "You've already had a run-in with Holliday. Goad him a little more! Challenge him a little more!"

"Aw, that's no good," exclaimed Ike. "All that'll do is get me into a fight with Holliday. It's all of 'em we want."

"Fix it so Holliday's provoked but can't do anything! When you challenge him, make sure you're not armed. Leave your gun at your hotel. Holliday won't draw on you if you're not armed. That would go against his code. But you'll have to make it plain that the next time you see him you *will* be heeled."

With a dubious expression, Frank Hall spoke up. "But how do we make sure the Earps get involved? And that kid?"

"As for the Earps, there's no way they're goin' to let their pal Doc go up against Ike. They'll be afraid he'll have one of his coughing jags. Don't worry about the Earps! They'll play into our hands nicely. I expect they've been hankering for a showdown. Once they're taken care of, who's to stop you from taking care of your business with your nemesis?"

Hall bristled. "My *what?*"

"Nemesis." Ringo chuckled. "Enemy!"

"Explain somethin', Ringo," said Hall suspiciously. "If this Tascosa kid is so nice—like you say, a friend of yours—how come you're so ready to let him be killed by goin' up against me?"

"Yes, he is my friend," said Ringo. He paused, letting a taunting smile stretch wide. "As for who gets killed, who's to say it will be Tascosa and not Frank Hall?"

Chapter Twenty-six
Invitation to a Ball

Having finished his day's work at the O.K. at six o'clock and a supper of chop suey at Sam Chung's Chinese Restaurant half an hour later, Chip Stone set his mind on spending the remainder of the evening cavorting at Diamond Annie's. Mounting a brown and white paint pony, he proceeded at a leisurely pace through the darkening purple dusk from Hop Town along Allen Street. Passing the Grand Hotel, he nearly rode down Ike Clanton.

With head bent low and a scowl on his face, Ike had stepped off the boardwalk to cut directly in front of the horse.

Jerking rein, Chip yelled, "Hey! Watch it!"

Staring daggers, Ike barked, "You watch it," and dodged across the street toward Hatch's Billiard Saloon where, Chip noted, Tom McLaury was leaning against a porch post, chewing on a toothpick and grinning.

"Ike's got some sweet disposition, eh?" chuckled Chip, patting his pony's neck and spurring him to a quicker pace.

When he dismounted at the Occidental, night was settling fast, the windows were ablaze with lights and the serving of supper was well underway. Cass Buford presided from her usual table in the company of Doc Holliday. "Evenin', Miss Buford, Mr. Holliday," Chip said, wisking off his battered hat. "Excuse me for intrudin' in on your supper, Miss Buford, but you wanted to know if'n I saw Ike Clanton in town? Well, I just spotted him. Nearly ran him down with my hoss! He's to be found at this very minute at Hatch's."

Doc Holliday's head jerked up. "Who's with him?"

"I saw Tom McLaury. Nobody else, though. Unless others was inside the billiard parlor."

"Was he armed?"

Chip's face crinkled quizzically. "Sorry, Mr. Holliday, but I din't notice."

"Thank you very much for telling me, Chip," said Cass as she picked up a purse and snapped it open. "Let me give you something for your trouble," she said, searching for a coin.

"Oh, think nothin' of it, ma'am," said Chip.

Cass smiled and closed the purse. "Well, have you had your supper yet?"

"I have, ma'am, thank you kindly."

"Then, step up to the bar and have a drink on the house."

"Thanks again, ma'am," said Chip, donning his hat, "but I'm on my way somewhere."

"Diamond Annie's, no doubt," Holliday chuckled as Chip hurried out. Leaning toward Cass, he asked, "How come you're interested in knowing the whereabouts of Ike Clanton? Are you worried about that incident last night between Ike and Tascosa?"

"You know Ike," Cass sighed. "He nurses grudges. And he's apt to settle 'em with a bullet in the back."

Holliday toyed with his coffee cup. "Where is Tascosa, by the way? How come he didn't join us for supper?"

"He's asleep upstairs. Been there all day." Her tone took on a scolding edge. "Says he couldn't sleep at all in the jail."

Holliday sipped the coffee. "Wyatt told me you were over bright and early this morning to fetch him," he said, dabbing his lips with a napkin. "Which is where I should be going right now," he went on, folding the napkin. "Virg and Wyatt ought to know that Ike's back in town." Rising, he lifted his black hat from a chair. "My advice to Tascosa, when you talk to him, is for him to stay put here in the Occidental and not go roaming around town tonight."

"I'm tellin' him more than that! I've got his belongings and his horse is tied up out back. When he wakes up, I'm going to tell him in no uncertain terms to get the hell out of town."

Holliday cracked a smile. "I'm a gambling man who's been known to go for long odds, Cass," he said, bending to kiss her cheek, "but take a bet on the likelihood of Tascosa running away from Ike Clanton? Uh-uh."

"It won't be running away," answered Cass with blazing eyes. "It'll be running *to* a better life. Away *from* hate!"

"To Tascosa," said Holliday, putting on the flat-brimmed black hat, "it'd be running."

Smoke from three cigars fogged the marshal's office when Holliday stepped in. "Good, you're all here," he declared with a nod to the brothers—Virgil behind his desk, Morgan tilted back in a chair with the *Epitaph* spread across his lap and Wyatt with gun-cleaning equipment and a pair of shotguns spread before him on a table. "Thought you'd want to know Ike Clanton's in town, last seen over at Hatch's in the company of Tom McLaury."

Picking up a double-barreled gun, Wyatt began rubbing it with an oiled cloth. "Anybody else with Ike?"

"The source of this information is the kid who works at the O.K. Corral," answered Holliday, drawing up a chair to Wyatt's table. "He says he only saw Ike and Tom."

Virgil Earp eased back and propped his feet on his desk. "Since when is Chip Stone collectin' information for Doc Holliday on the doings of the Clantons?"

"It was Cass Buford that Chip came to tell," said Holliday, examining a single-shot, pump-action shotgun. "Apparently she's upset over what happened last night—worried about Tascosa. I'm afraid Cass is head over heels in love with him."

Morgan Earp laid aside the newspaper and settled on his chair. "I've got patrol duty this evenin'," he said with a sigh. Standing, he adjusted the hang of his holster "I'll have a look-see around the town and count Clanton noses."

"Keep your distance, Morg," said Wyatt, assessing his work by peering down the barrels of the spotless double-fire shotgun.

"If it turns out to be more than Ike and Tom McLaury," said Virgil, "skeedaddle back here and let us know promptly."

With the sun down, the heat that had built during the day

quickly dissipated into a clear black sky scented by smoke of wood fires billowing up from chimneys. The handful of women on the streets wore long coats or heavy shawls. Many of the men had on wool-lined jackets or buttoned-up duster coats. And from the nostrils of their horses flowed long plumes of steam, as if the animals had fires in their bellies.

In the cold, sounds seemed to take on a brittle clarity — the clopping of hooves on the hard streets, the tinny banging of a saloon piano, the sawing strains of the stringed instruments of the orchestra accompanying the variety show at Schieffelin Hall, the bursts of laughter and eruptions of the applause from an appreciative audience, the bump and rattle of wagons and the clumping of his boot heels as Morgan Earp walked his beat.

Pushing open the door of Hatch's Billiard Saloon, he did not go in, noting as he closed the door again that Ike Clanton and Tom McLaury were engaged in a game at the table in the back and that neither was carrying a gun. After a patrol that took three-quarters of an hour and encountering no others of the Clanton gang, he returned to the marshal's office to declare, "It's as cold as a witch's tit out there, brothers, but peace and quiet and law and order reign supreme in Tombstone tonight!"

Wyatt grunted a laugh. "If that's so, it's the first time in history!"

"Since it's so heavenly out there," asserted Doc Holliday "might I suggest . . . a few hands of cards? Matchsticks for chips. A penny each."

"That suits me," declared Virgil, drawing a fresh deck from his drawer. "We're poor, underpaid lawmen, after all!"

At midnight when Lady Luck had proven even-handed, leaving each with about as many matches as the start, Morgan gazed at the night clock on the wall. "Time for another walk-around," he announced. "Any of you care to join me in a breath of fresh air?"

"At least as far as the lunch counter at the Alhambra," said Virgil, patting his belly. "Don't know about the rest of you, but I'm hungry."

"A bite sounds fine to me," said Wyatt. "Doc? Joining us?"

Counting his matches and calculating a gain of fifteen cents, Holliday frowned. "Barely enough winnings for a cup of coffee and a double slice of pie."

Striding shoulder to shoulder down the middle of deserted Fremont Street, they faced a cold, biting wind whipping off the Huachucas and arrived at the nearly empty Alhambra, red-faced and chilled. "Looks like the cold's put a crimp in business tonight, Case," said Wyatt to Casey Donovan, the all-night counterman whose round Irish face got its ruddiness from too much drink.

"Pretty slow even for a Tuesday night," said Casey.

"Make that Wednesday morning," said Holliday, nodding at the clock on the wall showing a quarter past twelve as he slid onto a stool with the door to his right and the Earp brothers in their black frock coats, black string ties and stiff black hats arrayed to his left like a line of crows on a fence.

Five minutes later, on a blast of chilled air, Ike Clanton stepped in. Closing the door, he leaned against it. "Well, look who's here," he said, grinning. His eyes flicked past Holliday to the counterman. "Casey, I'll be wantin' some steak and eggs with coffee." Advancing, he muttered, "Bring it to the table in the back. I don't want nobody coughin' on me whilst I eat."

Instantly inflamed, Holliday swung off the stool. "You son of a bitch of a cowboy," he shouted, parting his long coat to unencumber his holster, "get out your gun and get to work!"

Ike lifted his hands and whispered, "I don't have any gun!"

"You ain't heeled," growled Holliday, "go heel yourself."

"This man's provoking me unwarranted, Marshal," protested Ike, turning to Virgil. "I mean, can't a law-abidin' citizen have somethin' to eat late of a night without this tomfoolery?"

"I think it would be best," said Morgan Earp, easing from his stool and stepping between Holliday and Ike, "if you just went on your way, Ike."

"By what right are you throwin' me out?" thundered Ike.

Morgan parted his coat to reveal his policeman's badge. "By the power of this," he said, tapping it with a thumb.

"You're pretty tough behind that piece of tin," sneered Ike. "You all hide behind your tin badges," he said, raking the Earps with fuming, narrowed eyes. "None of yiz got the guts to come out from behind those bits of metal."

"You think so, huh?" yelled Morgan, ripping off his badge and slamming it onto the counter. "You can have all the fight you want

194

right now!"

"No gun," crowed Ike as he wiggled his upraised hands. "But I can promise you this. I'll be heeled tomorrow. And the minute any one of yiz, or all of yiz, make an appearance on the street tomorrow, the ball will commence."

Now Wyatt came down from his stool. "You listen to me, Ike Clanton," he said calmly. "My brothers and I are not going to take that last remark as a threat. We're going to credit what you just said to all the rotgut whiskey that's in you and hope that when you sober up in the light of day you'll see what a foolish and dangerous remark it was. For now, I suggest you get the hell out of here."

Chapter Twenty-seven
Heated Words

When Cass Buford entered her room just before four o'clock Wednesday morning, she was shocked to find Jim not in bed but half-dressed in his favorite wicker chair in the cold of the gallery. "Darling, what on earth are you doing out here in the freezing night air with nothing on but your britches?" she demanded scoldingly. "You'll catch your death of cold!"

Eyes fixed on the gray outline of the distant mountains against a black sky, Jim answered sharply. "What's my stuff doin' here?"

Hesitantly, Cass stroked his bare, cold shoulders. "I had them fetched from Fly's."

He shrugged off her touch. "You had no right."

"It wasn't safe for you to stay there any further," she said placatingly, drawing back. "It seemed best to move your things here for the time being. I also had your horse brought round back."

"God damn it, don't you see what you've done?" He pounded a fist on his knee. "Folks will think I skipped out of Fly's because of fear of Ike Clanton." Lurching to his feet, he spun round to face her with eyes burning with anger. "You've no business messin' in my affairs and takin' advantage of the situation to suit your own desires. I'm not movin' in with you. I told you!"

"That had nothing to do with it," she cried, wounded and spinning away from him into the bedroom. "For God's sake," she exclaimed, "I was thinking only of you."

"It was plumb stupid," he said, charging after her. "What did you

196

think I was going to do? Put up forever in this damned bedroom? Hide behind your skirts?"

In a burst of fury, she slapped his face. But immediately she clutched him to her breasts. "Ah, kid," she sobbed, "I'm so sorry! I only did what I thought was best. I couldn't stand the idea of you being hurt or . . . killed. I wanted to spare you. All I could think of was losing you. I wanted to get you out of this cursed town. I didn't want you ending up like Ethan!"

Jim held her tight. "I don't run, Cass." He was gentle in tone. Forgiving but insistent. "No matter what happens, I don't run."

Easing from his arms, she brushed away her tears. "No, of course." Taking his cool hand, she whispered, "Now come to bed."

Jim laughed. "I think I've had enough sleep."

"Sleeping," smiled Cass, "wasn't exactly what I had in mind."

Afterward, she watched him slumber, as all men seemed to do at such a time, while outside, the first glimmers of daylight were turning the sky a pale, heat-promising yellow.

At that moment Ike Clanton was downing a double whiskey at the Oriental. How many shots he'd swallowed before Ned Boyle had replaced Frank Leslie at the bar for the overnight shift, Ned did not know, but since midnight the number stood at seven. "All by yourself tonight, Ike," noted Ned, making conversation. "Where's your brothers?"

"They'll be here soon," answered Ike, his face twisting into a wild-eyed smirk. "Oh, they'll be here! Don't you worry none!" He gulped the whiskey and then wiggled a finger into the empty glass to indicate a refill was wanted. "Once they're gathered in town," he declared with a low rumbling laugh, "and the Earps make their appearance on the street. . . ." He downed the liquor and slammed the glass on the bar. In his mind's eye he pictured Finn and Billy stirring in their beds at the ranch ten miles west and the others rousing themselves as well—Ringo and Wes Fuller, Billy Claiborne, Tom McLaury, Frank Hall. He imagined them strapping on their guns. Then mounting their horses. Riding into town. All according to Ringo's plan. "Once the Earps show themselves, the ball will open."

At the Clanton ranch, everything was happening exactly as Ike imagined, though it had been a nervous, sleepless and restive night. Only Ringo appeared relaxed, confident in the plan he had laid out.

Satisfied with all he'd done to carry out that plan, Ike left the Oriental shortly after sunup, returning to his room at the Grand Hotel and standing before a mirror admiringly while buckling on the six-shooter whose very absence the night before had been so essential to Johnny Ringo's clever plan. The brazen provoking of Doc Holliday at the Alhambra in full view of the Earps had proceeded perfectly, Ike thought as he wolfed down breakfast at the Can Can. "All is set," he muttered gleefully as he ambled across Fourth Street to Brown's Hotel where Frank McLaury always put up.

"Cripes, you look awful," gasped Frank, gaping up from his own breakfast in the full dining room. He lowered his voice to a whisper. "You sure you're not too drunk for what's goin' to take place?"

Ike held out a rigid right arm. "Steady as a rock." He dropped the arm to his side and slapped his gun. "And rarin' to go." A delighted giggle rose in his throat. "Can't wait to get at them Earps!" he said exultantly.

"Keep your voice down," snapped McLaury. "And don't get ants in your pants! Last thing we want is you going off half cocked before the others get here." He peered at a grandfather's clock. "That'll prob'ly be ten o'clock at the earliest. So just hold your water, Ike!"

Now the time began to drag for Ike. Unlike Frank McLaury, who was content to park himself in a chair in front of Brown's and wait, he had no patience. It had always been a flaw, according to Old Man Clanton. How often had he listened to his old man ranting about flying off the handle? What was the number of times the old man had hauled off and belted him for it? But last night had been different, thought Ike as he lolled beside McLaury. Last night in carrying out Ringo's plan, he congratulated himself, he'd done just fine!

Ringo was the first to appear in town, nodding as if nothing was going on as he rode past Brown's alone and proceeded north on Fourth Street to dismount at the corner and go into the Capitol Saloon.

A few minutes later, Finn and Tom McLaury drew rein on their horses, dismounted and sat at the edge of the porch of the hotel without a word.

Next came the two Billys, Clanton and Claiborne. Riding in from the west on Fremont Street just before ten o'clock, they loped past Fly's, Bauer's Meat Market, Papago's provision store and the Capitol, then turned down Fourth, nodding at the foursome in front of Brown's and going on to Allen Street, tying up in front of Hatch's and disappearing inside.

Wes Fuller on a blocky chestnut mare and Frank Hall astride his pretty Appaloosa were last to put in an appearance. Turning off Allen a few minutes after eleven, they proceeded through the O.K. Corral, tethered their mounts next to Camillus Fly's studio and sauntered farther on, exiting to Fremont Street.

Observing them through the window of the O.K. office when they'd arrived was an astonished Chip Stone. "Holy hell," he muttered, "that was Frank Hall!"

Leaving the Capitol Saloon, Ringo strolled to the Oriental and arrived at half past eleven as Buckskin Frank Leslie was tying on a fresh apron and apologizing to Ned Boyle for being thirty minutes late in resuming his duties behind the bar. "Quiet night I trust?" he said.

"Pretty much," answered Ned, "although I was worried about Ike Clanton. He was here all night gettin' tanked-up."

"What's so unusual about that?"

"Nothin', I reckon," said Ned, heading for the door.

"Have a good day's sleep, Ned," remarked Ringo as Ned swept past.

"I always sleep like a rock," answered Ned, but as he strolled along Fremont Street and neared the marshal's office, he could not shake off the memory of Ike Clanton's curious turn of phrase. *Once they're gathered in town and the Earps make their appearance on the street . . . the ball will open.* After a moment of mulling over the possible meaning of the words, he pushed open the door to the marshal's office and found Wyatt Earp behind the desk.

Wyatt listened intently to what Ned had to say, thanked him, waited until he'd gone, rose calmly, crossed the office and took down the shotguns he'd cleaned the previous evening. At this hour, he surmised, his brothers were likely to be having a late breakfast at the nearby New York Coffee Shop.

With one glance at the weapons in their brother's hands, Virgil and Morgan were on their feet. "Ike Clanton's been makin' threats," said Wyatt as he passed out the shotguns. "Either of you know where Doc Holliday is at this hour?"

"Prob'ly at the Occidental," answered Virgil.

"Go and see, Morg," said Wyatt. "And be careful! Virg, you come with me. We'll see if we can locate Mr. Isaac Clanton."

The foursome at Brown's Hotel had separated, with Frank and Tom McLaury and Finn Clanton riding to join the two Billys at Hatch's on Allen and Ike heading up Fourth to connect with Wes Fuller and Frank Hall at the meat market on Fremont. Past the Can Can, Ike turned into an alley formed by the north side of the restaurant and the back of the Capitol Saloon.

Turning the opposite corner in the shadow of Shieffelin Hall, Wyatt tugged at Virgil's sleeve and whispered, "There's Ike." Dashing across Fourth, they bounded into the alley. "Stop where you are!" shouted Virgil.

Ike spun round.

"You been huntin' for me?" demanded Virgil.

Ike went for his gun, but the steady hand he'd shown to Frank McLaury faultered, slipping too low on the leather.

Before he could recover, Virgil swung the shotgun and struck the side of Ike's head. "You're under arrest," Virgil grunted, "for drawin' a gun inside town limits."

From in front of Bauer's Meat Market, Wes Fuller and Frank Hall gazed in disbelief as, arms clutched by an Earp on each side, Ike Clanton was marched east on Fremont Street to the courtroom of Justice of the Peace A.O. Wallace. "We'd better let the others know about this," declared Fuller, taking off at a run through the O.K. Corral. Bursting into Hatch's, he blurted, "The Earps have arrested Ike!"

"Those bastards," bellowed Finn. "That rips it! C'mon, boys. The time we've been waitin' for has come!"

Now leaning in the doorway of the O.K. office, Chip Stone watched with ever mounting amazement as the gang poured from Hatch's into Allen Street. "Geez," he gasped. "Hell's a poppin'." Bolting into the street, he tagged behind the gang, paused to observe them surging up Fourth Street and then dashed for the Occidental.

There, as expected, Morgan Earp had located Doc Holliday. At Cass Buford's table, he was chatting amiably with her and Jim Hardin as a waiter was about to place Doc's breakfast before him. "Leave the eatin' for later, Doc," Morgan declared. "Wyatt and Virgil are heading for a clash with Ike Clanton."

Bursting in as they were going out, Chip Stone slammed into them. "Somethin' big's goin' on," he blurted breathlessly. "The whole damned Clanton bunch is on a tear!"

"Where'd you see them?" demanded Morgan.

"Goin' up Fourth," gasped Chip. "There's Finn and Billy Clanton and the two McLaury boys, Billy Claiborne, Wes Fuller and—" His wide, blazing eyes fell on Jim Hardin. "And Frank Hall's with 'em, too, Tascosa!"

"That son of a bitch," yelled Jim, lunging toward the door. "He's here at last!"

"No, Tascosa," cried Cass, grasping his sleeve.

Shaking her off, Jim ran after Morgan Earp and Doc Holliday.

In a dash up Sixth Street, they reached Fremont as Wyatt and Virgil were shoving Ike through Justice of the Peace Wallace's front door. A block and a half away, the Clanton gang was advancing, their angry shouts preceding them.

Instantly, it seemed to Jim, they were all crowded into the small courtroom in a rolling, seething chaos of shouts. "You've threatened my life two or three times," bellowed Wyatt Earp. "I want this thing stopped."

Ike Clanton blared, "You're the ones that's lookin' for a fight."

"You damned dirty cow thief," shouted Wyatt. "If you're anxious for a fight, I'll meet you."

In return, Ike screamed, "I'll see you after I get through here."

But the flaring words were not what riveted Jim's attention. A face in the crowd compelled his gaze. He knew all the faces in the room save this one. Here was someone he'd never seen before. Yet he felt he knew him. Instinctually, deep in his gut, he knew him. This young, grinning, arrogant, staring-back smug face had to belong to the rattlesnake Frank Hall!

Presently, Judge Wallace restored order and heard the case

against Ike Clanton. Banging his gavel, he rendered his verdict. "Guilty! Twenty-five-dollar fine!"

Seconds later, the courtroom was emptied, and the seething factions milled in the center of Fremont Street where a crowd of the curious had gathered expectantly. "We can't settle this here with all these people gathered around," whispered Doc Holliday to the Earps. "Just hold your tempers, boys."

"We don't want any innocent bystanders gettin' hurt," Virgil shouted to the Clantons. "So why don't you boys just git outta here right now?"

Pressing a bloody kerchief to the spot on his head where Wyatt had slammed him with the shotgun, Ike Clanton shouted his answer. "Don't think fer a minute this is done with!"

"Not for a minute!" Wyatt shouted back.

Pulling at his brother, Billy Clanton said, "C'mon, Ike. You'd better get over to Dr. Gilligham's and have that head looked at."

As the Clantons backed west on Fremont, the Earps eased east to the corner of Sixth. "Well, gentlemen," said Doc Holliday as he lit a cheroot, "I don't know if this is the end of this little drama or merely intermission, but whatever it is, it calls for a drink! Perhaps several! Shall we retire to the Occidental? I'm buying."

On the way, Jim spoke sidewise to Holliday. "That was him, wasn't it? That was Frank Hall."

Fighting back a cough, Holliday muttered, "Yeah, it was him."

Chapter Twenty-eight
The Big Dance

With his thin face red with outrage and pulling at the corners of his gunfighter mustache, Sheriff John Behan strode into the Occidental and stormed to Wyatt Earp and his brothers leaning on the bar. "What the hell's going on around here. Wyatt?" he demanded.

"Just butt out of it, Johnny," said Wyatt quietly. "This affair is none of your business."

Boiling mad, Behan bellowed, "I am the sheriff of this county!"

Bunching Behan's shirt in his balled fist, Wyatt yanked him close. "Then, for crissakes, act like it for once," he snarled.

Shaken, Behan turned to Virgil. "Look, if you don't let up on the Clantons, there's goin' to be shootin'."

"They're askin' for it," said Wyatt, letting him go.

"The time's come for you to put a halter on those cowboys," said Virgil.

Smoothing his shirt, Behan pleaded. "Give me a few minutes. I'll have a word with Ike and see if I can put a damper on this situation."

"You do what you have to," answered Virgil with a sneer, "and we'll do what we must."

"Fifteen minutes," exclaimed Behan, darting out the door.

"Prob'ly the only reason that bastard came here," offered Wyatt, "was to spy on us for the Clantons."

Coming in as Behan left the saloon were Seamus Dolan and Johnny Deuce. "If there's anything I can do to assist you in this," said Seamus as he stepped up to the bar, "I stand ready!"

"Same here," declared Deuce.

"Thanks all the same," answered Wyatt, "but there's nothin' afoot we can't manage. You two stay out of it."

"Tascosa," said Deuce, clapping Jim on the shoulder, "is it true that Frank Hall's with the Clantons?"

"Appears so," said Jim.

"Be careful when you go up against him," said Deuce. "Hall's damned handy with a gun."

"We'll handle Hall," asserted Virgil Earp, turning to Jim. "You just keep your nose out of it."

Tight-lipped, Jim answered, "You let Hall get away once. He won't do it again."

Virgil smiled. "Talk like that can get you locked up again, kid. Take my advice and get the hell out of Tombstone."

With a sidelong glance at Cass Buford nervously fanning herself at her usual table, Jim muttered, "I don't run."

"For your information, gentlemen," interjected Seamus Dolan, "the Clanton gang is now convened in front of Bauer's Market. I saw them there not five minutes ago."

"Who's with them?" asked Wyatt.

"I say the McLaurys, Billy Claiborne, Wes Fuller, John Ringo and Finn Clanton." His eyes darted anxiously to Jim. "And Frank Hall was there."

"What about Ike and Billy?" asked Wyatt.

"Didn't see them."

With a bandage around his head and his brother Billy begging him to forget the Earps and return to their ranch, Ike Clanton at that moment was marching from the doctor's office to Bauer's Union Meat Market.

Awaiting him in the middle of Fremont Street in front of the market, he found his brother Finn, Frank and Tom McLaury, Billy Claiborne, Wes Fuller, Frank Hall and Johnny Ringo. Leading them off the street and around the corner of the market, he addressed Ringo angrily. "Looks like your plan ain't workin', Johnny."

"Why, it's working perfectly," said Ringo blithely as he leaned against the wall of the market, arms folded across his chest. "You've got them forced into a tight spot, Ike! They've been openly challenged. They'll have to take you up on it."

"Where are they now?" asked Ike. "Anybody know?"

"Last I seen, they was headin' for the Occidental," answered Wes Fuller.

"Well, let's make sure," said Ike. "Head down that way, Wes, and keep a watch. If you see 'em comin' this way, run back and let us know."

"Could be at their office," suggested Ringo, unlimbering his arms. "In that case they'd come down Fremont."

"Yeah, that's possible," said Ike. "So, Ringo, why don't you station yourself at the corner and keep a look out for them? The Capitol Saloon is your usual hangout, so the Earps won't think nothin' about it if they spot you there. If you spot them comin', hurry back here and let us know. How's that set with you?"

"From now on in, Ike," said Ringo, lurching toward Fremont Street, "it's your show." Reaching the Capitol, he observed John Behan scurrying up Fourth Street. "You look worried, Sheriff," he said as Behan reached the corner. "What's up?"

Breathing hard, Behan stopped to wipe his face with a yellow handkerchief. "You seen Ike Clanton?" he huffed.

"He and the boys are up the street at Bauer's."

"Thanks. Gotta talk to 'em," said Behan, hurrying on.

"You can talk," Ringo shouted after him, "but I don't think it'll do much good."

Wyatt Earp drew a gold watch from his vest pocket. "Seems to me Sheriff Behan's had plenty of time." He tucked away the watch and reached for his hat. "Brothers, shall we go and see if he's had any success?" As Virgil and Morgan rose, so did Jim and Doc Holliday. "Pardon me," said Wyatt firmly, "but the invitation doesn't include the two of you."

"This affair began last night with Ike Clanton and me," declared Holliday defiantly, "so, invited or not, I'm attending this party."

"Frank Hall's with that gang," said Jim angrily, "so there's no way you're goin' to keep me out of this, either!"

"This is lawmen's business," asserted Virgil.

"Then, deputize us," snapped Holliday.

"No way," said Wyatt.

"Don't be an ass, Wyatt," answered Holliday. "By my count, there are eight of them. Add Johnny Behan to their side, which is likely, and that's odds of three to one against you. With Tascosa and me on your side, they shift to even."

"Even?" Wyatt laughed. "How the hell do you calculate that?"

"Hell! I always was four times the man you are!"

"Don't be a fool, Wyatt," pleaded Seamus Dolan. "Doc's right. Don't walk into this outgunned."

"All right, Doc," sighed Wyatt. "You win. Consider yourself deputized."

"What about Tascosa?" asked Holliday.

"Not a chance," answered Wyatt.

Holliday's eyes skipped to Jim. "The kid's got himself set on taking on Hall one way or the other," he said. "Now's as good a time as any."

"No, Doc," asserted Wyatt.

"And what happens if this showdown with the Clantons turns out wrong? Suppose it's the Earps and not the Clantons that wind up on the losin' end? As sure as God made green apples, that gang will come after Tascosa. Do you want this kid facing those odds alone? All that aside, he's good with a gun at a time when our side is on the short side of the numbers in that equation."

"Time's awastin'," declared Virgil Earp.

"All right," sighed Wyatt. "Tascosa, you're also deputized."

"Good. Now let's go," barked Virgil.

Sipping beer at the Capitol Saloon, Johnny Ringo notices that, as they would in the face of an impending thunderstorm, the people of Tombstone have withdrawn from the streets. Like prairie wildfire, the news of what already has taken place between the Earps and the Clanton gang has swept through town. But that had been only Act One, thinks Ringo. Now, the curtain is about to lift for Act Two. Tombstone has become a stage upon which is about to unfold the climax of a tragedy worthy of Shakespeare, he thinks. Or, he muses, is it a comedy?

A few yards away, Sheriff Behan has failed in his attempt to persuade Ike Clanton and the others that now is not the time for a showdown with the Earps and strides angrily back toward Fourth Street in the hope that he might now dissuade the Earps.

With the sun past its zenith and the buildings on the west side of Fourth casting shadows across the street, Wes Fuller is watching five figures emerge from the Occidental: The Earps in their long black coats, black string ties and stiff black hats are armed with six-shooters and also carry shotguns, Doc Holliday in a gray coat totes one, as well, and the trail-dressed kid who has been gunning for Frank Hall wears a revolver. As they advance toward him, Fuller retreats into a doorway, thinking hard about what is about to transpire. A moment later, he mutters, "The hell with this. Ain't my fight!" He dashes across the intersection to the quiet and safety of the Russ House hotel.

Striding up Fourth, the Earps soon turn the corner at Fremont, walking slowly and cautiously past the Capitol Saloon.

Twisting sidewise at the Capitol bar and peering through the opened door, Ringo watches as they, Doc Holliday and the Tascosa Kid step into the street and form a skirmish line.

Through the large plate glass window of the *Epitaph*, John Clum looks on. He has witnessed the gathering of the Clanton gang and the pathetic pleadings of Sheriff Behan. As a responsible citizen, he is appalled by what he knows is about to happen. But he is nonetheless excited. The journalist in him realizes this will be a big news story.

Into his view from his left stride the Earps, Holliday and Jim Hardin.

They are stopped by Sheriff Behan beneath the awning of Bauer's Union Meat Market. "I must insist that you gentlemen turn around and go back," he demands, his voice carrying through the stillness of the deserted street.

"It's way too late for turnin' back, John," declares Wyatt Earp, sweeping Behan aside.

Viewed at an angle from his vantage point, Clum sees that the Clanton gang has taken up positions between Camillus Fly's Lodginghouse and adjoining studio, the Harwood residence and an adobe-walled assay office. Standing beside their horses and facing east on Fremont Street are Tom and Frank McLaury. Fanned out from them in the vacant lot on the east side of Fly's that opens at the rear into the O.K. Corral wait the three Clanton brothers—Ike, Finn and Billy—a jittery Billy Claiborne in his fancy twin-holstered gun rig and, to Clum's astonishment, Frank Hall, looking placid and cool as he drums his fingers on the grip of his holstered pistol.

They do not realize it, decides Clum, but they have boxed themselves in; the only escape being through the vacant lot next to Fly's, leading toward Allen Street through the O.K. Corral.

Less than six feet separates them from the Earps and their allies, Holliday and Hardin.

Now falls an awful stillness.

The voice of Virgil Earp shattered it. "You're all under arrest. Hand in your guns."

Like a cannon shot came Ike Clanton's answer. "Take 'em if you can, you son of a bitch! Get 'em boys!"

In Frank McLaury, the best shot of the bunch, Wyatt saw a flicker of movement. Whipping out his revolver, he fired at Frank.

In the same instant, drawing his pistol to arm's length and aiming at Wyatt, Billy Clanton fired.

Billy missed.

Wyatt's bullet ripped into Frank's belly.

Now a bullet from Morgan Earp's six-shooter tore into the wrist of Billy's gun arm and another into Billy's chest. Slammed against the side of the Harwood house, Billy slid to the ground. Switching his gun to his left hand, he fired at Virgil Earp, striking him in the calf and dropping him to the ground.

Gasping for breath and feverishly reloading his gun, Billy

watched his brother Finn running madly toward the O.K. Corral while Ike and Billy Claiborne abandoned the fight to run for the cover of Camillus Fly's photographic studio.

Also observing Ike's flight, Doc Holliday blasted with his shotgun, shattering Fly's window and door but leaving Ike and Claiborne unscathed to flee out the back in a footrace for the safety of Allen Street.

Grappling for the rifle in his saddle scabbard, Tom McLaury ducked behind his skittish bay horse. Bolting, it left him open to a chest-tearing second blast of Doc Holliday' s shotgun. Screaming in pain and gurgling blood, Tom staggered as far west as Third Street before dropping dead.

But Frank McLaury was not finished yet. Steadying a pistol, he aimed for Holliday in the same second that Holliday threw aside his shotgun and drew his handgun. With the simultaneous blast of their muzzles came a third shot — Morgan Earp's.

A bullet hole below his left ear, Frank McLaury spilled to the ground, dying as his shot found its mark in Holliday, drilling into Doc's hip.

Bullet-riddled, Billy Clanton clung tenaciously to life, stirring and lifting his gun in his shaking left hand. His target was Morgan Earp, and his bullet homed true, drilling Morgan in the shoulder. But Morgan returned fire, joined by a blast from Wyatt, both bullets slamming below Billy's ribs. Head slumping forward, Billy groaned with excruciating pain.

For thirty seconds there'd been a roaring of guns.

Now: silence.

As suddenly as the fight had started, it was over.

Ike and Finn Clanton were running for their lives.

As was Billy Claiborne, making a mockery of his claim to the mantle of Billy the Kid.

The McLaury brothers, reaping at last the seeds they had sown when they threw in with Old Man Clanton, lay dead.

Carried into the Harwood house, sixteen-year-old Billy Clanton, the son Old Man Clanton had prized above all his boys, suffered in extreme agony for half an hour before dying.

Morgan and Virgil Earp had been wounded.

And Doc Holliday.

Unscathed, Jim gaped at the carnage.

In that half-minute of mayhem, he'd done nothing. As bullets had flown and shotguns blasted, he'd searched in vain for Frank Hall. Now, in the enveloping silence, he saw him at last.

Scampering from the shelter of the back wall of Camillus Fly's studio and making a desperate, serpentine dash amidst the shielding stables and fences of the O.K. Corral, he reached his tethered Appaloosa, leapt into the saddle, thundered onto Allen Street and sped west.

Chapter Twenty-nine
What's a Friend For?

Desperate not to let Frank Hall escape, Jim's searching eyes spotted the skittish bay that had bolted to expose Tom McLaury to the spray of Doc Holliday's shotgun. Now calmly grazing on tufts of meager grass, the horse stood in an alley alongside Camillus Fly's buckshot-blasted photographic studio. Seizing the bay's slack reins, Jim vaulted into the saddle only to find himself impeded by people.

Wary, they were converging from the surrounding buildings on Fremont, pouring out of the nearby Capitol Saloon, dashing down the alleys and through lots from Fourth and hurrying across the O.K. Corral from Allen. Silent at first, then murmuring, they arrived to gape at the dead and bloodied men and then turn to talk to one another in a rumble of awe, disbelief and horror.

Jim could only curse and yell at them to get out of the way as he urged the horse through the maze of sheds and pens of the O.K. Reaching Allen at last, he booted the horse's ribs and thundered westward as more men, women and children crossing the street in a rush to the scene of the shootout scampered for safety onto the sidewalks.

Hall had a good lead on him; five minutes, maybe more, Jim reckoned. He also had the upper hand that belonged to the pursued rather than the pursuer—the luxury of knowing where he would be going. Plus the advantage of being on his own horse.

Past Hop Town and speeding over the western lip of the low

mesa that was Tombstone, Jim's borrowed bay plunged into the shimmering glare of desert cut by the road over which he'd driven so many of Josh Durkee's freighters with Felix Catlin jabbering at his side. Eyes fixed on a rooster tail of dust, he made out the fused shape of rider and horse — Frank Hall and his Appaloosa making hard toward the western horizon.

In that direction, Hall saw choices. He might leave the road and head across the desert. To the north lay Benson, where he was wanted. He could swing south toward Bisbee and the Mexican border and chance running into renegade Apaches. Either way, he was not equipped and provisioned for that kind of traveling.

Speeding after him, Jim was also mulling Hall's choices. If he kept to the road, he would come to the fork where he would have to decide whether to take the cut off to the Clanton ranch in hopes of outfitting for a long journey or the branch that led to the river and the goods stores in the mill towns beyond it. Going to the ranch made no sense, Jim decided. If he understood anything about the Earps, it was their tenacity. In the aftermath of what had just happened, the full weight of their vengeance soon would come down on the Clanton stronghold. If Hall were caught there and survived the Earps' fury, he surely would be arrested by them and turned over to the army to answer for the killing of their sergeant. Hall's only real choice, Jim figured, was to make for the San Pedro. But with a cold, sinking feeling in his belly, he also realized that once across the San Pedro, Hall soon could be into the rugged, shielding ranges of the Whetstones or the Huachucas that he knew so well.

Squinting through the glare and Hall's dust cloud, Jim saw the gap between him and Hall widening. "The bastard's spotted us, hoss," he yelled. Pummeling the bay's ribs with his heels and whipping its flanks with the reins, he bent forward and pleaded into its swept-back ears. "Got to get that snake this side of the river, hoss! C'mon, hoss!" Apparently Tom McLaury had been a shrewd judge of horse flesh, thought Jim, grinning exultantly as the game bay surged.

As the distance between him and the trailing rider closed rapidly, Frank Hall twisted in his saddle and peered back for the first time with concern. Not until he was well out of Tombstone had he realized that he was being followed. Having seen Virgil and Morgan Earp and Doc Holliday wounded, he reasoned that this purposeful figure behind him astride Tom McLaury's horse was not Wyatt Earp, who would have concentrated first on seeing to the conditions of his brothers and friend Holliday. Therefore, the man following him, Hall decided, had to be a friend of his own. Ike Clanton, perhaps. Or Finn. Wes Fuller, maybe. Or even Johnny Ringo. Now he realized he was wrong.

This dogged pursuer had to be someone else.

But who?

Then with a flash of clarity, he knew.

This had to be Lou Garrard's avenger! The Tascosa Kid.

With the gap between them narrowing, Jim could make out the object of his pursuit quite plainly now—the brown patches of the Appaloosa's hide, the glint of sunlight on Hall's spurs as they flailed the horse's sides, the curve of Hall's haunches as he leaned forward almost flat in the saddle, the dark streak of soaking sweat down the middle of the back of Hall's blue shirt.

Closing fast, Jim winced from the sting of spraying dirt and pebbles whipped into the air by the hooves of the Appaloosa's churning legs, their pounding and the straining breath of the bay barely drowned out by the rush of hot wind past his ears.

Drawing nearer and coming up on Hall's right, he could see every detail of him—weathered tan hat blown back and held by a leather thong that looked like a raw cut beneath the sharp line of Hall's jaw, flapping red neckerchief looking like a tail, the sweaty blue shirt rippling with the force of the racing wind, bullet-studded loops of a black gunbelt, the elegant curls and swirls etched into the shiny leather holster lashed by a rawhide string to the faded blue-denim curve of Hall's right thigh, the dark walnut grip of a pistol and then the blur of Hall's hand as he reached for it.

More than likely this was the same gun that Hall had used to kill Lou Garrard, thought Jim as he reined the bay sharply to the left.

Hall fired and missed wildly, but his pursuer's evasive move served to widen the gap between them. Jerking the Appaloosa sharply right, he expanded the distance by spurring the horse into plunging from the smooth hard road into a gulley and up into the brushy, cactus-encrusted desert. Fixing his attention on an out-

213

cropping of shelf rock a hundred yards away, he reckoned he could easily drop this pestering, vengeance-minded and foolish kid from there with his Winchester rifle.

Surprised by Hall's maneuver, Jim lost time and distance before he managed to wheel the bay from the road. He gave up more space and minutes fighting through brush and cactus that caught his clothing and slashed the horse's flesh while Hall's plucky Appaloosa broke free out of range of a Colt pistol and onto a patch of stony inclined ground that appeared to afford Hall a clear run to the objective that Jim now recognized. Reaching it, Hall would have good cover and would be shooting down. "Can't let that happen," whispered Jim as he pulled rein on McLaury's horse.

Recalling the Apache attack upon him, Seamus Dolan and Johnny Deuce, Jim drew from its scabbard the rifle that McLaury had been trying vainly to get into his hands when the horse had spooked and left him uncovered and open to Holliday's shotgun blast. "Easy now, horse," Jim muttered while cocking the rifle. "Hold perfectly still!"

Leveling the rifle, he sighted not on Frank Hall but on the Appaloosa that seemed to be dancing as it pawed and pranced upon the loose and slippery footing of the rocky incline.

Two shots in quick succession brought it down.

Thrown, Hall slammed the ground hard but rolled clear of the flailing legs and the thrashing, horrifying last seconds of the Appaloosa's life. Galloping forward, Jim pointed the rifle at Hall, who was struggling to get to his feet. "Got you now, you son of a bitch," yelled Jim as he reined in the bay.

Dazed and with a twisting look of hate on his scratched and bleeding face, Hall jerked up trembling hands. "Don't shoot," he begged. "I give up!"

"Just stand where you are, snake," answered Jim. Holding the rifle in both hands and pointing it at Hall's chest, he swung his left leg over the bay's neck and slid to the ground. "Back up," he said, poking the rifle toward Hall. "Ten paces."

Eyes narrowed in puzzlement, Hall slowly retreated.

"Far enough," said Jim.

Emitting a nervous giggle, Hall said, "Listen, Tascosa—"

"Shut up!" shouted Jim. "Only my friends can call me that."

"I can explain what happened between me and your pal Lou," pleaded Hall. "I think you got the wrong story!"

"You shot him didn't you?"

"I shot him, sure, but you ought to know why."

"The hell with why. All I know is, Lou's gun was holstered! Like yours is now. You never gave him a chance to draw it. Why not? Because you knew he was better with a gun than you could ever be. Is that it?"

Hall stared, his lips moving wordlessly.

"In all my days, I never knew anybody as good with a gun as Lou Garrard," said Jim. "Save one." Throwing aside the rifle with his left hand, he dropped his right loosely to his holster, the fingers curled. "That one is somebody Lou taught." He cracked a smile. "Guess who!"

With chilling understanding, Hall went for his gun.

Jim got to his Colt first, drilling one shot through Hall's heart. Slipping the gun into its holster, he stepped forward and stared down at Hall's half-open but lifeless eyes.

"That settles it, Lou," he muttered as he turned and walked away. "I didn't hold back. I gave it my all. After all, what's a friend for?"

Chapter Thirty
Yesterday's News

The next afternoon, Jim slumped into his favorite wicker chair on the gallery outside Cass Buford's bedroom above the Occidental and gazed at the headline in the *Epitaph*.

YESTERDAY'S TRAGEDY
Three Men Hurled into
Eternity in the Dura-
tion of a Moment

Below the banner, John Clum had written: "Stormy as were the early days of Tombstone, nothing ever occurred equal to the event of yesterday."

"I'll say," Jim chuckled, lifting his eyes momentarily to the azure sky and the distant mountains drenched in pink late-afternoon sunlight.

Poking her head through the open door, Cass said, "Did you say somethin' to me, honey?"

"Just talkin' to myself," said Jim.

Looking down at the paper again, his eyes skipped to another heading.

THE EARP BROTHERS JUSTIFIED

"The feeling of the best class of our citizens is that the marshal was entirely justified in his efforts to disarm these men and that being fired upon they had to defend themselves," the news article continued. "It was a case of kill or be killed."

Ike Clanton, the paper noted, had been arrested and jailed, and a warrant had been issued for Billy Claiborne.

How Clum must have enjoyed writing that, Jim thought as he folded the newspaper and laid it in his lap. The cowboy element that Clum despised had been put in its place at last.

Having learned of Jim's shooting of Frank Hall as his paper was going to press and also having satisfied himself that neither Jim Hardin nor Frank Hall had taken an active part in the main event of Wednesday afternoon in the environs of Camillus Fly's photographic studio, Mr. Clum made no mention in his two-column story of their private duel in the desert. Besides, there'd been a midnight inquiry into the shooting of Frank Hall. Held in his brother Virgil's office by Wyatt after assuring himself that the wounds suffered by his brothers and Doc Holliday were minor, the hearing disposed of what Wyatt called a sideshow quite nicely with a verdict that Jim had killed Hall in self-defense. It being a purely personal matter having nothing to do with the major event on Fremont Street, Clum had decided it was not worth pulling his newspaper apart for. The item could await the next edition's "Death's Doings" column.

"Seeing as how you came forward and reported what you did," Wyatt Earp declared in rendering his verdict, "and making note that you brought Hall's body along and thus allowed me to see for myself that he was shot from the front and had fired his own gun, I shall not attempt to hold you. *But . . .*" He rose from behind his brother's desk. Reaching out, he gathered the ends of Jim's blue neckerchief and twisted them into a ball under Jim's chin. "Just like I did up in Dodge City, I'm telling you — and telling you for the last time — to get your ass out of my town." He released the knot. "For your own damned good! The man you've killed has plenty of friends in this territory. And sooner or later one of 'em is going to come after you just as you went after Hall. You don't hold the patent on revenge, kid! Now, whether or not anybody comes gunning for you, I don't really care personally. I've never have held you in much esteem. But if you're to be gunned down by some vengeful-minded owlhoot, I don't want it happening here. My brothers and I are going to have our hands full enough dealing with the friends of those we killed this afternoon, so we don't want you around complicating matters."

"That's no legal cause for you to run me out of Tombstone," Jim protested, loosening his tie.

"Maybe you're right," answered Wyatt, drawing a cheroot from his vest pocket. "Maybe there is no legal justification," he went on as he lit up. "But if I see your face in this town past sunset tomorrow, I'm going to rethink my verdict in the death of Frank Hall and issue a warrant for your arrest on suspicion of murder."

Jim exploded. "You ain't got a shred of evidence to charge me with murder!"

"Maybe I got none now," said Earp, blowing a plume of smoke into Jim's face, "but I sure as hell will have *plenty* if I set my mind to the task. And who do you think a jury of twelve good men and true will believe? You?" He whisked the cheroot from his lips and grinned triumphantly. "Or . . . Wyatt Earp?"

So that's that, thought Jim as he laid aside John Clum's paper and rose to return to Cass's bedroom.

A meager bundle, his belongings rested beside her as she sat on her bed, smiling at him tenderly.

"Sun'll be down soon," he said, crossing to the bed. "Better be goin'."

"Wyatt's right," Cass said, clutching his hand and pressing it between hers. "It's best that you go." She was fighting back tears now, and her throaty voice was even more so. "This old dame is gonna miss you, you know." Abruptly, she raised his hand to her lips. "Promise me you'll write."

"Guaranteed," he said, swallowing hard and withdrawing his hand. Picking up his things, he smiled down at her. "Look for a letter from San Francisco!"

Chapter Thirty-one
Promise Kept

It was more than a year before Cass Buford opened the letter with Jim's promised postmark. Inside: big, boyish script on one sheet of pale blue paper.

UNION SQUARE HOTEL
San Francisco, California

Dear Cass,

I take up my pen in the hopes that you are well and doin good. I am doin fine.

I am sorry I did not write to you sooner but I have been busy. When I got here I found myself a job with one of the big freightin outfits unloadin goods from the ships that come in to the docks from all over the world. But soon I got promoted and now I am workin in the office of the firm and makin very good money.

This letter is bein written at one of the fancy hotels they have here. I'm stayin here for a few days because come Saturday I am goin to be gettin married. Boy I'll bet that comes as a big surprise to you! You would like my sweetheart very much. Her name is Susan Veatch and she is the daughter of the man who owns the freightin company I work for. She is a very pretty gal and I will send you a pitcher of her and me from the weddin. But enuf about me.

How are you? How are things in Tombstone? I think about you and my friends Seamus and Jonny Deuce a lot. Say hello to them for me. Do you ever see Ringo?

I must close now because there is to be a party that some of my new found friends are throwin in my honor on the occasion of my weddin.

Your friend,

Jim Hardin also known

as Tascosa

P.S.

Will you do me a favor? When you go to Boot Hill to visit the grave of your brother Ethan will you please have a look at the plot of my pal Lou Garrard and put flowers there?

Chapter Thirty-two
Return Post

Occidental Saloon
Tombstone, Arizona Territory
November 18, 1882

My Dearest Tascosa,

Thank you for your letter. I shall treasure it always. I send you my sincerest congratulations and heartfelt best wishes on the occasion of your marriage.

I am quite well and business is thriving.

Much has happened since you left Tombstone, and I regret that there is some sad news to report to you. Your friend Felix Catlin passed away last week. He died peacefully in his sleep and was afforded a grand funeral by Josh Durkee, always a most generous and kind-hearted man, as you know. At the services, Josh asked about you, but as I had not heard from you at that time I could only tell Josh that knowing you as I did I was sure you were prospering, as I see by your letter, you clearly are.

Other occurrences since you left Tombstone I shall put down as best I can in the sequence in which they took place.

The first of these happened three days after Christmas last year when there was an attempt on the life of Virgil Earp. He was caught in an ambush on Allen Street and riddled with buckshot from at least five guns. Suspicion fell immediately on Curly Bill Brocius, who had been seen in town that day, but a posse that Wyatt organized could not find him. The attack left Virgil a cripple, and he has now left Tombstone for good.

Then on the night of March 17 this year Morgan Earp was killed as he was playing a game of pool in Bob Hatch's place. A hail of bullets crashed through the window from Allen Street and one hit Morg in the back. Wyatt was there at the time and carried Morg into Bob's office. A doctor was sent for, but it was useless. The bullet was lodged in the spine. Morgan died the next morning.

This shooting was also blamed on those like Curly Bill, the two Clanton boys, Ike and Finn, and other cowboys who wanted to get revenge for what happened last October. But there was never any direct proof.

However, that didn't stop Wyatt from going after those he thought did the shootings of his brothers. He caught up with Curly Bill at Iron Springs and killed him with a shotgun. That put Sheriff Behan on Wyatt's tail, as you can well imagine. But Behan is not likely to get his hands on Wyatt, for Wyatt has now left Tombstone for Colorado, and the governor up there will not honor Sheriff Behan's requests for Wyatt's return.

By the way, Doc Holliday is also up there with Wyatt. His health is worse, and I am amazed Doc has lived this long.

Of course, all of this new trouble was the result of the big shootout last year, which everybody in town still talks about and takes sides over with some saying the Earps were right and some saying the Clantons were set up to be killed.

The ones who think the Clanton gang got led into their big showdown with the Earps hold that it was Johnny Ringo that was the brain behind it. The theory goes that Ringo somehow managed to get Ike Clanton to provoke the Earps into coming after him by getting Ike to pick a fight with Doc Holliday.

I find that idea far-fetched, but there are plenty of folks who buy it. Whether it's what happened or not we'll never know because Ringo is dead. They found his body propped up against an oak tree in Turkey Creek Canyon. The cause of death was a slug from a forty-five that was in Ringo's hand. The ruling was that Ringo had committed suicide. But some people point out that there were no traces of gun powder around the wound, so how could Ringo have shot himself and not leave powder burns?

That mystery has led to speculation that Ringo was killed for what he did in causing last year's gunfight. Those who hold to Ringo being murdered say Billy Claiborne could have done it. Billy was known for saying Ringo had set up the whole thing.

We'll never find out from Billy if he did shoot Ringo because Billy was also shot and killed, only with no mystery as to who did it. Buckskin Frank Leslie shot Billy the Kid (ha, ha!) a couple of days ago outside the Oriental. Billy had been all likkered up and, when Frank bounced him, went for his two guns. Frank was quicker, and when he came back into the saloon he said, "He died nice."

There are also some people in Tombstone who believe that it was your old friend Johnny Deuce who plugged Ringo. But we'll probably never find out if that's the truth because that crazy hardcase from the Clanton gang, Pony Deal, is bragging that he evened the score for Ringo by killing Deuce. I can't say if Deuce is dead or not, but nobody's seen him around for a while. As for Ike and Finn Clanton, they laid low for quite a spell after they got cold feet about going up against the Earps and both saved their skins by hightailing it through the O.K. Corral. But with the Earps out of the way now, they're back conducting their old trade — cattle rustling.

Seamus Dolan is doing very well working at the *Epitaph,* but John Clum is no longer his boss. Mr. Clum sold the newspaper last May and, like you, moved to California. He never told me why he was going, but I believe it was because of the vendetta that was launched against the Earps. As Clum had been their prime backer and ally, I expect Clum feared he might be marked for revenge next.

Seamus sends his regards. But get this! Seamus says he's writing a book about all the things that went on while you were with us in Tombstone and all about what led up to the gunfight last October. He says he's going to give the book the title of "Gunfight at the O.K. Corral." Ridiculous, isn't it? We all know that nothing happened *in* the corral. It all took place around Camillus Fly's boardinghouse and photo studio. When I pointed this out to Seamus, he just gave me one of his withering looks and said, "Well I sure as hell can't call the book 'Gunfight at Camillus Fly's Place,' can I?"

It's supper time at the Occidental and I must go to work, so that's about it for now, Tascosa, except to say that I miss having you around for supper and *you know what* afterwards!

Be happy with your bride!

Love and kisses,

    Your friend,

    Cass